A MOTHER'S BROKEN PROMISE

RACHEL VELASQUEZ

December 1, 2018

ASIN: 1978417020

ISBN 9781978417021

Daughters of OM Publishing

Edition 2

ISBN 978-1-957815-01-5

DEDICATION

I dedicate this first to my Lord and Savior, Yeshua HaMashiach. He has taught me so much about parenting and love. I see the growth in me and am honored that He has chosen me as His.

I also dedicate this to all the parents and children. You are loved! Nothing can separate us from YHVH's love. If we stay focused on Him then all things, blessings and promises will manifest.

Have childlike faith

CONTENTS

A Mother's Broken Promise

1 THE PARTY

Frankie sat at the window looking out; he was smiling. He was in deep thought, with a memory that was slowly fading and one that he did not want ever to forget. He could see her face, beautiful and smiling, waving at him from the car as he walked away and off to school. She always waved with the 'I Love You' sign; never once did she ever miss a chance to do so. Finally, he turned and walked away. Just before he walked out of sight, he turned, and there she was, still waving and blowing him kisses. Mom did this every school day. She would always wait for them to get out of sight before driving away. "Frankie! Come on. We must finish getting ready for the party," yelled his brother Samuel.

Frankie struggled to keep the memory fresh. It was hard to ignore his big brother yelling at what seemed right into his ear. Finally, with her memory fading, he turned to his brother. "I don't want to go," he answered. "Come on. You don't want dad to come to fetch you." Samuel responded. Samuel was the son that always did as he was told, but Frankie, on the other hand, always put up a fight. "Why do I have to go to the stupid party?" he asked. "I just want to stay here in my room alone!" "You know that this is one of mom's favorite days," Samuel insisted as he walked over to his brother. "I can't; I just can't!" Frankie's voice broke, and tears rolled down his face. "I never want to celebrate anything ever again!" Frankie cried, "I just want my mommy!" Samuel slid beside his brother and put his arm around him, "I know how you feel, but we have to be brave for dad." He hugged his little brother and dried his tears. Samuel was only two years older, but mommy had always said he was 'an old soul.' Samuel was only nine, but he knew that he had to be strong for Frankie.

Samuel took seven-year-old Frankie by his hand and led him downstairs.

They saw all the food and hearts as they walked down the stairs. "Samuel?" Frankie continued, "How do we get mommy back? She has been gone too long. I miss her so much. I do not want to see people here at our house without mommy." Samuel felt his stomach tighten, and he fought back the tears. He cleared his throat before he began, "I am trying to help daddy find a way. We just don't know how to get her back yet." Samuel held Frankie's hand for numerous reasons; he was afraid that Frankie would run back upstairs and hide in his room or trip down the stairs due to the tears rolling down his face. Samuel knew that his little brother was very upset and not paying attention. They paused, wiped tears away, and straightened up their clothes as they reached the bottom of the stairs. Samuel ran his fingers through their hair and practiced their smiles. They had to swallow lumps in their throats and blink away, eyes full of tears as they looked at each other.

They saw their dad looking sadder than a lost puppy as they entered the living room. Seth cleared his throat, "There you are. I was wondering when you were coming down. You both look so handsome and strong. We have a lot to do. Are you ready?" Seth had remembered his wife, almost willing her to walk through those doors. He smiled at his boys and headed to the kitchen. "Now, you know that your mommy would want everything perfect, so let's get to work." Seth encouraged his boys. Seth could see her rushing around, ensuring that everything was just right. She was the perfect hostess. Frances Grace was a beautiful, young, articulate woman, the love of his life and soul mate. Seth's heart skipped a beat every time he thought of his wife. He was jerked out of his daydream by the boys wondering where to put the food. They needed direction that Seth himself was unsure he could give. It had been almost two years since that day she disappeared. He had only agreed to go along with the party at his family and friends' urging, 'this was supposed to help them deal with her loss.' They all seemed to have given up on her return, but he was still waiting for news. He would not give up, not ever. Frances Grace was the mother of his children, and he would never give up looking for her. Not just for his own sake but for the boys' sake. He had never seen a woman so in love with her babies the way she loved her boys.

The doorbell rang, and it was the guests starting to arrive. Today was Valentine's Day; they had celebrated with friends and family for the past 12 years. Frances Grace believed that Valentine's Day was a day to celebrate the love between her and her husband and celebrate the love she felt for family and friends. Although she hated red, she wore it just for Valentine's Day and Christmas. He smiled as he recalled that Christmas was her favorite time of year. She would always say, 'no one will ever see me in red any other day.' Frances Grace believed in family, and she would always say, "without family, you are one lonely person." Although she had always dreamt of being a mommy, she didn't want much more than that. Her children, husband, and family were the most important people in her life. She was a joy to be around and a joy to have.

As the family and friends arrived, the boys were cordial and smiled when someone spoke to them. They went through the motions, but everyone could see how miserable they were. Their aunts and uncles attempted to cheer them up, but nothing seemed to work. They had all hoped that the memory of their mother's party would bring them joy. There was laughter throughout the house and the family's stories, but the boys did not notice any. Finally, one of their aunts noticed that Frankie looked out the window and seemed to be in a trance. She patted his head and brushed his hair with her fingers, but he did not move, so she quietly walked away. Rae was Frances Grace's older sister. Rae thought this was the saddest thing she had witnessed in a long time. Rae's heart broke as she watched the boys in their pain. Unfortunately, she worked long hours, so she had not been able to help much.

Finally, the long evening ended as the guests made their way home. "Will this party ever end?" Frankie asked Samuel. "Hopefully, everyone will leave soon," Samuel answered. The boys never thought that today would happen without their mommy. The boys never agreed that having a party without their mommy was a good idea. Never once were they asked if they would like to do this. No, all the adults just decided that it would be best. The boys had overheard the family say, "the boys need family around so they can move on," but this is not what they needed. What they needed was for the family not to give up so quickly. They received hugs as they watched people getting ready to leave; the boys both smiled and prayed for the night to end. As the last person left, Frankie ran upstairs; Seth and Samuel started to clean up the mess, which always follows a party. People had offered to help, but Seth reassured them that he could clean up. Glasses and spills everywhere, plates on every table, cookie crumbs on the floor, cake smeared all over the couch, trash cans full of junk, and the emptiness seemed to take everyone into their thoughts.

Seth remembered that Frances Grace always sang and danced around as she cleaned up after the parties. He would always stand back and admire her. She was light on her toes and had a voice of an angel. She never spoke an ill word of anyone, never complained about the mess, and would smile at him when she would notice that he was only an observer. Instead, she would dance around him and smile as she serenaded him. As she giggled, he squirmed. He was not willing to float around the house as she would. What a beautiful sight, he remembered. But where was she? Who took her? Why did they take her away? "I have to find her," he thought to himself.

Samuel was helping today, but he was usually always tucked into bed when his mommy was here. She would sing a song, kiss him, pull his covers up to his chin, and whisper, "I love you forever." He remembered hearing his mommy singing and giggling as he drifted off to sleep. He had never gotten up to see her clean because he always listened and obeyed. She had the most beautiful voice, and he had always loved to hear her sing. He remembered her soft sweet angelic voice, softly singing him to sleep. He could almost hear her singing; suddenly, a glass slipped out of his hand. He came back to reality and looked at his dad in shock. "Don't move," Seth warned and immediately came over and cleaned up the glass. As he cleaned, he comforted Samuel, "don't worry, we are all tired, and accidents happen." When he had finished picking up the glass, he picked up Samuel and carried him off to bed. "You should be in bed, young man." "Daddy, I need to help you." He attempted to argue, but Seth did not listen. As Samuel got ready for bed, Seth peeked in on Frankie and returned to Samuel. He tucked his son into bed and kissed his cheek, "goodnight, sweet boy." As his dad walked out of the room, Samuel silently wept. When the door closed, he got up and knelt, "Dear Jesus, I only have one request, please bring my mommy home. I'm sorry I haven't always said my prayers. I have been very angry with you. Why did you let my mommy disappear? Who took her? She would never have left us all alone. She promised to pick us up. She never broke a promise before. Please promise me, Jesus, that you will bring her back. We need her here; we are all so unhappy. She was your light that was bright in everyone's life. I need my mommy. Please bring her back, to make us happy again. Please, Jesus, bring her back, Amen." He climbed back into bed. He cried as he closed his eyes and drifted off to sleep.

Frankie had run up the stairs and thrown himself on the bed. Tears soaked his pillow as he tried to muffle his sobbing. Tonight, was the first party they had had since his mommy had disappeared. Everything was full of her memories. He could smell her perfume and hear her voice, and Frankie thought he saw her tonight. He had been looking out the window in the family room; when he saw an image of her in the window, she had disappeared as he got closer. Frankie missed her so much. He was only five years old when she disappeared. Frankie had always felt her presence everywhere he went. He was so afraid that he would forget what she looked like. Frankie kept a picture of her on his nightstand, but when his daddy would turn out the light, he would get her picture and sleep next to it. His tears soaked his pillow as he heard his daddy entering the room. Seth came over and sat next to him. "Do you want to sleep with me tonight?" he asked. "No, I'm okay, daddy." "Are you sure?" Frankie nodded, 'no.' Seth leaned over and kissed his cheek, "goodnight, sweet little one, you can come jump in if you change your mind." As his dad walked out of the room, Frankie silently cried as he held his mommy's picture. "Oh, mommy, please tell me how we can help you come home." He begged as he held on to her picture. Frankie said his prayers before falling asleep, "Dear Jesus, I know that I do not ask for anything else but my mommy to come home. Please keep her safe and bring her home soon. You know that I am so sad and miss her very much. My mommy must be very scared. Please keep her safe and bring her home. Amen."

Seth headed downstairs to continue to clean up. When he reached the bottom of the stairs, he paused and listened. Seth closed his eyes and could hear his wife singing. He could smell her fragrance. Seth knew he had to open his eyes, but he wasn't ready. Seth was unsure how long he had enjoyed his memory when suddenly he felt someone watching him. He opened his eyes, and there in front of him stood his beautiful wife smiling at him. As Seth reached out, she waved goodbye, "I love you," he heard her say. The memory seemed so real. Did he see her? Seth shook his head, wiped tears away, and finished cleaning up. Before Seth climbed into bed after he had checked in on the boys, they were both sound asleep, but he knew that they were dreaming of her. As he drifted off to sleep, he wondered if they would ever see her again.

A week had passed since the party. Frankie was upstairs in his bedroom, and suddenly, he could smell roses. He turned to look, but no one was there in his room. Frankie remembered that his mommy loved roses. He rushed out of his bedroom; no one was in the hall. Frankie ran into his brother's room; Samuel was not there. He went downstairs, where the rose fragrance was even more potent. He called out, "Mommy?" He headed toward her art room; mommy's art room door had not been opened since she disappeared. "Mommy?" he called as he turned the doorknob and opened the door. "Mommy," he whispered as he saw her image. She was very faint, like a ghost, he thought. "Mommy, I miss you so much," he whispered, afraid that she would disappear. She turned and smiled at him. As he stepped toward her, she looked at him so lovingly. "Mommy, please don't go," he pleaded. She seemed to float towards him. She reached out and lightly swept his hair aside. She had always done that. "I will be back, baby. I love you forever." She disappeared right in front of him. Frankie thought that he had been daydreaming.

He always imagined her sitting next to him, but this seemed real. Frankie could still feel her touch on his forehead where she had straightened his hair. He could still smell the roses. Frankie had many questions. Was this a dream? Am I going crazy? Did this happen? Where is everyone? Am I here alone? Is mommy a ghost? So many thoughts were running through his head. "Daddy! Daddy!" he called out as he ran through the house.

Seth heard his son's screams and rushed out of his den. He could smell roses and felt quite confused as he reached Frankie. "I saw mommy! I did, I did, I really saw her!" Frankie exclaimed. Seth listened to Frankie's story and wanted to believe him, but this did not seem possible. He could not deny that he, too, could smell roses, and there were no roses in the house.

Samuel had been outside feeding the dog. He had heard all the commotion and rushed inside. "What's going on?" he asked. As Frankie filled him in, Samuel was smiling. Samuel listened, very interested in the details of Frankie's story. Samuel could see exactly what Frankie was describing. Then Frankie told them about seeing her in the window at the party, and then today again, Samuel thought he should also talk about his experience at the party. "I saw mommy at the party, too. She was watching everyone and smiling at me. SHE BLEW ME KISSES when I walked towards her and waved 'I love you.' I turned to call you daddy, but when I looked back, she was gone." Seth smiled at his boys, "We all miss her very much. We all want her to come home. We will find her and bring her home where she belongs. Do not ever give up hope." Seth hugged his boys and held them tight. "Your mommy loves you both so very much. I know she is trying to find her way home. We are all going to work together and bring her home. I do believe she is trying to give us a sign."

A Mother's Broken Promise

Seth couldn't believe what had just happened. They were all seeing his wife and smelling her everywhere. Seth firmly thought it was a sign giving him more hope. Seth knew that she would be coming home very soon. He did not know where she was or how she would come home but felt deep in his heart that she would be home one day soon

2 SHE AWAKENS

She had been in a medically induced coma for over 12 months and had remained in a coma. Alice was the wife of a plastic surgeon. She was in a horrible accidental fire that had burned over 30 percent of her body. Alice fell down the stairs and suffered severe head trauma in her fight to escape the fire. The surgeon had opted to induce the coma so she would not suffer so much. Every day, Jack had been by her side, helping with her physical therapy and changing dressings. He read to her from her favorite books every day. Jack held her hand and spoke to her every day, reminding her of her life. He continually pleaded with her to come back to him. Jack was always there, except for days when he saw patients himself.

Alice had been dreaming a beautiful dream and playing with her baby boy. He was so tiny and beautiful, dressed in little, tiny jeans and wore a cowboy hat and boots. She was singing a lullaby to him. He yawned and closed his eyes as she held him close. As she awoke and opened her eyes, she looked at the doctor at her bedside. She blinked her eyes, not sure where she was. "Doctor where am I?" she asked. Jack looked up, "Oh darling, you're awake." Alice looked at him, confused at his remark, "do I know you?" He was so disappointed! He had sat there, helping her all these months, hoping to avoid this response. Talking to her, massaging her body, doing therapy, reading, and telling her how much he loved her. He had hoped that she would not have any memory loss, but that was not the case. "Alice, you were in a terrible accident." He answered, "Do you remember anything?" Alice looked into his face, but nothing came to her. "I was just dreaming about my beautiful baby boy," she stammered. "Where is he?" she asked. "Darling, we don't have a baby." He answered almost in tears. "That's not true," she cried. It seemed so real to her. It felt like she had held this baby. She could still smell him and see his beautiful little face. "Darling, you need to rest. You have been through a lot." He attempted to comfort her, but she pulled away. "I don't know you. Please don't touch me." She insisted. Jack called for the nurse and doctor to come in. Alice was so upset that they decided it was best to give her something to relax. The doctor ordered a sedative.

Jack talked with Dr. Stevens about the probability that Alice would not get her full memory back. She has had such a traumatic injury and recovery period. She may go into shock with the changes in her life. Alice had to have numerous surgeries for the swelling in her brain and skin grafts. She had flat-lined multiple times in her recovery, so her brain may be protecting her and possibly even taking her to a happier place. Dr. Stevens reminded Jack that he would need to be patient with her, give her some space, and pray for the best.

Alice opened her eyes again, attempting to fight the medication but was fighting a losing battle. As she lay in her bed and drifted off, she could think about the baby boy. Alice began to dream again and dreamt of the day the baby was born. The room was painted a baby blue, had machines everywhere, the doctors were wearing masks, the nurses were hurrying around, but her baby was in her arms; she paid them no mind. What a beautiful tiny baby; he smiled at her, and she at him. She brushed his forehead with her finger and kissed his cheek. She took a deep breath and took it all in; then, the doctor wanted to take him. She cried, "No, please, don't take him away." He reassured her that he just needed to check and weigh him. She looked on and wanted him back. Something didn't feel right to her; as she looked at her baby, she asked, "Is everything ok?" No one answered her. "Oh no," she thought, "I have to wake up." She started to cry and forced herself to awaken. As she opened her eyes, she saw she was alone. She looked around the room, and nothing seemed familiar. This was not a hospital room. It looked like a bedroom. This room was not a hospital with beautiful wooden floors, a large comfortable bed, high ceilings, and long beautiful drapes. She remembered hospital rooms; she had her baby in a hospital. Where was she? She attempted to move her legs, but they seemed so heavy, and she felt like she could barely move her arms. What was going on? She didn't want to cry out just in case the same people would return.

"I have to remember," she thought to herself. "Why doesn't this room look familiar?" she asked softly. "Can I move my body?" she wondered, "No" was the answer to her question. This feeling was the strangest thing to her; maybe she needed to call out. "No," she thought, "I will just wait a little longer and see what I can do." It was probably the medication she was given when she became upset. "This time, I will make sure I stay calm and ask questions when someone returns to check on me," she thought. It felt like her body was numb, but her mind seemed to be working fine. I can move my head, see everything in the room, and my mind seems sharp, but I can't move any other parts of my body. She tried to remember the fire as she lay there, but nothing came to mind. She attempted to reflect on the fall, but nothing came to mind. This room seemed so strange and unfamiliar. The only memory that she believed she remembered was the baby. Tears filled her eyes as she thought about the baby, "maybe he died in the fire," she felt herself losing it again. She took a deep breath and slowed down her breathing. "No, my baby is alive," she thought to herself. "I will not give up this beautiful memory, no matter what."

Alice heard someone walking into her room. She closed her eyes and pretended to be asleep. It was a woman; Alice could smell her perfume. It was a strong scent, some scent that she did not like. Alice wondered if she could trust this woman. Maybe she should open her eyes, but fear overtook her, and she kept them closed. The nurse came over and felt for her pulse. "Slow down your pulse and your breathing," she thought. The nurse reached out and softly touched Alice's shoulder, "Mrs. Alexander, are you awake?" Alice did not want to respond. She slightly moved her head. "Mrs. Alexander?" the nurse continued, "I only want to help you." But Alice refused to open her eyes. She heard the nurse move to the opposite side of the room. She listened; the nurse picked up something and moved back towards Alice. She sat at the foot of the bed and softly began to speak, "I know how frightened you feel. When you awakened and did not recognize anyone in the room. It must have been so terrifying for you. Then have the doctor, and I come in only to calm you down with medication. I'm sure this only makes you trust me even less." She was silent for a few minutes to see if Alice would respond, but Alice held firm and did not move. She continued to take slow deep breaths and tried not to move too much. Then the nurse continued, "My name is Valerie, but you may call me Val if you like. I have been here for about six months. My understanding is that Dr. Alexander brought you home after they removed you from the medically induced coma, and you didn't awaken. He spends all his free time here with you. He is gone right now; he has patients to see. I am here as your nurse. Dr. Alexander had been hoping that you would awaken when he was home. He was hoping to be the first to talk with you. Dr. Alexander left today disappointed that you did not remember him and that it upset you so much. He likes for me to read to you every day. Is there something you would like to hear if you are awake?"

She paused and waited for an answer. Alice just remained quiet.

As Valerie began to read from 'Romeo and Juliet' Alice listened. Alice liked the story, but she did not feel like this was one of her favorite books. Alice strained to remember her favorite book, but all she could think about were children's books. "How strange," Alice thought to herself. Alice struggled with whether to trust or not to trust Valerie.

"Hello?" Alice quietly spoke, "where am I?" Alice startled Valerie, and she was not expecting to hear Alice speak, "Mrs. Alexander, you are in your home." "I don't remember anything about this room. It seems so unfamiliar." Alice continued, "Did you call me Mrs. Alexander?" Valerie was now standing beside Alice, "yes, Mrs. Alexander, do you remember anything at all?" Alice shook her head, afraid to speak of the baby again. "Shall I call Dr. Alexander and tell him that you are awake?" Valerie asked. Alice didn't want Valerie to see the fear she was feeling. "No, please do not," she begged. Valerie shook her head to reassure Alice.

"It's okay; I will sit here with you until you are ready to call him. Is there anything I can get you?" Alice suddenly noticed that she seemed parched, "May I please have a glass of water?" Valerie quickly moved toward the window, reached for a water pitcher, and poured a glass, "Here you go." As Alice took a sip, the water felt so good going down. She took another drink, and as her throat became moisturized, she suddenly felt hungry. "May I have something to eat?" "Sure, what would you like?" Valerie asked. Alice shook her head, "I don't know." Finally, Valerie asked, "Would you like a sandwich, soup, or something more filling?" Alice shook her head, "Anything would be fine." It seemed so strange that she could not think of anything she wanted. "May I have fruit too?" Valerie walked to an intercom and spoke to the cook.

"Please bring Mrs. Alexander a turkey sandwich and fruit salad. Do not call Dr. Alexander," she instructed. Valerie turned and headed to the bathroom, and she brought back a basin and towel. As she wrung out the towel, Alice could see the steam.

Valerie spoke softly, "Mrs. Alexander, may I help you with this?" "No, thank you, I would like to try myself," Alice responded as Valerie helped her sit up. Alice tried to move her arms, but they were so heavy. She shifted her eyes to Valerie for an answer. Valerie quickly reached for her arm and put the towel in her hand. Alice was very clumsy in wiping her face, but she did it alone. This was quite an accomplishment. Alice smiled at Valerie. Valerie was quite the nurse; she had slipped lots of pillows behind her to help with sitting up.

Now she could see her hands sitting up, and it all seemed so strange. Her hands did not look familiar to her. As she touched her fingers, palm, and the back of her hand, she wondered, this can't be me. Valerie spoke softly, "Mrs. Alexander, you had many surgeries. The burns you sustained were severe. Mrs. Alexander?" Alice looked at her, "please call me," she paused. She did not remember her first name. "Alice?" Valerie asked. "Yes, Alice?" she questioned. The name Alice did not seem familiar at all. She felt that her name was something else but what? The warmth of the towel felt so good to her skin, but she was not sure why. 'Is my face disfigured?' She thought. She battled with the idea of looking in a mirror. Maybe after lunch, she would give it a try.

The cook knocked and entered the room; she looked at Alice with love and concern. "I have been waiting to make you something to eat for such a long time." Alice smiled at her, but she did not remember the cook. "I hope you enjoy this. Your husband had given me a list of your favorite foods with directions on how to fix them." Alice thanked her and struggled to eat her first meal in who knows how long. She still had an I.V. in her arm but was attempting to eat. The smell of the fresh bread made her feel comfortable. The fresh bread and turkey felt good going down as she took small bites. It made her throat feel a little scratchy, but it was delicious. The fruit salad was so sweet; she suddenly remembered the baby. He was now about two years old, giggling as he ate the fruit. Alice knew that she had stopped eating, and tears rolled down her face. "Alice? Are you okay?" Valerie asked as she reached out for Alice's hand.

Alice looked at her and struggled to stop the sobbing, "I had a baby, I know it. I have this vivid memory of him." Valerie put her arm around Alice, "Don't worry, Alice. I will try to help you get all the answers. You will not be alone." Alice watched Valerie's face; she seemed very sincere in her eyes and smile. Alice calmed down and finished her meal. "Valerie, do you think I am Alice?" "Of course, as long as I have known you, Dr. Alexander did have to fill me in on your history, but there is no doubt about it." "Valerie, did he tell you if we had a baby? Did he die?" Alice pleaded, praying that he was not dead. "Look, Alice, you should rest. I am not sure why you have this memory, but there is no baby as far as I know." She was trying to keep Alice from panicking. Valerie continued, "Why don't you lay back and rest. What made this memory come back to you? Go ahead, tell me what you recall."

Alice felt her heart jump with glee. "Valerie, I keep dreaming of this baby boy. He is so beautiful and tiny, and I feel like he looks like me. He smiled at me, and I looked at him as I held him. I also saw him when he was about two years old. We were eating fruit. He was giggling, and so was I. I can smell his scent; I brushed his forehead and still feel him in my arms." "Is it possible that I have someone else's memory?

Can this be someone else's child? Is it a nephew?" Alice looked at Valerie, who was at a loss for words. Finally, Valerie spoke with much caution, "Alice, if this memory is not real. Do you believe in ghosts? Is it possible that someone in this house had a child?" Alice looked at her like she had seen a ghost, "it is my baby, not some else's," she insisted. "Dr. Alexander has never told me about a baby, Alice," Valerie continued, "do you believe in ghosts?" Alice thought for a moment, "I don't know. Maybe I do need to rest." At least this would give her time to dream about this beautiful baby. Not having to answer any more questions would be good too. She closed her eyes and drifted off to sleep. It felt good to think that she had someone on her side who would look out for her and listen.

Valerie watched Alice and wondered if a baby was haunting her. Maybe she did have a baby that died. 'What if he was not Alice's? Maybe she remembered a relative's baby. She recalled how the doctor would sit and talk to Alice. Dr. Alexander always spoke to Alice while she was in her coma and would tell her about their lives. Maybe he was just being practical, knowing that she would have memory loss and need help remembering. It was very odd but logical.'

Valerie recalled that one day when she had walked into the room, Dr. Alexander was holding Alice's hand. He was telling her about their wedding day. She was dressed in a beautiful white gown, and all their friends were present. They had a small reception at the town hall with a band that played their song. He had recalled that as they danced and gazed into each other's eyes, they repeated their vows. 'I always promise to love and hold you, in sickness and health, poverty or wealth, until death does us part.' He had said, 'My darling, I will be here for you. I promise to be patient with your recovery. I love you more than life.' He sounded sincere and loving, and she felt like she had walked into something so private that she hurried out of the room. When she had returned an hour later, he was still holding her hand but had laid down his head on her arm. She had quietly worked around him, taking Alice's pulse and temperature.

Valerie remembered that Alice was crying one day not too long ago before she had awakened from the coma. She had wondered what made her cry. There were numerous times that Alice would be smiling and seemed so content. She wondered if these were the times that she was dreaming about this baby. Valerie had always admired that Alice never seemed to wince at the discomfort during her therapy sessions. 'She must be courageous,' she had thought. Valerie was always curious about coma patients and what they thought or felt. Valerie thought this might be a perfect study, but now she thought that all she wanted to do was ease Alice's pain.

Valerie dreaded telling Dr. Alexander that Alice had awakened and insisted that he not be disturbed. She knew who her employer was and what his instructions were, but she felt a sense of loyalty to her patient. Alice needed to see that she could trust Valerie for her to be effective in aiding Alice's recovery. She would just have to face the consequences.

Alice had fallen back asleep and looked so peaceful. Valerie noticed the time and knew Dr. Alexander would be walking in the door at any moment. Just then, he opens the front door. She turns and prepares herself. As he entered, he asked, "How is she doing?" "She is resting; she had quite an exhausting day," Valerie responded. Dr. Alexander was at his wife's bedside; he looked over at Valerie, puzzled. "Dr. Alexander, she woke up at noon and insisted that we not bother you. She had lunch and fell back asleep." "You did the right thing, Valerie. Was she still confused? Did her memory…." He asked but drifted off before finishing his question. "She could not remember anything. She was still confused; she didn't recognize the room or the cook." Valerie responded. He smiled at her, "She wouldn't have recognized either. You see, Janie was recently hired. This room is new to her; I bought a new house after the fire. I just couldn't take her back into the house where the accident happened." Valerie saw the sadness in his eyes and voice.

He sat at Alice's side all night, hoping to have a moment with her if she awakened.

The Envelope

3 KEEP ON SMILING

Frankie sat in class daydreaming. Mrs. Jones noticed that he was not improving in this department. When the bell rang at the end of the day, Mrs. Jones asked Frankie, "Frankie is your dad picking you up today?" "No, the sitter is supposed to be here, but he is getting off early today." He smiled a shy smile. "Can you take this home for him?" "Sure," he smiled, took the envelope, and ran out the door. Anne Marie was the sitter; she was in college and picked up the boys after school. She was nice but not someone that Frankie would have picked. Ann Marie was always busy with homework and calling her friends; Ann Marie didn't have time for Frankie and his problems. On the other hand, Samuel liked her because she was fun and flirty.

Samuel flew into the house; he was on a mission. He ran up to his room, closed and locked the door behind him. Frankie chased him, but he was much smaller and could not keep up with him. Anne Marie headed into the kitchen; she always made an afterschool snack for the boys. Ann Marie went into the pantry to get the peanut butter. She noticed yellow roses in a vase on the kitchen table. She smiled, she had never seen flowers in the house before, and they smelled so good. Next, she found the rice cakes and peanut butter. She also grabbed some apples, and these were Frankie's favorite. She always got a kick out of his smile when he ate his apple slices. As she called out to the boys to come down, she noticed that the front door was still open. Neither of the boys came down. Ann Marie called out again and headed towards the open door. She could see a dog sniffing around her car. Ann Marie walked out and looked around, but the boys were not there.

She was feeling a little panicked as she headed back inside. She had not noticed them leaving the house, but she was a little distracted with making their snack.

"Frankie? Samuel?" she hollered. They had always answered or come running when she called, "where could they be?" she wondered. "Frankie! Samuel!" she now screamed out their names with a sense of urgency. As she rounded the corner to run upstairs, the boys appeared on the stairwell. "Where were you guys? Why didn't you come down?" Samuel looked puzzled, "What's going on? We were upstairs getting some things together." Anne Marie headed back into the kitchen as she put the plates on the table for the boys. "It's your favorite, Frankie." He smiled a huge smile and smugly responded, "Well, that was yesterday's favorite, but I'll still eat it." Samuel gave him a quick smile and sat down. "OK, boys, who brought the roses?" Ann Marie asked. "I thought you did," Samuel stammered. "Frankie? What do you know about these flowers?" Anne Marie asked again. "Well, they are mommy's favorite," he answered. "Mommy always said she would always have them in her house." He added. "Maybe dad brought them," Samuel said. Frankie smiled and added, "I think mommy did."

Anne Marie always felt uncomfortable in the house. However, the comment made the hair on the back of her neck stand on end. She tried to shrug off Frankie's statement, and she did not want to have that kind of conversation with him. She changed the subject as quickly as she could. "What were you boys doing upstairs?" Samuel answered first, "Well, I am working on a school project." "I thought I was supposed to be helping you with homework?" Anne Marie questioned. "Well, it will take me a couple of weeks to do, so I thought I would just do it myself." Samuel hoped that she would not push the issue. "May I see it?" she asked. "Maybe next week," he insisted. "Frankie? What were you doing?" He lit up as he spoke very slowly, "I was talking to mommy." Anne Marie was now very fearful that she would be having a conversation that would be uncomfortable. "What do you mean, Frankie?" She prayed that he would just drop it. Instead, Frankie smiled and shrugged his shoulders. Samuel's eyes were wide with amazement, "Frankie, how were you trying to talk to mommy?" "Never mind, I don't want to talk about it. I'm hungry. When will daddy be home?" Samuel reached for Frankie's hand, "Little brother, please tell me." Samuel's eyes welled up with tears, "Please." Frankie pulled away and looked at his big brother, "Who do you think brought the flowers?" "Daddy, he must have brought them in while we were in school." Frankie smiled ear to ear; he shook his head, "No, silly, mommy did."

Anne Marie had no choice but to walk out and call Seth. "Seth? Are you almost home?" she asked. "Is everything ok?" he asked. "Yes, but Frankie needs to talk to you and says he is starving. Shall I start something, or are you bringing dinner?" "Thanks, but I thought we could go out to dinner tonight," Seth answered. "Can you let the boys know I will be home in a few minutes, and we can discuss what we want for dinner?" Seth continued, "are you sure you are, okay? You sound funny." "Yes, I will let them know. They will be so excited." She said as she hung up the phone. She took a deep breath and started back into the house.

Frankie was smiling as he gazed out into the yard. He watched his mommy; she was working out in her flower garden. She always wore her funny hat and one of her purple dresses. She sang to her flowers and giggled because she thought it was funny. Frankie leaned toward the glass and slowly put his hand out to touch her. She looked over at him and waved, 'I love you.' Frankie waved back and smiled.

"Keep on smiling," he said. Samuel looked over at his brother and saw him gazing out. "I miss her too," he said. "Look," Frankie said, pointing outside. "Samuel, look, can you see her?" Samuel thought he did, but he knew he didn't, "I think I want to." "Look, Samuel, she is by the roses." Frankie pointed again, "I think I can," Samuel stated as he stared at what he believed was his mommy.

"Frankie, how long have you seen her?" he asked. "Always," Frankie whispered. Neither changed their vision for fear that she would be gone. Samuel put his hand on Frankie's shoulder. "Keep on smiling," Frankie whispered. "As long as you keep smiling, mommy will stay with us. If you frown or cry, she disappears." Samuel looked on, trying hard to keep smiling but feeling like crying. Samuel couldn't believe his eyes. He did see his mommy. She was wearing her favorite hat, she had numerous, but this one was special. Mommy had found it at an old rummage sale; she said it belonged to the lady who was our city's founder. Mommy had told us that she felt like she had time traveled when she was wearing the hat. Mommy felt connected to times of old, back in the frontier days. Dad had always teased her and said that she was too gullible and that she would probably buy oceanfront property in the desert. They always giggled about this, and she would say, "Well, at least I would have the best land in the desert!" She was always laughing and smiling.

Anne Marie walked into the house and called the boys as she came into the kitchen, "Your dad will be here in a few minutes. Where do you guys want to go for dinner? Boys? Frankie? Samuel?" The boys heard Anne Marie, but not wanting to turn, they responded in unison, "I want to stay home." "What are you looking at?" she asked. "Nothing," they again answered in unison. "Come on, let's clean up, boys." She urged them to help, but neither boy moved. "Your dad will be here any minute. Come on now and help clean up." Nothing made them move; they were unwilling to give up this precious moment.

Seth opened the door and called out to the boys, "Hey guys, I'm home! Hey, where is everyone?" Anne Marie slowly walked towards the boys and looked out the window; she could not see what had their attention. She turned as Seth walked into the kitchen. She shook her head and said, "They have been gazing out for a few minutes, and I can't get them to look away." Seth walked toward the boys. He asked, "Hey guys, what are you looking at?" The boys did not move or answer. Seth walked up behind them and looked outside but saw nothing. He placed his hands on their shoulders and shook them. "No, daddy!" Frankie cried, "Mommy, please don't go!" Frankie put both hands on the window, trying to reach out. "Mommy!" he screamed. Samuel turned to look at his dad, tears welling up, and threw his arms around him. Frankie continued to call, "Mommy! Mommy!" Seth gathered Frankie in his arms and looked at Anne Marie for answers, but she was in tears too.

Seth tried to comfort the boys, but there would be no comforting tonight. They were no longer hungry or interested in going out for dinner. The boys were so upset that they sat up all night crying and calling out for their mom. Seth thought it would be best for the boys to sleep with him. After they had cried themselves dry, they sobbed until their voices were so hoarse that the sound was gone. They finally slept from exhaustion. Seth was at a loss as to what had triggered this. He lay between the boys with each in an arm. Seth eventually drifted off to sleep when he realized that he could smell roses. Seth opened his eyes and looked around. He had left on the light and felt that he would not be able to sleep if it was on. He forced his eyes shut and attempted to drift off.

He would be staying home tomorrow; it was a good thing he was the boss because they would not have made it these last two years with him missing so much work. He closed his eyes and prayed, 'Thank you, God, for my two wonderful boys. Keep my beautiful wife Frances Grace safe from harm. Keep my business strong. Give me the strength to help these two beautiful blessings until their mommy can come home. Thank you for Anne Marie; give her the strength to deal with days like today. Thank you for family and friends but keep them from pushing me too much. Thank you for Frances Grace. Bring her home safe and sound. Amen.' His prayer was very similar every night. Tonight, was not the first night this thing happened, but it was the worst.

The boys usually calmed down within a couple of hours, but it was almost three in the morning tonight. The boys had a special connection with their mom that not all children have. He had to stay strong and be supportive of his precious little ones. He believed that she was trying to reach out as hard as it sometimes was.

4 NIGHTMARE BEGINS

Seth was at work, and the boys were in school when this nightmare came to pass. Frankie and Samuel had been waiting for a very long time, it had been an hour, and their mom did not pick them up. The boys had gone into the office and asked to call home. The school attendant lady, Carolyn, had attempted to contact the house and France Grace's cell phone, but there was no answer. They then tried to call Seth at work, but the receptionist had forwarded the calls to the answering service due to the entire office's conference meeting. The answering service did not page Seth due to human error.

The school finally called the police; they took the boys home when they arrived, but no one was there. They found a fresh batch of cookies on the counter, the door was ajar, 'Buddy' their shepherd mix, was in the front yard, and the boys were troubled. Frankie started crying, and Samuel looked everywhere for his mom. When the police asked the boys about their mom, Frankie said, "Mommy promised to pick me up and said we would decorate some cookies. She never breaks a promise to me." Samuel kept very quiet; he had a terrible feeling. This horrible nightmare still had not ended. Seth remembered that day like it was yesterday, and the pain he felt was still very fresh.

Seth finally drifted off to sleep. Most nights, he dreamt the same dream. He was at work when the call came from the police department. 'Mr. Laurel, we need you to come home.' He had dropped everything and rushed home. There were police cars everywhere; as the officer met him, he asked, "Mr. Laurel, have you seen your wife or heard from her?" Those words made him numb and nauseous, and he immediately asked about his boys. "What do you mean? She should be home with the boys. Where are my boys?" Seth forced his way into the house. He called out for his wife and boys, but neither answered. An officer tried to hold him back, but Seth pushed through into the living room. He was trying to get answers, but no one was talking.

All the police wanted to know was if Seth knew where his wife was. 'Tell me where my family is' he was struggling with an officer. He was led into the family room and sat down. He was hearing them talk but was not retaining the information. He felt that he was not in his own body, and the world was spinning around. There was a terrible pounding in his head. He heard an officer say, 'do you understand?' Seth did not understand anything; his mind was racing with thoughts of his family. 'Where's my family?' he asked, tears rolling down his face. Then he heard someone say, 'the boys are safe. They are at the police station.' Seth wanted to go to them immediately, but the officers had more questions.

He told them that he would answer all their questions, but he needed to see his boys. As they drove him to the station, his thoughts were on his wife. 'Where could she be?' She had never missed picking up the boys; Francie was so punctual. Nothing would ever keep her from being there for them. 'Dear Heavenly Father, please keep her safe from all harm and bring her home.' He prayed this over and over until he reached the police station. He ran inside and held his boys. They all cried and held each other; he reassured them that the officers were looking for their mommy and that she would be okay. They gave him a chance to call family to pick up the boys. He was questioned for 12 hours and finally released. They asked ridiculous questions like: Does your wife have any enemies? Was she having an affair? Are you having an affair?

He knew they needed to find out everything they could, but if they had known her, they never would have asked such things. They had gone through the entire house, phone records and questioned neighbors with a fine-tooth comb but had no leads. No one saw anything or heard anything. Everyone that knew Frances Grace knew that she would never leave on her own. This case was of foul play, which was immediately the presumption by everyone involved. The police could not find her; there was no trace. Every night was the same at home, lots of crying and screaming. Seth wished he could awaken from this nightmare. He had taken a polygraph test and passed with flying colors. Police finally had taken Seth off the suspect list.

Frankie and Seth had similar but just little different nightmares.

Frankie dreamed so many different nightmares. As he drifted off to sleep, he dreamt they had breakfast and discussed the day. Mommy said, "Don't forget we are decorating cookies today." She was preparing for Valentine's Day and had decorated a few. "Mommy, promise you won't decorate them yourself." Frankie pleaded. She laughed and wrinkled her nose, "I don't know, maybe I should get it all done, and then we can play games after school." she teased him. "Mommy?" he whined. She was laughing, "Okay, okay, I promise! I will pick you up right after school, so be ready to make a frosting mess." She was smiling at both boys. They finished eating their breakfast and left for school. She pulled up to the school and walked them to the school guard so they could cross by themselves. He would turn and see his mommy waving, 'I love you.' Frankie turned before going out of sight, and Mommy was waving and blowing kisses.

The day was uneventful, but he got a tummy ache after lunch, and his teacher had told him that he needed to stay unless he felt like throwing up. He did not feel like that, so he remained until the end of the day. While he was sitting and waiting for his mommy, he thought, 'mommy is never late.' He was trying to be patient but finally asked Samuel, "Why do you think mommy isn't here?" "Frankie, she probably just had to pull the final batch of cookies out of the oven." Samuel offered.

It was now starting to get dark, so they went inside to call home. Carolyn, the friendly office lady, had tried to call, but no one answered. She looked apprehensive and asked them to wait by the principal's door. The policeman came and said that he would take them home. Frankie was very excited to be riding in the police car. He looked at everything, but Samuel was very quiet.

When the car stopped in front of the house, they saw Buddy in the front yard. He was not supposed to be there. Samuel ran over and grabbed him, and he led him to the backyard. The police officer looked at Frankie and said, "Frankie, you stay here." Samuel went into the house and came out quickly, he was telling Frankie something, but he did not understand him. Frankie was feeling very sick and sat down in the front yard. Samuel ran to him and said, "I couldn't find mommy inside."

The police officer was calling someone in his car. Then he started asking lots of questions, 'Where do you think your mom could be? Where is your dad? Do you know who she may be with?' All the questions were making Frankie dizzy. The police officer asked the boys to sit in the car. They saw neighbors coming over to see what was going on. More police officers arrived, talking to everyone who came over. They were knocking on doors and talking to neighbors. Then the officer came back and said he was taking them to the police station.

Frankie started crying, and Samuel asked, "Are we under arrest?" The officer shook his head 'no.' Then Samuel asked, "Why can't we stay in our house?" The officer answered, "We can't get a hold of either your mom or dad so we will take you to a safe place." "Our house is safe," Samuel insisted. When they arrived at the station, the boys were taken to a special room, and a nice lady brought soda and cookies. Frankie had not stopped crying and kept asking for his mom and dad. Frankie kept saying that his mommy would be waiting at the house and that he needed to see her. Frankie was so upset that he sobbed and cried, screamed, and howled, 'Oh mommy, I need you to come home now! Let me see my mommy!' Frankie looked at Samuel and thought that he was so brave.

Frankie tried to stop crying, but he missed and needed his mommy. Both boys heard their dad and ran to the door. Their daddy held them tight, and they all cried together. Seth told both boys, "don't worry, mommy just got lost. She will be with us real soon. She loves you both so very much. The police are looking for her and trying to do everything they can to help her come home." He then was asked to call someone to pick up the boys because they needed to talk to him. Frankie immediately put up a fight and started to cry again. His daddy reassured him that he would be home soon and would check in on them both.

Samuel drifted off to sleep every night after his prayers. He always had the same nightmare; he sat with his brother, waiting for his mommy. Frankie asked Samuel, 'why isn't mommy here?' but Samuel didn't have any answers. He was worried; mommy was never late. She was the one that was always early and waiting for the boys to get out of school. Sometimes, while he was in class, he would glance out the window and see her sitting in the car, singing, and smiling.

That day, when she didn't come to pick them up, he looked out and wondered if she was taking out the last batch of cookies. He had smiled at the thought of her pulling out the cookies and hanging up her apron. She had her favorite apron on, which the boys had given her for Christmas the year before she went missing. It had a picture of the boys making goofy faces; she loved it and wore it.

When the boys decided to go inside and call home, Samuel knew that something was very wrong. The phone was ringing too much, and when mommy did not answer, he felt very panicked. Then everything was a whirlwind. The police came and took them to the house, the dog was out in the front yard, and mommy was not home. The police talked to the boys, but Samuel could not hear anything. His head was pounding, and he felt like he would throw up. Frankie was crying, and he was feeling like crying too. Samuel didn't know what to do for him. He was feeling awful, too but knew he had to keep it together so his little brother would not lose all hope. When Samuel finally saw his dad at the police station, he felt much better and cried. He wasn't crying because he was sad but feeling so relieved that finally, he saw one of his parents. Samuel had been so worried that something had happened to both of his parents. Samuel was so concerned about his mommy and prayed that she would be home by the time they got there.

When the police had asked his dad to stay longer; they requested to have his relatives pick them up, he started to cry, and the tears just ran down his face. He felt so alone again, unsure if he could leave and be alone. The boy's Auntie Rae had picked them up, she was mommy's sister, and they were so much alike. Auntie Rae wanted to take them to her house, but the boys insisted on going home, 'what if mommy is there?' Frankie asked. Samuel said, 'we have to be there when she gets home.' Auntie Rae knew that she would not win this fight, she drove to the house, and it was dark and very spooky.

As Samuel cried himself to sleep, he dreamt about his mommy that frightful night. He saw her taking out cookies from the oven, the doorbell rang, and when she went to the door, someone had taken her against her will. The man was dressed in black and had put something on her face, and she fell asleep. He then put her in his trunk. He was not very careful with her. Samuel was feeling very angry and scared for his mommy. He saw her head hit the car when he threw her in. Samuel wanted to reach out and choke him, but Samuel knew he was only dreaming.

Samuel awoke sweating and crying. Samuel was still awake when dad came home. He pretended to be asleep so he would not worry about him. Seth had sat at the edge of the bed. He was crying and kissed Samuel's forehead. Seth whispered, "Don't worry, sweet one, I will find your mommy and bring her home." When he had left Samuel's room, Samuel just cried and cried and cried until he was so numb that he could no longer cry. The tears had dried up, and Samuel no longer had tears to shed. He feared that people would think he did not miss his mommy because he could no longer cry. Samuel thought about his mommy every day, and his tears would not come every day. When he woke up, he was crying but tearless. He would sob, and his heart would break every day. 'Oh, mommy, I miss you and need you every day. Please find your way home.' His body would go numb, his heart ached, and his throat would dry up and ache, his eyes filled with tears that never left. Finally, he would awaken with so much pain cutting clear through to his soul.

Every morning was the same for Frankie. As Frankie opened his eyes, he heard his mommy's voice, "I'm coming home, baby. I love you." He opened his eyes and looked up to heaven, "Dear Jesus, please let today be when mommy comes home. Amen." He jumped out of bed and ran downstairs, yelling, "Mommy? Mommy?" Seth would turn and say, "Good morning, little one. Did you say your prayers this morning?" "Yes, I prayed that today would be the day mommy comes home." He replied, "It will happen. I know it will." Frankie would sit down for breakfast, saddened that she was not there. Seth would always smile and nod in agreement.

Every morning was the same for Samuel. He would set his alarm to awaken before anyone else. Samuel would be up early and out in the garden when his dad and Frankie were downstairs. It was time for him to talk with mommy; he sat outside on her bench and could feel her presence. "Mommy, we all miss you. I know that you will come home when you can. Frankie is waiting for you to make him cookies. Auntie Rae brings cookies over, but he won't eat any. He says that no one makes his cookies as you do. Daddy needs you too, mommy. I can hear him cry at night. He does not know I am awake. I can't sleep at night because I worry that you are being hurt." He would share every event from the day before. He would spend as much time as was allowed before breakfast. He quickly learned that he had more time by getting his homework and backpack ready the night before.

Seth would awaken from his nightmare and reach for Frances Grace. Her pillow was always empty and cold. He felt lost and didn't know if he could go through his day. "Oh Francie, how can I get you back? I have looked everywhere; there is no sign of you. The boys need and miss you. Please, God, bring her back safe." He cried every morning, afternoon, and night. He did not believe he could go on but knew that he needed to for his boys. He would take a hot shower to mask the tears; the boys would always say he was burning up. He knew that he could not give up for their sake, nor for his own sake, neither.

The nightmare continued throughout the day. Frankie was always looking around the corner, looking for her. He would turn and look over his shoulder every few minutes. His teacher was very concerned about him; Frankie did not seem to be getting any better. She feared that he might be getting worse. The loss of a parent was tough for children, but Frankie was not dealing with the loss. He was waiting for his mommy to come back. To him, she was just missing. He knew that she had disappeared and got lost but knew in his heart that she was coming home. He thought that he would have to help her find her way home.

Samuel continued to look for his mom all day, every day. He would look behind doors, in dark rooms, hallways, and around every corner. Samuel knew he had to do his part to help find her. He looked in every car, truck, or van on his way home. He was constantly scanning to see if he could see her somewhere.

Seth's business was suffering from him not being there all the time. He spent half of his day looking for his wife. He went to every nearby town and looked at every hospital and shelter. He searched everywhere he possibly could. He was spending a few hours working to be home early for his boys in the afternoon. His team was trying to succeed, but Seth was the leader and knew everything about his business. His team needed him at work, but his kids and wife were more important. Finding his wife was so significant for him and his boys. She is out there, and we just need to find her. The nightmare continues.

5 DAY OF DECISIONS

Alice awoke bright and early, the sun was shining through the curtains, and she heard horses. She enjoyed that sound; it was a familiar sound. How Alice wished she could remember if they were her horses. Alice looked around the room and saw a handsome face but one that she did not remember. This man had called her 'Darling' just the other day; he seemed so concerned that she did not recognize him. He was the man she thought must be her doctor since he was wearing his lab jacket. 'If he lived here, why was he dressed like that?' she wondered.

She was afraid to awake him for fear of how he may react, and she did not want to talk to him right now. She was feeling sick to her stomach with fear of needing to figure out who she was and where this place could be. Maybe this was time to face the music and get some answers. She cleared her throat and softly spoke, "Hello? Are you awake?" She watched him, but he did not stir. She decided that she needed to reach out to him but was afraid to touch this stranger. She lifted her hand and placed it on his, and he startled and jumped. He was looking at her with amazement and tender eyes.

He asked, "Would you like something to eat? Are you hungry? Do you need a drink of water?" He squeezed her hand, but she pulled away. "I'm sorry," she apologized, "I am still trying to figure out who, why, where, and what's going on." He smiled and quietly spoke, "I'm your husband, and you have had a traumatic injury. It will take some time, but you will remember our lives together. May I get you something to eat?" Alice looked at him puzzled, "I am not hungry. I did eat some lunch yesterday." He smiled, "I'm glad. I hope the cook made your favorites. I had left her a list of things you enjoyed eating." "Yes, she made a delicious sandwich and fruit salad. Did I know her before my accident?" she asked.

Jack was glad that he and his wife were talking without medicating her. He replied, "No, Janie is new. She came to work for us when I purchased this new house. I was afraid that it would be too traumatic for you to see the same faces at our home where the accident happened. I hope that is okay with you." "I do not remember anyone from before," Alice replied. "How long have I been here?" She asked. Jack explained, "Well, it's about two years since the accident, and about six months ago, the doctor thought it would be best to bring you home."

"I heard horses. Are those yours?" Alice asked. Jack smiled, "Those are our horses. You used to ride before this happened." "How many horses do you have?" Alice continued, "Are they all for riding?" Jack knew this would take some explaining, "Well, you have your favorites, and some are wild. You wanted to save the wild stallions, so you bought a dozen. We have someone to care for them, but you loved to be outside with them." "I think I remember loving horses," she struggled to remember, "I am not sure." Jack came closer to Alice, "Would you like to see them later today?" Alice was smiling at the thought of seeing the beautiful horses, "I would."

Jack walked over to the intercom and spoke to Janie, "Janie, could you please bring up some breakfast for us." Alice watched him and wished she could remember something, anything. Jack walked back to Alice and sat next to her. He watched her with amazement, "Alice, is there anything else I can answer for you?" Alice wanted a million questions answered but knew this was not the time. "No, I think I need to take it slow. I should walk around and see if anything refreshes my memory. Possibly the horses will help with my recovery. Is it possible to see my medical doctor so I can find out what my issues are?" "Well, I can fill you in." Jack quietly offered. Alice interjected, "I would like to speak to my doctor, and I hope it doesn't offend you." Jack nodded his head but wished she would allow him to do more.

Janie knocked and entered the room. She had prepared blueberry pancakes, easy over eggs, ham, and fresh fruit. It was quite a display, and Alice was very impressed. Alice did not remember if she liked these foods, but they smelled delicious. It had been so long since she had eaten food; an IV was not the same. She giggled at the thought of eating all this food. She suddenly felt famished. Jack watched her very closely, and he smiled when he heard Alice giggle.

As she took a bite, she realized that she loved blueberry pancakes. She gobbled up the blueberry pancakes and then took a bite of the ham, it was not as pleasing, but she did like it. However, when Alice tasted the eggs, she did not like them. They made her gag. 'Wow,' she thought, 'I have a gag reflex.' Jack looked at her quite surprised, "What's the matter? Don't you like the eggs? You used to eat them all the time." She smiled at him bashfully, "Maybe my taste buds have changed?" She most definitely loved the fruit; it was so sweet and pleasing to her palate. She wondered to herself how anyone could like eggs like that. It was such a distasteful and unpleasant texture. As Alice finished her breakfast, she realized that Jack had been watching her very quietly, making her uneasy. Alice squirmed in her bed, and it was time to get out and get some fresh air. "Why don't you show me around after breakfast." She quietly stated. His eyes lit up, and he smiled, "I would love to."

Valerie knocked and entered, "I'm sorry, am I interrupting? I can come back later." She stated. "No, please come in," Alice responded. "I would love it if you could help me get dressed. I would like to go out and get some fresh air." Valerie entered and started to pull out some dresses. As she showed Alice the dresses, Alice shook her head 'no.' She did not like anything in the closet. Jack got up and excused himself. He looked apprehensive. "Is there anything different in there?" Alice asked Valerie. Valerie shrugged her shoulders and continued to look for something to please Alice. Valerie pulled out every dress, and none pleased Alice. Valerie then pulled out blouses and skirts. Again, nothing seemed to appease Alice. Then Valerie pulled out a pink skirt and a white blouse. Alice's eyes lit up, "yes, that is what I will wear today. Thank you, Valerie! That is exactly what I feel like." Valerie eyed Alice: she wondered if these were all new clothes that Dr. Alexander had purchased.

Valerie helped Alice undress, and as Alice saw her body for the first time, tears filled her eyes. She asked for a mirror. Valerie attempted to explain to Alice that her scars were from the accidental fire, but Alice didn't listen. She reached for the mirror near her bed. Valerie attempted to stop her, but Alice gave her a look that made Valerie realize there was no stopping her. Alice's eyes filled with tears as she gazed upon her scarred face. Alice did not recognize this woman, 'who am I?' Alice wondered. She saw that her eyes were kind and had sympathy for the vision of the woman that looked back at her in the mirror.

Alice put down the mirror and slid her hand over her body, inch by inch, centimeter by centimeter. She ran her fingers over every scar that she saw. Alice closed her eyes and ran her fingers between the scarring, and her heart broke. Tears flowed down her cheeks, her heart broken, and her fingers numb from the sensation. Alice gathered her thoughts and took a deep breath, "I am ready for my shower." Valerie quietly helped her off the bed and into the bathroom. Alice started to shake from her anxiety. She looked at Valerie and attempted a smile, but it was challenging to keep from shaking. Finally, Valerie asked, "How warm?" Alice shrugged, "Hot? Maybe?" she honestly had no idea. Valerie warmed up the shower and reached in to see how hot it was, "If it's too hot, it may burn you. Let's start a little cooler, then warm it up if you prefer." Alice nodded in agreement. When Alice stepped into the shower, she asked Valerie to step out.

Alice started sobbing uncontrollably. She held on to the wall for support and then sat on the floor, continuing to cry. Alice didn't want Valerie to witness her breakdown, but now it was time to get it together and finish showering. As she washed, the tears flowed with no end in sight. As Alice shampooed her hair, she found some scars on her head. 'What happened to me?' she wondered to herself. 'Why did this happen to me? Oh, Lord, give me the strength to carry on.' Alice cried, "Dear Jesus, please give me the strength to find myself. Help me to remember my life and to feel fulfilled. Help me to accept what I am today." She prayed out loud.

Valerie knocked at the door, "Mrs. Alexander, are you okay? Is there something I can do for you?" Alice wanted to be left alone but knew that was not an option. "Can you please get my towel?" She asked. Valerie entered and grabbed the towel from across the room. As she walked toward Alice, Valerie saw that Alice had been crying. Valerie wrapped the towel around Alice, held her close, squeezed her, and smiled. "It's okay to call me Alice. You know that?" Valerie smiled and responded, "You know you can lean on me whenever you need to." They smiled at each other without another word. Valerie helped Alice to dress.

Alice was struggling with being a stranger in this house. She looked around the house as she was being wheeled around by

Valerie. Suddenly Alice felt that she needed a little space. "Can we head to the stables? I want to see the horses." Valerie ensured that she avoided all the holes, but it was still a rough ride to the stables. Alice took a deep breath, enjoying the fresh air. "Valerie, have you ever seen a more beautiful sight?" Alice continued, "Oh my goodness, these are beautiful creatures." Tears started to roll down her face again. "I don't remember any of these horses. Why can't I remember?" Alice asked. Valerie reached out a hand, "Come on. Maybe if you touch them, you may recall something." "I feel afraid," Alice answered. "You are a natural with animals," Valerie continued, "I can see it in your eyes." Alice smiled, "What if I scare them with my," she paused, "condition."

The stable hand, Erik, walked up just as Alice was standing up. "You will help them; they have missed you very much." Alice turned to face Erik, "How do you know they missed me?" She asked. Erik smiled and quietly answered, "They tell me." Alice could see that he was a gentle, caring man. She immediately liked him. "What are their names?" she asked as they walked towards the horses. Erik looked at her puzzled, "You do not remember Mrs. Alexander?" Alice shook her head no. "Mrs. Alexander, I am so sorry; I had not spoken to your husband. I did not know. I am so sorry." Erik stammered. "It's okay," Alice answered.

Valerie and Erik both held on to Alice as they approached the horses. Alice reached out her hand, and one of the horses came to her. He was huge, solid, and beautiful. "His name is King." Erik stated, "He is the biggest one. He was the one that alerted us to the fire. He saved your life." Alice reached out to him. He came right up to her and neighed. He put his face into hers and almost seemed to say, 'I am happy you are here.' Alice held herself up and hugged this beautiful animal. "King, thank you so much for saving my life. I hope you will be my friend. Correction, I hope that you will be my best friend. I am sorry that I do not remember you." King seemed to understand and nudged Alice with his nose. She giggled and leaned toward King, a gentle giant. Alice stepped away from King and suddenly felt faint. The stable started to spin, and Alice lost her balance.

Valerie and Erik immediately were upon her. They helped her to the wheelchair, and Valerie rushed her back into the house.

Alice knew that she had overexerted herself, but the fresh air felt good. Alice was disappointed that not even the horses brought her memory back. The good news was that she had a good cry and felt a little better. Alice lay in her bed, where she had been for the last six months, but she was awake and thinking this time about the fire, the horses, the fresh air, the food, Jack but mostly thinking about the precious baby. She knew with all her being that she had held that baby. This memory was the only memory that she had. There was nothing else that came to mind. The food was unfamiliar, the shower did not seem normal, and nothing was familiar but the baby. She could smell him, feel him close to her and hear him. He had such a sweet voice. This memory gave her comfort and peace. Alice closed her eyes and prayed, "Lord, I know this baby is mine. Please help me find him." Then, she drifted off to sleep.

6 THE BEGINNING

Seth sat in his bedroom, staring out the window. He remembered when he first saw her. They were in different high schools, and she was a few years younger, so he had not paid much attention to her. On the other hand, Francie always said it was 'love at first sight.' Francie's side of the story was that she fell in love the first time she saw him at a football game in 8th grade. Seth was athletic and played all sports, but it was at a track meet when he first remembered seeing her. He ran the hurdles and sprint events, and she ran distance events. Francie was a little social bug and knew everyone; she knew most of his classmates. Francie went out for track but was not the fastest runner or the best jumper. She loved to run but just for fun. Most people would tell you that Francie did not have an ounce of competitiveness. She was just happy visiting with the kids from the other teams. Francie and her best friends were all social bugs. It was in April at a track meet that she saw Seth. He was on the bus talking with his friends.

Francie talked with Gayle, one of his classmates, when suddenly both the girls were running. Gayle had taken Francie's hat and ran into the bus, tossed the hat at Seth, and laughed. You see, Gayle knew that Francie was head over heels for Seth. Gayle intended to get the two to talk. Francie ran onto the bus, and to her surprise, there sat Seth wearing her hat. She looked at Seth, then at Gayle. She was at a loss for words which was very unusual for her. Francie gave Seth a shy smile and quietly asked for her hat, "May I have my hat please?" He smiled and shook his head at Gayle, "I wondered if this was something I wanted to wear as a fashion statement." He leaned over and handed her the goofy-looking hat. He noticed that she lit up as he gave her the hat. He saw her dark brown eyes that seemed to sparkle and a smile that brightened the bus. Gayle was grinning as Francie glared at her and stomped off the bus. She was so embarrassed by this incident. At one of Seth's events, he noticed that this young lady sat behind some of his friends, watching him from a distance. He had to smile when he saw the goofy hat.

Seth was busy with life, so he didn't think about that little girl again. At least not for some time, and then one day, many years later, she happened into his life. They met at a social event, and he couldn't take his eyes off this beautiful, poised young woman. She stood talking to his best friend, Lee. As he made his way toward her, he wondered if she was there with someone else. Francie had her back to him and didn't know that he was on his way to speak to her. She was surprised to see Seth. They spoke briefly that night, but he intended to sweep her off her feet. Instead, he watched as she talked to others at the party. She so elegantly walked from one guest to another. He noticed how she smiled and laughed as she visited with guests. She was wearing a purple dress and heels. She looked so confident, and everyone greeted her with a kiss on the cheek as she approached them.

Seth never once saw her with another man, so he decided to get her number. He was not the kind of man that walked up to ladies and got phone numbers, but this young lady was not like most. As he approached her, he started to worry, 'what if she doesn't give out her number to old friends?' he wondered. 'Well then, I will just have to get it from someone we both know.' He convinced himself that it was possible. "Hello again, Francie," he managed. She turned and faced him, "Hello Seth, are you enjoying yourself?" "Yes, I am. This is a fantastic party. Are you in charge of it all?" he asked. She giggled, "No, but I know who is in charge. I just helped with the food and was allowed to attend." "You catered this event?" he asked in awe of the accomplishment. "My friend has a catering business, and I help out." She added, "Here, try these." As she handed him a tasty-looking morsel, Seth looked at it and took a bite, "Wow, what is it? It is delicious." Francie smiled, "I call it, A little taste of heaven. One night, I looked for something to eat and found some chocolates and carrots. I put them together, and there you have A little taste of heaven. Of course, there are other ingredients, but I can't give that away."

Seth shook his head in approval, "look, the reason I came over, I was hoping to get to your number and hopefully take you to dinner some time." Francie smiled, "well, I don't give my number out to strangers." Seth immediately added, "The good thing is that I am not a stranger. We have spoken before many years ago." She slipped her hand into her pocket, located near her hip, and pulled out a little card, "This is my business card, and you can usually reach me at this number." She turned and walked away without another word.

He watched her walk away with amazement. 'How could someone so elegant and beautiful not be married' he wondered. He watched her for the rest of the night, keeping his distance so as not to scare her. He mingled with the other guests but never took his eyes off her. Finally, towards to end of the night, he looked at the business card. He was shocked to see that it was a catering business card. 'A Little Taste of Heaven' was the name of the business. He smiled to himself; she is modest enough not to boast of her business, a very clever young lady. It was a stunning card, different shades of purple, and there was a pink flower in the corner. He had never seen this flower before, but he would be looking to see what it was.

Francie played hard to get and avoided his calls. For a week, he called once a day and sometimes twice. Finally, one day he showed up at her apartment with flowers and planned to invite her to dinner. Francie opened the door and was shocked to see Seth standing there in his blue jeans, T-shirt, and a bouquet of daisies. He was muscular and dark-skinned. He smiled, "Hello Francie, may I come in?" "I'm sorry, I don't normally allow strangers in my house." She smiled and opened the door wider. She stood in the doorway wearing shorts and a T-shirt.

"These are for you," Seth handed her the flowers. "Thank you! They're beautiful," she replied, "Please come in." Seth stepped in and removed his shoes. She watched him closely, "Won't you have a seat?" she motioned to the living area. "Let me put these in some water, please; make yourself comfortable." "I apologize for showing up unannounced, but I have left numerous messages in my defense." Seth stated. "I'm glad you came; may I get you something to drink?" she offered. She returned from the kitchen with a couple of glasses of water. They chatted for hours, and he thought he might as well ask the question. "Would you do me the honor of going to dinner with me tomorrow?"

The date he set was the very next day, Valentine's Day. Francie was surprised and clumsily answered, "Are you sure?" He smiled and said, "I did drive two hours to ask you since you haven't been returning my calls." "I have been so very busy," she replied. "Surely, you must have had a moment?" She enjoyed the torture, "I had to study, sleep and work." "Sleep?" he asked. "Of course!" she replied. "Now, why would anyone need to sleep?" he inquired. "I require ten hours of sleep to retain all the knowledge I am absorbing during my busy day." She was teasing him.

"Well, I traveled two hours to inquire about tomorrow night. So, are you free?" Francie thought for a moment, "Hmmm, let me see. I have classes then at the library and work until 10 pm. I do need my beauty sleep. So, no, I don't think I am available." She said with a grin. Seth smiled back at her, "Well, I guess I will ask my girlfriend to go instead." Her eyes widened, "How dare you, sir, invite a lady to another's night." Seth was grinning from ear to ear, "Well, you know, I thought if I could have just one night to see if you were worth my time. Maybe then, I could consider traveling more often to the city." Francie knew she was in deep trouble. She had not anticipated the response; she knew this man would give her quite the fight. But, on the other hand, she was impressed with the banter.

Valentine's Day. He was so excited and wondered if she was just as enthusiastic as he. He had no idea that she, on the other hand, was wishing she had never agreed to a date. She was so nervous. She had dreamed of this day since the first day she had seen him the football game. Francie liked to tease him, she always told the story of how she had fallen in love with him, and it was love at first sight for her but not for her knight in shining armor. Francie had dreamt of him every night and knew that she would marry her knight in shining armor one day. Although they had not had contact in years, she thought of him constantly. Since the night they met at the social, he thought of her every day, every hour, and every minute and fell head over heels in love with her. She was a brilliant, kind, strong-willed, funny, happy young lady.

Valentine's Day was date night. Seth drove up to her apartment, and as he walked up to her door, he could hear her music playing. She listened to country music; even that did not make him turn and run away. Seth did not like country music; as a matter of fact, you could say he despised it. He wondered if she would be ready as he knocked on the door. The door opened, and there she stood, gorgeous in her red dress. She smiled, "wasn't sure you were coming?" she teased. He did not enjoy being teased, but her smile made it okay. He responded quickly with a smirk, "Why wouldn't I come? I asked you out tonight." She giggled, "Well, it sure took long enough, don't you think?" She invited Seth in for a moment. Then, she turned to the hall closet and pulled out a white sweater. Seth quickly stepped forward and helped her with the sweater. She smiled and slipped into her sweater. The weather was nice, but evenings were always a little chilly.

The drive to the restaurant was a little quiet. Francie started first, "Say something." Seth smiled and replied, "You say something." They laughed, and the ice was broken. Francie started with, "How was your drive here, my knight in shining armor?" Seth laughed, "Well, the stallion was a little slower than I anticipated.

He needed a drink before arriving here. He galloped some and broke out into a dead run when he smelled the roses out in front of your house." Frances continued to toy with him, "Hopefully, he didn't eat all of them; those are my prize roses." "No, just the ones in the front yard." Seth teased back. Francie let out a giggle that made Seth smile.

The reservation was at an Italian restaurant called "Mio Amore." Seth had requested the best table, so they sat in a corner away from others. He had spent some time planning and brought unique flowers to the restaurant before picking her up. Seth had special ordered, mauve-colored roses a week before, anticipating that Francie would be available. He had hoped and prayed that she would not decline the invitation.

As they enjoyed their meal, they chatted about everything. Hours seemed only to be moments. They discussed life since high school, college, careers, and family. Both came from large families, she had eight siblings, and Seth had thirteen. She was living on her own, which her folks hated. They thought Francie should live at home since she wasn't married, but she had to live her own life, not her parents. She was studying medicine with a dream to help children. Seth was working as an engineer and wanted to start his own company. She even admitted that she would love to have a dozen children. She laughed as she spoke of little children filling the house with their giggles and little feet running all over.

Francie enjoyed life more than anyone he had ever met and was always smiling and laughing. Seth knew that this young lady was the one he wanted to spend the rest of his life with. He knew that he did not want to leave this beautiful lady again. Seth whispered, "Will you marry me?" Francie didn't miss a beat, "Why, sir, are you sure you are asking the right girl? I thought your original plans were with your girlfriend?" He smiled and continued quite seriously, "Frances Grace, I know it is sudden, but you are all I have thought about since the social. I can't stop thinking of you; your giggle makes me smile, and your laugh makes me laugh. Would you please do me the honor of marrying me?" as he dropped down to one knee. Francie was filled with such emotions that tears streamed down her face, "I will," she whispered. Everyone in the restaurant applauded. The owner was an old friend of Seth's and brought out wine for everyone in the place. Seth had invited his closest friends to witness this wonderful event. What a beautiful night that was.

They had a small ceremony. Seth didn't like dressing up, so Francie, the kind, thoughtful, loving lady she was, stated that she didn't need a big wedding. Instead, she made her wedding dress which she had been dreaming of for years. The dress was white with lace and ivory beads, making her look like royalty walking down the aisle. She wore her grandmother's veil. Seth watched her closely to make sure she didn't turn and run away. Francie glided down the aisle. Her train was long and adorned with tiny pink and purple roses. Behind her followed her four-year-old little niece. Little Becky was so cute; Francie adored her niece and insisted that Becky was the only one that she would have help her into her next chapter of life. Becky followed in her dress that her Auntie Francie had made just for her. It was pink with lace, and her hair was curly, so she looked like Shirley Temple with her dimples in full bloom.

They only had their parents, immediate family, and four best friends at their wedding ceremony. The reception, on the other hand, was not so small. The whole extended family and friends packed the town hall. More people than Seth had anticipated, but Francie knew precisely who she had invited. Francie made sure that every guest was made to feel special. She personally spoke and thanked each of them for coming to her life-changing event. The food was excellent, and everyone seemed to have a wonderful time. The night went well and without any complications; if there were any, Seth was not aware.

They had decided to wait on the honeymoon until she was done with school. Two years later, they planned to go away, but things would take a turn that would prevent them from going away, as with most well laid out plans. As the months approached and Francie finished her studies, she became pregnant and had a difficult time. Unfortunately, this precious life was not to be. She miscarried three months into the pregnancy. She named the baby Hope. Francie took it very hard; Seth was very disappointed but tried to keep up a positive outlook. Francie withdrew from friends and family. She never wanted anyone to see her sad, so she pulled away. She bounced back after a few months and started planning another honeymoon. She had reserved a cruise to the Bahamas. The weather was great, and the trip would be good for them both.

The Bahamas brought some much-needed time alone; it was serene and peaceful, and the sands were white with crystal blue waters. It was very relaxing to be away from everything, and Seth saw that he had his wife back in full bloom. Francie did every excursion available. She swam with dolphins, snorkeled, swam with the sea tortoises, ate everything in sight, and laughed again like she used to. "She seemed to enjoy the dancing probably the most," he thought.

Francie became pregnant on this trip. She was so happy, and she glowed like a firefly. Francie was being so careful with this pregnancy. She ate all the right foods, exercised, and saw her doctor. Francie was keeping close tabs on everything she felt. She did not want to tell anyone that she was pregnant until she knew that there would be no complications. Francie finally decided that it was time to announce to the family when she was five months along, and much to her surprise, the family, already knew that she was expecting. She couldn't believe that they had not approached her. They were trying to respect her privacy, which they usually didn't do, but because of the miscarriage, they didn't want to add to her stress.

Francie carried the baby to full term. She was so happy and never complained about the weight gain, the pain, or the discomfort. She was in heaven. They had agreed that his name would be Joseph if it were a boy. He came one summer night. The water broke, and Francie went into labor. Once at the hospital, the doctors monitored everything very closely.

Joseph was born at midnight; he was a healthy baby boy. Francie had had some complications, so they stayed a few extra days in the hospital. She held her baby boy as much as they would allow her. When they brought Joey home, he turned blue, and we rushed him back to the emergency room. He had only been home but a few hours. They discovered that he had a heart condition; Francie had held him until Joey took his last breath. She had sat in a rocker, tears flowed freely, and she kissed him often. She had begged God to spare his life, but God had other intentions for little Joey. He wanted this little angel to return to heaven, and his work was done here on earth. Unfortunately, Joey passed away that night. The funeral was difficult, and Francie was devastated. She cried for weeks, and she was inconsolable. Seth was worried about Francie, who was not looking good. She was not eating, drinking, or sleeping. Seth was so concerned that he took her to the emergency room. They immediately hooked her up to an IV and kept her for a few days. When she came home, she was looking so much better. She was even starting to talk again. Seth had prayed to God that He give her strength to carry on.

Francie had prayed for strength as well. She asked God to forgive her for being so unhappy about losing her babies. She had promised that if he would bless her with other babies and allow her to raise them, she would make sure that they followed His example. God being the wonderful God that He is, allowed her to have two beautiful, wonderful baby boys.

Francie was blessed twice and never stopped thanking God for her blessings. Francie was a loving, forgiving, passionate mother. She never let her boys want for anything. Francie was so attentive. She was the woman he had fallen in love with and even more.

She was his rock, his love, his soul mate, and the mother of his children. She was everything you could ever ask for in a life partner. She was strong, stubborn, and full of energy, loved life, and loved their babies with so much passion that you could see her glow. She kept her promise to God and raised them to love and trust Him.

She had stopped working when she became pregnant with Samuel. She did not have any complications with him. Having a July baby meant that she would not have to suffer through the hot summer months. Seth believed, the day Samuel was born, 'God opened the heavens and sent down the best little angel he had.' Seth adored his son and his wife. They felt so blessed and didn't seem that life could get any better. Both he and Francie were so thankful that they had a healthy baby. As Samuel grew, he was the spitting image of his father. He slept through the night from the first day home. He was everything that Seth could have ever asked for.

Francie was so excited one day when Seth had come home for lunch. She was glowing. She sat down with the boys and smiled. Seth asked, "What's going on?" Francie almost couldn't hold it in, "God has blessed us again!" she exclaimed. Seth smiled and hugged his wife. Francie talked about a hundred miles an hour, explaining what the doctor had said. She was about four months along, and this would be an October baby. As the months passed, she got so big but never complained. The summer months were the hottest that had been recorded. Francie did not complain once. She held on and treasured every moment. This baby was active, he kicked like a soccer player, and his little knuckles pushed through like a boxer. Francie lovingly said that there was a hurricane brewing inside. She would be giggling every time the baby kicked and punched. There were times that Seth walked into the house, and she and Samuel would be laughing and telling baby Frankie that he was winning. Samuel was so excited that they had a little brother for him. Samuel was the one that named his little brother. He thought that since he and his daddy shared the same first letter, then mommy and his little brother should share the first letter too. Samuel had thought of numerous names like Fabian, Freddy, Fernando, Flip, and Frankie. He liked Frankie best because it was almost like mommy's name.

Frankie's birthday was quite eventful. He wasn't about to make things easy. Francie went into labor two days before, and her water broke as she arrived at the hospital. Francie was immediately put on an ultrasound to check and see if there was enough amniotic fluid. Thank goodness there was because he threatened to come out but changed his mind. Francie never complained. She smiled through all the challenges, kept a positive attitude, and sang to her baby boy every day. Samuel was allowed to come and visit. He was so concerned about his mommy and baby brother. Frankie decided that it was time, so he gave a good contraction and started working his way out. The nurse had just been in the room and said it would be another couple of hours, but Frankie had other intentions. They called the nurse back, and as she walked in; Frankie was crowning. The nurse immediately called for the doctor, who was just stepping out of the hospital but ran back inside.

Frankie was a healthy little boy who made his mommy so happy. Francie was so pleased that she had two precious baby boys and a husband that adored her. Francie didn't want to let go of this tiny boy, but they had to take and clean him up. When he was returned to her arms, she was the happiest Seth had ever seen her. She had Samuel climb up onto the bed and see his little brother. They both looked so happy.

Seth was so blessed and felt that they had everything they needed. Two healthy little boys that adored their mommy, and she adored them. They went everywhere together. She never left them with anyone. Not that others couldn't watch or care for them; she never wanted to leave them behind. She took them along when she had doctor visits. The boys would sit in the reception area reading books. She took them grocery shopping, and they helped her find things she needed. She took them shopping, and they gave her their opinion on clothes and such.

When they first went off to school, she would sit all day outside, waiting for them to finish up. Finally, Seth had to put an end to the madness. He begged and pleaded that she come home or shop while the boys attended school. It took some time for her to be at ease with both the boys in school. She had her fears but slowly started to be able to go home and relax. Of course, she volunteered more than any other parent did, but it was good for her to see that everyone at the school was friendly and safe.

She gave up her medical career to be with the little blessings they had. She loved being a mother more than breathing. She always said, "No amount of money will ever keep me from my family." She just had not anticipated being ripped away from their lives.

What dreams they had. It seemed so long ago. Seth firmly believed Francie would never have left on her own; she loved her boys more than life. Yet, Seth never stopped looking for her. He looked over his shoulder every time he heard a giggle or a voice that resembled hers. Seth always looked in hospitals for the admission of a Jane Doe. He would spend hours at the parks, looking to see if he would see her. He also always looked down ravines, creeks, rivers, and around every corner.

7 ALICE'S HORSES

Alice quickly learned that the only time she would be alone would be to spend time with her horses. Someone was always with her when she was in the house, on the porch, yard, and car. She was feeling overwhelmed with all the information she was told.

Jack felt he had to try to help Alice remember. He feared that she might never remember if he didn't attempt to help her. Unfortunately, all the pictures of them had burned in the fire, so there were no pictures to try to jog her memory. Jack was a surgeon who was adopted, and he had lost touch with his adoptive parents early in life. This memory was very painful, so he didn't want to talk about how and why, so that subject was closed for discussion. Alice was an orphan and turned out into the streets at age 18. She had worked as a waitress while going to nursing school. Jack told Alice that she had been a nurse at the hospital where he used to work. They accidentally ran into each other in the hall as they rushed to their assignments. When he first laid eyes on her, he was astonished at her beauty and elegance. She had been so embarrassed about the incident that she avoided him for weeks.

Alice thought that she had had the loneliest life she could imagine. 'How could I have been so unfortunate as not to have any family?' she wondered, 'Why hadn't I been adopted?' 'Was I a horrible child?' She had so many questions and may never have answers. Yet, she wanted a family more than ever now.

Alice pitied Jack's life. She wondered why he had lost contact with the only family he had. Alice had no one and longed to have someone. As she watched Jack talking about their life together, she wondered if she had genuinely been in love with him when they married. Did she marry him from a need to have a family? Was she desperate or so lonely that she married this poor man? Was he desperate to have someone in his life? She had too many questions that she was afraid to ask.

Alice decided that she needed a break from all this memory jogging. "I think I would like to go see my horses. I feel well enough to go on my own if you are not offended?" She stated. Jack was a little surprised, "If that will make you happy, please go." He half wished she would not go without him. "I feel strong enough. Besides, Erik is out there, and he can help if I have trouble. And you are only a call away." She insisted.

Alice walked out of the house feeling free. She took in a deep breath and smelled the fresh air. The smell of fresh-cut grass seemed familiar, but she didn't remember mowing a lawn. It all looked so beautiful. The yard was very nicely trimmed, the hedges were cut just right, and the flower garden had a few flowers blooming, but she didn't recognize any of them. As she strolled toward the stalls, she could hear the horses neighing. It was a calming sound.

Alice approached the stalls and hesitated a moment. She suddenly had a slight fear of the horses. She knew if she felt fear, the horses would sense it. She took a deep breath, gathered her senses, and searched for every ounce of bravery. She walked closer, and her fear seemed to dissipate.

King was the first to greet her. "Hello King, how are you this lovely morning?" She reached out for him. "I was a little afraid at first, but now I am not!" She admired his strength and beauty. She made her way to the others and greeted them, although she didn't remember their names. Alice loved them all and hoped she would learn their names with time. She didn't realize that she had spent a few hours, and it was now lunchtime. Alice did not feel hungry but thought she had better take a break for lunch. She had every intention of returning just as soon as she could.

She sat down for lunch with Jack on the patio. He had the table set by the time she reached him. He had flowers in the middle of the table and requested fried chicken, mashed potatoes, green beans, biscuits, and sweet tea. Lunch was delicious, and Janie was an excellent cook. She had brought out some freshly baked pecan pie, and it was over the moon. Pecan pie was a favorite for her. As they sat and visited, he filled her in about the ranch. She learned that they owned everything up to the creek and as far as her eyes could see. The creek was a good half-mile from the house, and he warned her not to cross the creek because he had observed some bears on the other side of the creek. They had not made their way over to their property as far as he knew. He instructed her to stay away and not be alone if she wandered near the creek. They discussed the flower garden and its contents. She learned that it was not kept up just because he didn't want to put in flowers that she would not enjoy. The flower garden would be a project for her.

After lunch, she headed back to her horses. She helped Erik with feeding and brushing them. She worked on her horse etiquette and language.

Charlie Brown was a brown, scrawny horse who was very gentle. He had been rescued, and no one had ridden him yet. Erik said, "He is waiting for you, Mrs. Alexander." Black Beauty was just that; she was a beautiful black Choctaw mare.

She was young and was to become one of the riding horses. She was highly-strung, and yet she allowed Alice to touch her. Erik was surprised because she did not allow anyone near her. Eric struggled to bathe and brush her. Lola reminded Alice of a showgirl. She was beautiful and had the longest eyelashes she had seen on any horse. Lola was cream-colored and had a long mane with a star on her forehead. Alice wondered why she wasn't named Star instead. Leo resembled a lion due to his mane. Erik explained that every time he washed and brushed his mane, it was so full that he had to braid it to control it.

Buddy Boy was a rescued mustang. He was magnificent and loved to play. Buddy Boy must have thought he was still a colt. He was dark brown and muscular and looked like he was on steroids. Sadie was a black and white mustang mare. She had a white patch on her chest and down her face; she was playful and flirty. Sadie came up to Alice and nudged her a few times. She was beautiful and strong. Crystal was a white mustang with a long mane and long legs. She was swift and not very friendly. Annie was fat and probably ate all the others' food. However, she was gentle and seemed just a little lazy. Danny was a white stallion and was the third-largest horse. He was not too fond of anyone touching him but was a magnificent animal. Ephraim was a scrawny-looking creature that looked malnourished. Erik said that the veterinarian stated that he was doing fine but was just so skinny. Good Ole Boy was the oldest. He was a mustang that was on his last leg. He hobbled around and was very gentle. Spartacus was the second-largest horse and a most magnificent creature to behold. He was stunning in beauty, size, and a masculine stud. Lucky Day was just over two years old. He was found with the group but did not seem to have a mother. He was a spotted appaloosa.

For the most part, all the horses seemed to take to Alice. She was gentle and quiet when working with them. Alice forgot her troubles while she worked with the horses. She was eager to learn all about them and was hopeful that she would be riding them soon.

Alice had lost track of time, and it was suddenly dark outside. She looked at Erik quite surprised and smiled, "I guess I will be expected inside soon." She started to walk away from Erik when he added, "Mrs. Alexander, I hope you have had an enjoyable day today. I hope that you will be riding soon. It will be my honor to help you remember." Alice turned and smiled, "Thank you for your help, Erik. I truly appreciate it. I will see you tomorrow morning. Is six too early?" "No, that will be perfect. I let all the horses out for a run, and the sun should be rising at that time. That will be quite a sight for you." He returned the smile.

Alice walked back to the house and felt a sense of freedom and renewal. She was starting to think that she could survive anything. Alice was nervous about meeting her husband inside and having to explain her time with the horses and Erik. But however nervous, she felt the horses most helped her relax and feel like a natural person.

Alice opened the door and could smell something extraordinary. She walked through the house looking for someone, anyone but no one. Alice could hear voices but was not sure where they were. She finally spoke up, "Hello? Where is everyone?" Jack entered from the kitchen. "Hello," he said, "How was your day?" She smiled at him, "It was terrific. Sorry that I got so preoccupied with the horses. I lost track of time and just realized how late it was." "Well, that's the way it always was. I was used to that, and you were always so happy, so it never bothered me." "I know that I do feel good. There were no memories jogged, though." Alice felt guilty. "Don't feel bad; sometimes these things take time." He hoped that this would comfort her. "Dinner is almost ready if you want to freshen up before dinner." Jack offered, "You do smell a little rancid." He smiled.

Alice headed towards her room to change and freshen up. As she walked toward her room, she thought, 'How strange that she didn't spend much time with her husband.' She stopped at the door and slowly opened it, 'It feels strange walking into the room alone,' she thought. As she changed her clothes, she noticed her scarring again. She paused a moment and took a deep breath. She slowly felt the scars on her face. She was wondering what she looked like before the fire. 'No wonder the horses are nice to me; I must scare them.' She thought. Her hair was growing well, but there were spots where there was no hair, and she attempted to pull her hair over those spots but was not too successful. She could see from her eyes that she had a very caring, nurturing, and loving soul.

Alice followed her nose to the dining room. The table was set with beautiful china, "Is this a special occasion?" she asked Jack. He smiled, "Every day I have you alive is a special occasion." She returned the smile, but something made her uneasy. Alice quickly changed the subject, "What do we have for dinner tonight?" Jack turned to the table and explained that it was her favorite dish, Chicken Scaloppini with Prosciutto, Mozzarella, mashed potatoes, and Coconut cake. Alice looked at the fantastic plate, but nothing seemed familiar. As they sat and ate the meal, she thought, 'This chicken is disgusting.' But she lied not to upset her husband, "Oh, this is very delicious. I can't wait to dig into the cake; it smells so good." Somehow, she felt like she would prefer to start with dessert. She carefully asked, "Jack, did I ever eat my dessert first?" Jack looked quite surprised by the question, "Gosh, never! You always felt that the meal had to be eaten as it was supposed to; salad first, main course, then dessert." 'How sad,' she thought to herself. "It seems that you should enjoy a meal as you would like to enjoy it." Alice was hoping that this comment would not create a problem. Jack just smiled and remained quiet, "We can enjoy a meal anyway you would like." Alice could not keep her eyes off the cake as they finished their main course. She smiled and reached for the cake as she took her last bite. She tasted the cake and smiled from ear to ear. "Now, this is some dessert! Did I always love dessert?" she asked Jack. "Dessert is something that you thought every meal had to have." He replied. "So that is a 'yes,' right?" she asked him. Jack smiled, "Yes, that is a yes."

"Is this my recipe or someone else's? Was I a good cook? Did I like to cook?" Jack was not ready for the bombardment of questions, "Yes, it is your recipe, and you love to cook." "Jack, is there any literature about people that had been in comas, forgetting to do things that they love? I can't remember enjoying cooking, and the smells are unfamiliar to me." Alice had a worried look on her face. Jack had a sad look, "There are no guarantees, but let me reassure you that we will do everything possible to help you remember our lives together." Alice was finishing her cake but wanted another piece. She reached toward the cake but stopped herself. She didn't want to seem greedy.

She looked at Jack and started to talk about the horses. "It is hard to believe that they are so gentle with me. Why don't I remember buying, riding, or caring for them?" "Do you think that I will remember how to ride them? Do you think I am ready to ride?" Jack could not believe his ears, 'what was his wife thinking?' he was starting to fear that she would be pushing too hard. "Look, I know you want to get everything back to normal, but these things take time. If you rush into things, you may hurt yourself. You can't be thinking about riding any time soon. Are you listening to me?" Alice was not listening; she was trying to figure out how to remember. She thought that if she pushed herself into different situations, maybe she would bring back some memories. She looked at Jack, "I know you are worried about me, but I survived a fire and head trauma. What could be worse?" "Death," Jack forced out. Alice was surprised by his answer, "Why would you say that?" "Death is the worst thing that could happen if you fall off one of the horses. Head trauma you have already had, and we can deal with that, but I could not deal with losing you." Alice shook her head, "I promise not to ride tomorrow. Don't worry. I will be careful."

They had sat for hours in the living room, but there was not much conversation. Alice sat there thinking about the horses, and she wondered if he rode. "Jack, do you ride?" He suddenly looked up, "No, I have never been very interested in riding those animals. That is your thing." Alice looked a little puzzled, "Why did you get the horses for me?" Jack smiled, "You used to ride at the orphanage and always said you wanted to do it again. So, I thought they would be therapeutic. We got them just before the accident, so you hadn't ridden them." "That is so odd; did we do many things separately?" Alice hoped that she would be getting some good information. "Well, I was so busy with my medical practice that I just didn't have time to learn to do some of the things you enjoyed doing. Our schedules were very different." Jack explained. "It seems so sad that we didn't spend time together. Were we in love?" she asked. "Of course; we were the best of friends. We did a lot of other things together. We used to travel and enjoyed going out to eat." Alice was looking at him, but nothing came to her.

She glanced at the clock and noticed that it was after 10 pm. "Well, I need to get some rest. I promised Erik that I would be out at six tomorrow morning to help with the horses." Jack smiled, "Let's turn in, and we can have breakfast early before I leave for work." "That would be fine," Alice responded. "See you tomorrow." She said and headed to her room. Jack stood alone, watching her walk away. He had hoped that he would at least get a hug, but she was gone.

As Alice prepared for bed, she wondered if she would remember the horses tomorrow. Alice knelt on her knees, "Dear Lord, I do not remember you, but I feel close to you. I know that I was in an accident, but I do not remember anything. I do not necessarily want to remember the fire, but I want to know who I am. Please help me to remember. I know that I am a mother and I feel and believe it is true. I do have a memory of a baby from my dreams. If this is my baby, please help me get back to him. Take care of my baby wherever he may be. Please give me patience. Please give Jack patience too. Thank you. Amen." As she rose, she felt her heart fill with joy.

Alice dreamt of the baby all night. This time, her dream was more explicit. She saw this beautiful baby and big brother. They were beautiful boys. She dreamt of sitting on the floor playing with the boys and heard them giggle. She giggled herself and awoke, giggling. It was two in the morning, and she felt such peace. She closed her eyes and prayed, "Thank you, God, my heart is full." She drifted off to sleep and, once again, dreamt of these boys. She played all night with them. She ran and laughed. She gave them rides on swings and sat with them to eat. It was just the three of them. Her heart rejoiced as she played with the boys. They had dark hair and brown eyes. They smiled, and the dream brightened, even filled with happiness. Alice wished that she would never awaken from this beautiful dream.

8 BROWNIES

It had been a very typical day for the boys at school. Ann Marie had picked them up from school and was getting the snack ready. Ann Marie planned on a warm snack that she hoped would make the boys feel better. Ann Marie hoped that brownies would be a different type of treat that neither would mind nor expect. She had asked Seth if it were okay to spoil them today. She had found Frances Grace's recipes and thought this would be a great treat. Both boys were in their appropriate rooms but started to smell the baking seep into their rooms.

Samuel was working on a project that he had been working on for a few weeks. However, he was not allowing anyone to look at it. Instead, Samuel would hide it in his secret spot in his room when he left. Samuel was working on a gift for his mommy, whose birthday was coming up at the beginning of April. Samuel was very secretive because he wanted to ensure only his mommy saw this.

Frankie was in his room working on his homework. He wanted to be outside after his snack, so he didn't want to have to do homework later. Frankie sat working on his Math and Spelling but seemed very distracted. He was not able to get things done as fast as usual. Frankie kept looking at the time and wondered if he was going downstairs soon. He looked at his homework and knew he better buckle down and get things down. Frankie sat looking at his pages and got to work. He loved math and remembered his mommy showing him how easy it was to learn. She had also played spelling games with him to teach him how to remember to spell. She would always make up songs that used words to explain what the word meant and spell it out. It was so easy to remember her songs.

Ann Marie called up to the boys to come down. Both the boys lifted their heads and started putting things away. Frankie finished up his homework and put it into his backpack. Samuel hid his project in his secret spot. Both boys opened their doors and stepped into the hallway. They took a deep breath and immediately knew what the snack was. They hurried down the stairs and walked into the kitchen. Ann Marie was serving up the brownies with some ice cream.

Frankie hollered, "STOP!" Ann Marie froze, and she looked at him. "No ice cream for me, please." "What? No ice cream? It's the ice cream that makes brownies the best." She responded. Frankie looked at her and said, "If these are my mommy's brownies, nothing else is needed." "This is your mommy's recipe, but" she attempted to finish, but Frankie was faster than she, "NO buts about it. My mommy makes the best brownies in the world."

Samuel smiled at them and removed the ice cream off his brownie. Ann Marie saw him and smiled at him. "You too?" she asked him. "It's okay; I just don't want it on the brownie." He replied. Samuel took a bite and smiled at her, "They are good." Ann Marie was amazed to hear that they were good, not great. "Just good?" she asked. Samuel shook his head yes. She could see that he was emotional and did not push the issue.

Frankie took a bite and looked at Ann Marie, "These are not my mommy's brownies. They do not taste like hers. You must have done something wrong." Frankie insisted. Ann Marie smiled and did not even attempt to clarify or ask any more from either boy. "Sorry, I was hoping that I could make them like your mommy." Frankie shook his head and pushed the plate away, "Can I have something else? I do not like this." He continued, "I think you forgot to put in the love. Only my mommy knows how to do that. No one else will ever be able to make them like her." Ann Marie asked, "What would you like?" she was very disappointed. Frankie shook his head and looked away, "I changed my mind. I don't want anything."

Samuel was watching Frankie, "Frankie, it's okay. You don't have to eat any." Frankie looked at his big brother and asked, "Do you think I can go outside now?" Samuel shook his head, "You need to wait until I finish, and then we can go outside together." "I don't want to wait for you or anyone." Frankie stood up and walked towards the back door. "Frankie, wait a minute, I will come with you." Samuel turned to Ann Marie and gave her a small smile, "I am so sorry. It was a very hard day."

Ann Marie watched them as they walked towards the garden. She thought to herself, 'These boys are so sad, and they do not want to forget their mom, so they are keeping everyone at a distance. They refused to admit that her brownie recipe was made right. I wish I could help these poor boys more than I feel I am doing.' She turned to get her phone to call Seth when the door opened. She turned and saw Seth standing in the doorway. "Wow, those brownies smell so good." He stated. She smiled and said, "Well, I think it was too much for the boys to handle. They both claimed that they were not as good as their mom's." Seth walked over and took a taste, "these are very good. Good job!" He noticed that the boys were out in the garden. "Look, Ann Marie, don't worry; I appreciate your effort. It does mean a lot." Ann Marie replied, "I wish I could do more." "You are doing just fine; please don't stress. Thanks, and have a good night." And with that, he headed out the door.

A Mother's Broken Promise

As he reached the boys, he heard their conversation. "Frankie, you were a little mean to Ann Marie. I think you should go and apologize to her." Samuel had put his hand on his little brother's shoulder. "I do not have to apologize! Those brownies were rotten! She should not be trying to be like mommy. She will never be my mommy!" "Ann Marie was only trying to help you feel better," Seth interjected. Frankie's head turned so fast to his daddy, "She made me feel worse!" Seth put his arms around his boys, "I love you both, and Ann Marie tries hard to help us. She is not trying to be your mommy. She hoped you would smile for a change by making you a sweet treat." Frankie was now crying, and Samuel was close to tears. "I don't care!" Frankie cried, "I do not need anyone to try to make me feel better; I need someone to bring my mommy home!" Seth knew that this was not a conversation anyone could handle today.

Seth thought to himself, 'Just walk them back inside,' but this was her spot, and he knew this was where they needed to be. He stepped over the bench and sat between them. "What should we do for dinner?" he asked, hoping to change the subject. Frankie was the first to respond, "I'm sorry, daddy, I know I was not nice to Ann Marie, but she tried to make mommy's brownies and then put ice cream on them. They were ruined! She doesn't know how to put love in them like mommy." Samuel added, "They were good, but they didn't taste the same." "I know, sometimes people try too hard. They think that things that remind you of her will make you feel better. Someday, it will be better, but until then, let us try to be nicer so we don't hurt other people's feelings. You don't have to like it, but at least try not to say bad things." Samuel and Frankie leaned on their daddy and cried.

Frankie suddenly started laughing; he looked at Samuel and pointed, "Mommy, Mommy." The two boys saw their mommy smiling at them and blowing kisses. Seth looked but saw nothing. "Daddy, you must believe. If you don't, then you can't see her." "I want to believe, but I am an adult, and it's hard for me to make-believe." "Oh, daddy, it's not make-believe. It is real!" Frankie insisted. "Daddy, try to be happy. Just try to forget all the sadness. Have a smile on your face, and mommy will be there." Samuel added. Seth tried to smile, but all he thought was, 'How can I smile when my boys are hurting so much.' He tried to force a smile, but he knew it was not a smile. He closed his eyes, and suddenly he could smell roses. He half-opened his eyes and prayed he would see her. He saw nothing but did smell the roses, which were not in bloom.

They sat there until the sunset, no words were spoken, but suddenly, there she was. Seth's heart skipped a beat, he not only smelled her roses, but he was watching her. She slowly moved from one rose bush to another and smiled at them. She waived her signature wave, 'I love you,' and smiled at them. Seth was speechless; he watched his beautiful wife tend to her roses. She then slowly moved towards them. Francie reached out and touched each one. She swept Frankie's hair from his forehead and lightly touched his cheek. Francie grazed Seth's cheek across to his lips and smiled, 'I love you.' She put her hand on Samuel's head, ruffled his hair, and lightly touched his cheek. And then, she was gone as quickly as she appeared. It had cooled off in the early evening, and the boys knew it was time to go inside. All three boys rose without a word and silently walked inside the warm kitchen.

Ann Marie had put away the ice cream and brownies. The kitchen still smelled of freshly baked brownies. "Well, it's dinner time. What would we like tonight?" Seth asked. "I want spaghetti and meatballs," Frankie answered. "That would be fine with me," Samuel added. "Alright, do we want to make it or go out?" The boys looked at each other and answered in unison, "Let's make it!" "Okay, Samuel, you get the noodles out while I get the pot ready. Frankie, you get the meatballs out of the freezer." Seth instructed. They all went to work like a well-oiled machine. As Frankie reached for the meatballs, he said, "These are the last of mommy's meatballs, daddy." Seth turned and smiled at him, "I guess we better enjoy them then." Seth filled the pot with water and started the stove and oven.

Samuel opened the box of noodles and set it close to his dad. Frankie placed the meatballs near the stove and then opened the pantry to get the loaf of bread for garlic bread. Frankie turned and opened the refrigerator and pulled out the lettuce and tomatoes. Samuel joined him and pulled out the carrots and cheese. Next, Seth reached for the radish and cucumbers. Frankie then asked, "Daddy, do you want cranberries and sunflower seeds like mommy likes?" Samuel asked, "Do you want avocado like mommy?" Seth smiled at them, "Of course, it's the only way to have salad, right?" They all laughed; this was precisely what they needed tonight.

As they worked together, they laughed and giggled. The only one missing was the only lady in their lives that made them laugh and feel important. Seth did all the chopping, but the boys added all the ingredients to the salad and had fun tossing it. They then prepared the loaf with butter and garlic then Seth placed it in the oven. Then off to set the table, they marched like good little helpers. Seth did roll call for mom, "We are burning daylight; move forward, little cowboys. Come on now, ride those ponies. Frankie, Sammy, Seth!" They laughed as they galloped along. The table was set, the oven timer went off, and the noodles were ready. The sauce was prepared with the meatballs. When all food was served and at the table, the boys bowed their heads and prayed in unison, "Thank you, Lord, for this meal and blessing. Please bless the less fortunate and keep them safe. Amen." Frankie added, "Please let mommy eat a good meal and be safe. Bring her home soon. Amen." They had been holding hands, and each gave a little squeeze. They had not prayed together in some time, and it felt good. They had been angry with God for allowing the beautiful lady in their lives to have disappeared.

They enjoyed this meal more than they had in a very long time and chatted about school and friends. They discussed tomorrow's events and planned out their days for the next few days. Seth even brought up going to the cabin when school let out for spring break. "I thought we should take a trip to the cabin and stay over spring break." They looked at each other and nodded in agreement that it was a good idea. They had not been to the cabin since before Francie went missing. Seth was relieved that the boys agreed to go out to the cabin.

Tonight's dessert would be ice cream. As the boys cleaned up the dishes and put away the leftovers, they knew they had had a breakthrough. Each felt a sense of growth and satisfaction. As they pulled out the toppings for the ice cream, they laughed about the silly things they did and said. They each liked different toppings, so everything was on the kitchen island. Frankie wanted two scoops with peanuts and chocolate drizzle. Samuel wanted two scoops with chocolate, caramel drizzle, and whip cream. Seth only wanted one scoop with bananas, caramel, and peanuts. Finally, they headed to the game room to watch TV and enjoy their treat.

They snuggled up together, watching the discovery channel and shark week. The boys had not watched TV in a very long time. They usually just went up to their rooms and did their own thing. As the evening ended, it was time to head to bed. Samuel said, "Papa, can we do this again tomorrow?" Frankie nodded in agreement. "Of course, we can do it anytime you want." Seth reassured them, "Ok, time to brush your teeth." Seth hated to have the night end. It was so much better than having them both crying. He hugged them and pointed upstairs. Without a word, the boys went up and got ready for bed. Seth cleaned up the kitchen when he heard a whisper, "I love you, and I always will." He turned, but there was no one. He finished up and locked up the house. He looked out to the garden and spoke to her, "I will love you forever." He turned and shut off the lights, set the alarms, and headed up to see his boys.

Frankie was in bed and had his mommy's picture at his side. "Daddy, is it okay that I like to sleep with mommy's picture?" "Yes, of course. I know that she must feel safe knowing that you hold her close to your heart." Seth answered. Frankie smiled at his daddy, "Today started as a bad day, but it is a good day." "Did you say your prayers?" "Yes, I did," Frankie answered. "Goodnight, sweet little one. I love you so very much." Seth tucked him in and kissed his forehead. Frankie closed his eyes as his dad walked out and whispered, "Goodnight, mommy! I love you and want to see you. I had a very good day today. Goodnight, my mommy, sleep tight. See you soon." He closed his eyes and dreamt of his mommy. They played games and laughed in his dream, which made Frankie very happy. He slept all night for the first time.

Samuel was still on his knees, saying his prayers. "Dear Jesus, today was a very good day. Thank you for helping us feel better. Please keep my mommy safe and bring her home soon. Thank you for letting mommy come to us. Please help daddy be happy more often. I know he misses her too. Please help my little brother understand that you will bring her home soon. Please help him to be happy too. Thank you, Jesus. Amen." Seth entered the room and tucked him in. "I enjoyed today very much. I hope we all laugh more too." Samuel smiled and said, "Mommy is coming home soon. I can feel it." Seth hugged him and kissed his forehead, "Goodnight, sweet boy." When his papa walked out and turned off the light, Samuel closed his eyes and begged God to let him dream of his mommy. As he drifted off to sleep, he dreamt of his mommy. They all played together, and Samuel slept like he had not slept in a couple of years. He dreamt of playing and laughing with his entire family all night long.

Seth closed the door behind him and fell to his knees; tears streamed down his face, "Dear Lord, thank you for today. It was wonderful to see my beautiful wife. I pray that it was a sign that she is okay and will be home soon. Thank you for helping my boys feel good, if only for today. It was a wonderful day in the end. Thank you for the laughter. Please give me the faith of a child. I need to know that she is doing fine and will be back soon. Thank you, Jesus, thank you so very much. Amen." Tears did not stop streaming down his cheeks. He was so happy that he did not have to hear his boys cry all night long. As he got ready for bed, tears streamed down his cheeks, and he felt so happy that he had the faith of his children. If he had not believed, he might not have seen her. The night was silent, and all was calm. The boys slept through the night, and so did he. Seth dreamt of his beautiful wife and boys all together again.

The Laurel home was silent and calm for the first time in years. There were no nightmares, no crying, no screaming, and no being up all night. Instead, peace and heavenly dreams filled the minds of everyone in the house. It was the first night that all the boys had a good night's sleep. They slept so soundly that even the dog had a good night's sleep.

9 THE STABLES

Alice awoke after a good night's sleep. She had the best night's sleep since coming out of the coma. She heard a familiar voice as she awakened, "Good morning, Alice. Are you feeling stronger today?" Valerie asked as she took Alice's vitals. "Good morning, Valerie. I feel so good today. I would like to be at the stables by six." Valerie asked very cautiously, "Alice, are you planning on riding today?" "No, not planning to," she responded. She had set the alarm for 4:45 and expected to have breakfast with Jack. As she showered and dressed for her day, she was excited to spend the day at the stables. She slipped into riding jeans and a polo and grabbed a sweater just in case it was chilly. As she headed out of her room, "Valerie, have you ever ridden a horse? You are welcome to join me today." Valerie smiled, "Thank you. I will be happy to come out and watch."

She headed to the kitchen, where she could hear voices. As she entered, she greeted Erik, "Hello Erik, are you ready to show me everything I need to know?" Erik smiled and responded, "I am and look forward to teaching such a quick study." "Good morning, Jack," Alice greeted him as she saw him standing in the back. "Good morning, you are looking stunning, Mrs. Alexander." Alice smiled a shy smile, "Oh, stop it. Good morning, Janie. What's for breakfast?" Janie smiled, "Good morning, Mrs. Alexander. I thought you would enjoy some waffles and eggs. We also have fruit and juices. Please enjoy."

As everyone gathered in the kitchen, they sat down and enjoyed breakfast. Today was a family-style breakfast, and Alice enjoyed the closeness. There was laughter and interesting conversation. They discussed the weather currently. It was cool, but it would get much warmer by lunchtime. Old Chief was an older horse and had been at the vet hospital. He was coming home today, and he may be difficult. They discussed bears, a couple had been sighted by the creek, but there was no sighting on the property. They discussed getting some dogs; they thought they might keep the bears off the property. Alice had wanted to get puppies, but that did not go over very well. They thought the bears would eat them as a tasty little morsel. Valerie was worried that Alice may overdo it today. Alice just smiled and said, "Don't worry, Erik will keep an eye on me, and Valerie, you can come out and check on me or join me. Jack, please don't worry. I will stop if I start to feel tired, I promise." "Janie, you outdid yourself with this wonderful breakfast. Thank you so much." Janie was very grateful, "Thank you, Mrs. Alexander. Glad you enjoyed your breakfast." They all picked up their plates and placed them in the sink as the group left.

Jack grabbed Alice's hand, "Please promise me to be very careful today." Alice smiled at him, "I will." Jack wanted to lean over and kiss her cheek but decided that maybe it was too early. Alice asked, "What time do you see patients?" "My first patient is at seven, but it will take me over an hour to get there," Jack answered. "Have a good day," Alice added as she headed out of the door towards the stables. Jack watched her leave and wondered if she really would be careful today.

Alice felt so happy as she headed to the stables. She had a good night's sleep and wonderful dreams. Alice knew that these two little baby boys were alive, and she wanted to find them. Alice would use the horses to gain her memory. Today would be the first day to get closer to her recovery. She caught up to Erik and started asking questions. "When do the horses eat?" "We will let them out for a run but need to round them up since the bears lurk nearby. They will eat once we get them back into their stables."

They had reached the stables. They opened the gates as they greeted the horses, and the horses knew what to do. They ran into the meadow and played. It was fun to watch the horses running and kicking up their hooves. It was clear that they enjoyed stretching their legs. They all played as if they were colts. Erik and Alice worked on cleaning out the stalls. They replenished the water and placed fresh straw in each stall. It had been about an hour when Erik whistled. Alice looked up and saw him standing at the edge, and he whistled again. As she walked toward him, she could see that he had a concerned look on his face.

Alice stepped up to Erik and asked, "What's going on?" "I heard something and looked out, but none of the horses were in sight. I may need to go searching for them. It would be best if you went back to the house and waited for me to return, Mrs. Alexander." He explained. "Will you go in the truck?" she asked. "Yes, that will be the safest thing to do." He had not taken his eyes off the meadow. "I can finish up the stalls while you are gone." She insisted. "Mrs. Alexander, I fear that the bears have come onto the property. I would prefer that you be safe in the house instead. I will call for help and bring a couple of other ranchers to help me if I need it."

Alice was worried, "Can you outrun the bears in that old truck?" "Oh yes, please do not worry about me. I will be fine; I have my cell phone, and I will call the house when I find the horses. I do not want you to worry about the horses." Erik was heading toward the truck. Alice headed to the house and almost ran as she hurried. She was worried about the bears attacking the horses.

Alice reached the house and turned to see if she could see Erik in the truck, but she could not make him out. Alice walked in and explained to Janie and Valerie that Erik would be calling the house to let them know when he found the horses. The three ladies stood on the patio looking out towards the meadow when they heard the phone ring; Janie ran to answer it. Valerie and Alice could not see anything; they were also looking for the bears. Janie returned, but it had not been Erik. Alice asked, "Is there a pair of binoculars?" As she searched the grounds for the horses and Erik, she noticed something far away but could not make out what it was.

Valerie brought the binoculars to Alice. As she looked around, she saw the bears. They were strolling across the creek on the other side. They were not looking like they were too concerned about anything. Suddenly, she saw Erik corralling the horses back to the stables in the pickup truck. She had wanted to help, but Valerie thought it might not be safe with the horses running back. As Alice watched all the horses running, she suddenly had a flashback.

She was riding a horse, but she was just a kid. She was riding along a creek when the horse reared up, and she flew off. She had fallen in the stream, and the water was frigid. As she got up to get back up on the horse, she saw that the horse was limping. It had a broken leg. She suddenly lost the memory, and as she tried to regain the memory, she felt so sad that she started to cry. She was not sure why she was feeling like this, but she was very emotional. Maybe it was because she had a memory of herself. She looked at Valerie and explained the memory she had. Valerie had a million questions, 'How old were you? Did you see your face? Did it feel like it was your horse or someone else's? Did this place seem familiar to you? Did you think it was your property? As she continued to ask questions, Alice's mind tried to remember. But unfortunately, nothing else came to mind. It was just a quick memory with no actual details.

Erik was bringing the horses into the stables when Alice decided to go out and help. Valerie insisted on coming with her to make sure she was safe. As they gathered in the stables, she could see the worry on Erik's face. He was concerned that the bears were getting bolder. He saw bear tracks on the property. He thought that the horses had just been scared off but had not been in any real threat from the bears. As the horses were safely tucked into each stall, they were very excited about the morning's events. They were all neighing and carrying on. Alice could see that they were all discussing the bears. She spoke to each one and calmed them down. Alice spoke in a very soft, soothing voice, brushed, and kissed their necks. Alice sang a little lullaby for each one. She was unsure how she remembered this song but was happy that she was feeling calm. Finally, the horses had all settled down and were quiet again.

Erik decided that he needed to call Mr. Alexander. As he spoke to Mr. Alexander, he stated that we needed the dogs immediately so the bears would not come any closer or onto the property again. Suddenly, Alice had a funny thought, what if the bears only wanted to go and use the pool? Wouldn't it be funny to watch them swim? She imagined them in the pool swimming around but not just swimming, doing backflips and such off the diving board. That would be a funny sight! Alice could hear Mr. Alexander saying that he was giving the go-ahead on the dogs. She was getting excited. The idea of dogs excited her. She wasn't sure if she had had dogs before, but Alice felt she loved dogs.

As they finished up in the stables, Alice was feeling giddy. She was so excited that she almost couldn't hide her excitement.

Alice was full of questions. "What kind of dogs? How many can we get? Will they come inside the house? Do you think I can have them sleep in my room?" Erik hated to break her bubble, but he stated, "Mrs. Alexander, these will be working dogs. They do not come inside or act like pets." "Why couldn't we get a puppy? He could grow up with the horses and be used to him." Then Valerie smiled at Alice, Alice knew that she was possibly acting like a child, but she didn't care. She wanted a puppy, and it would be a great companion for her. Alice wondered if she had had a dog when she was a kid, or did she have a dog before her accident?

Erik, Valerie, and Alice went into town to meet someone about getting some dogs. The man had some hunting dogs. He had five American Blue Gascon hounds. As soon as Alice saw these dogs, she fell in love with them. She wanted them all. As Erik talked details to Mr. Jenkins, she played with the dogs. They seemed to take to her immediately. Erik looked over at Alice and smiled. She suddenly realized that she was no longer self-conscience about how she looked. The dogs seemed to accept her for her gentleness and were not afraid of her. One of Alice's fears was that she would scare animals and people away.

Alice's face was pretty scarred up. She had yet to look in a mirror but had felt all the scars. She was afraid to look in a mirror. Today, she would finally look at herself—no more fear. "I must be brave to be able to find the boys from my dreams." she thought to herself.

10 IT IS A GOOD MORNING

After a good night's sleep, the boys woke up.

Samuel was the first to get up. As he arose, he sat upon the edge of the bed and said, "Jesus, today we move forward to finding mommy. You showed us that she is alive, and we are ready to find her. Show us what to do." He jumped out of bed and ran to take his shower. Then, he sang, "I love you in the morning. I'll love you in the afternoon. I love you in the evening. I love you every day. I will always love you, my sweet baby boy." This song was a song his mommy would sing every day. He could almost hear her singing to them. "I love you in the morning. I'll love you in the afternoon. I love you in the evening. I love you every day. I will always love you, my sweet baby boy."

Seth was the next to stir. He heard the shower going, so he headed into his bathroom. Seth stood at the vanity and smiled. He thought, "I know I saw my wife last night. I want to see her again. How do I do that, God? My boys need their mommy. I need my wife. What do I need to do? Tell me what to do, God. I will do anything!" Seth could hear Samuel singing in the shower. He smiled and hummed along to his son's little lullaby.

Frankie could hear his brother Samuel singing, and he smiled as he imagined his mommy singing the song. He closed his eyes and could see his mommy singing and smiling. As Frankie opened his eyes, he knew that today would be a great day. He hurried and jumped out of bed, grabbed his clothes, and headed to the bathroom.

Frankie immediately started singing along with his brother. He brushed his teeth while he hummed along. His brother finished his shower, and Frankie ran out and into the hallway. Frankie skipped down the hall when his dad came out of his room. Seth said, "Somebody is in a great mood!" Seth reached out and grabbed his youngest son, spun him around, and tickled Frankie. Frankie giggled as he threw his arms out. Samuel came into the hallway to see his brother being spun around. Samuel ran and jumped on his daddy's back. As they all dropped to the floor in laughter, Seth tickled both of his boys. They giggled until they could no longer laugh, and laughter turned to tears of joy.

After what seemed like hours of laughter, they gathered themselves and prepared for breakfast. "Who wants sausage and eggs?" asked Seth. "I do!" the boys said in unison. Samuel headed to set the table as Frankie grabbed the napkins. Seth headed to the refrigerator for the sausage and eggs. They discussed the day's events. Frankie wanted to go out and do some gardening for his mommy. Samuel thought they should get some groceries. Seth suggested, "Why can't we do both things. Let's get groceries first, and then we can work out in the garden until evening." He was hoping that he could see his lovely wife again. "How do you want your eggs?" he asked his boys. Frankie answered first, "May I have three-minute eggs like mommy makes?" "I have never made them, but I can try," Seth responded. Samuel added, "I'd like mine scrambled. Frankie, don't you think it would be easier if daddy made them all scrambled?" "I guess so," Frankie answered. "I can wait until mommy comes home to make me my special eggs." Frankie smiled and added, "It won't be too long." Seth cringed when he heard the last remark. He silently prayed, "Lord, please let that be real soon. Don't make my baby boy wait too long."

A Mother's Broken Promise

As the boys enjoyed breakfast, they talked about their dreams. Frankie laughed and said, "I was dreaming about mommy all night long. We played at the park like we used to. Mommy was laughing when I jumped in the mud, and it was raining in my dream. She called me her little piggy. She was laughing, hugging, and kissing me. I was dreaming of her singing me to sleep before I woke up. It was nice to dream of mommy. I hadn't had a happy dream in a long time. Daddy, as a matter of fact, that's why I am so happy this morning."

Samuel smiled at his little brother and winked at him. Then he continued with his dream, "I was dreaming of the time we went camping. Remember how funny mommy was? She was so worried about us getting bug bites. She kept spraying us and making sure we were not getting bitten. Then she made sure we were not cold by putting a few layers on us. I remember feeling like a snowman that couldn't move his arms. Frankie's little arms were sticking straight out, and he couldn't move. Daddy finally convinced mommy that we were okay, and she eventually took one layer off us. We were making S'mores, and Frankie got his all over his clothes. Mommy just laughed, took off the dirty clothes, and put on new layers. Daddy, you were laughing the entire time. The whole camping area sounded like a boom box when you laughed so loud. I laughed because mommy was giggling when she saw us eating the S'mores. When I woke up, I could still hear all the laughing."

Seth smiled and said, "those are great dreams. I slept so well last night that all I could think about was how great last night was." He didn't want to share his dream. He had dreamt of his wife when she was pregnant with the boys and how happy she was. He would save that dream and share it with them when they needed to have their spirits lifted. He could see that they were so pleased. Suddenly he had a great idea. "Boys, what do you think about going camping?"

The boys' eyes lit up. "When can we go?" they asked almost in unison. "How about we go during spring break?" Seth asked. "When is that?" Frankie asked. "It should be in April," replied Samuel. "That is so far away," Frankie added, "Why can't we go sooner?" "It may be too chilly right now," Seth replied. "Daddy, can we go tomorrow?" Frankie asked with a sense of urgency. "No, Frankie. I have to make sure I get all my work done and have current projects finished before we go." Samuel looked at his daddy, then at Frankie, "It may be too cold for us, and we need mommy to put all the layers on us." he giggled as he finished the sentence. Frankie smiled and added, "I guess I can wait."

Seth was happy that his older son was so grown up. He wished that he didn't have to grow up so quickly, but it had helped under the circumstances. Seth thought to himself, 'If only Samuel could just concentrate on being a kid.' He had so much work to get done. He decided to get started to be done and enjoy the break with the boys. Spring break would arrive before he knew it, and he could not break a promise to the boys. As he rushed to get the boys off to school, he noticed the note sticking out of Frankie's backpack. He asked Frankie, "What is this?" Frankie smiled and said, "Oh yeah, I forgot all about it. My teacher sent it home to you."

Seth dropped the boys off and reminded them that Ann Marie would pick them up right after school. When he arrived at work, he went into his office to read the letter from Frankie's backpack. He realized that tears were running down his face as he sat reading it. He read,

"Dear Mr. Laurel,

It is with great concern that I write this note to you. I believe that you need to get professional help for Frankie. He is unable to concentrate at school. I find him daydreaming too often. He will, at times, burst into tears for no apparent reason. He has also told me that he is talking to his mother. I have found him talking to himself every day, and he is not interacting with the other children. He has become very withdrawn. I am reaching out to you first before alerting the school officials to this disturbing behavior. I hope that you will be willing to meet with me after school. Please reach out at my extension 321 at the school number.

Sincerely,

Mrs. Jones"

Seth reached for the phone and dialed the school number. He knew that he would get the voicemail, but he was determined to make time for his boys. So, as he heard the teacher's voicemail, he prepared for his message, "Mrs. Jones, Thank you for sending the note home with Frankie. I will be by your office at 5 pm. If that is not a good time for you, please call me at 555-4321."

It was a typical day for the boys at school. Samuel enjoyed math and science, but recess was the most fun. He loved to run outside, even on a cold winter day. Recess was in the middle of the morning, so when Samuel went out to play, he knew that he would get to see Frankie. He tried to keep an eye on his little brother every day. When he saw Frankie, he went up to see how his day was going. Frankie was looking better today than most days. Frankie smiled at Samuel and said, "today is the best day! I was in class, and I could see mommy watching me." Samuel smiled and decided that he should talk to Frankie. "Frankie, do you think mommy is watching you?" "Yes!" he answered. Samuel sat down on the bench and pulled his little brother next to him. "Listen, Frankie, I know that you see mommy, but Mrs. Jones doesn't. She is an adult, and she may not believe you. She might even think that you are making up stories." "I wouldn't lie, Samuel." Frankie insisted. "I know, but teachers don't always understand what you are going through. They only worry if you are doing okay."

Samuel was wise beyond his years. He knew that when he saw the letter that Frankie had in his backpack was not a good letter. "Frankie, I want you to try not to be looking outside all the time. You need to get all your schoolwork done in class if you can. Do you think you can try hard today?" Frankie smiled, "Sure, I can try really hard." Samuel walked his little brother back to class when the recess bell rang. Frankie looked at Samuel and said, "I will get all the work done first, then look at mommy." Samuel knew that his little brother would keep his word. He looked over his shoulder and smiled as he walked back to his classroom. He knew that today was a new day for them all.

11 THE TEACHER'S OFFICE

Seth finished work a little earlier than usual but rushed over to the school to meet with Mrs. Jones. As he waited in the hallway, he remembered the first day he and Francie had brought Samuel to school. It was a day of anxiety. The day you leave your firstborn, or any child for that matter, for the first time is a day that you look forward to but also dread. He could hear Francie making sure that Samuel would be excited about meeting his new classmates. She kept encouraging him for weeks, and he was so excited. However, the day that they had to leave Frankie was quite different. She wasn't ready to let her last baby go and worried if he was too young. Frankie, on the other hand, was ready. He had been asking for two years if you could go to school with his big brother. Frankie was very bright. He learned everything that his big brother was learning. Frankie was more than prepared, but he was mommy's baby. As independent as he wanted to be, mommy was hanging on as tight as possible. Then, Seth heard someone clear their voice which jolted Seth out of his memories.

Mrs. Jones was standing at the entry of her classroom. "Mr. Laurel, please come in. I am so sorry to bring you in, but I wanted to see what you have been experiencing at home. I am very concerned about Frankie." Seth smiled a nervous smile. "I am glad that you reached out to me first. We have had a tough time at home but didn't realize it was affecting Frankie at school. I have not noticed his grades suffering." Mrs. Jones smiled, "Frankie is an excellent student, but he daydreams too much. He is even talking to his mother sometimes and will not engage during class. He is very withdrawn, and I see him at recess sitting on the bench talking to himself."

Seth didn't know what to say, "you know, some kids have a great imagination. He happens to be one of those." He didn't want to tell her that they all have had situations where they see his wife. "I will talk with him tonight. Is he getting his work done in class that he should?" Mrs. Jones wasn't impressed at all with his answer. "Mr. Laurel, I feel that Frankie needs to be evaluated by a school psychologist. I can plan for that next week. I feel that Frankie has had too much to deal with and needs help." Seth was now getting angry, "Mrs. Jones, I said I would speak with Frankie tonight. I do not believe that he needs to speak to anyone else. He has had too much trauma speaking to counselors that tell him how he should feel. Last night we had our first night of sleeping through the night. I do not want my boys to go backward. So, I am asking that you give us a little more time. We are planning on getting away for Spring Break. The boys are so excited. Please do not harm my little boy by forcing him to speak to another counselor. Give me until after Spring Break. I have a good feeling about this." Mrs. Jones thought for a minute and shook her head. "Okay, I will give you time but will be watching him very closely."

As Seth left, he thanked Mrs. Jones and felt some relief. He wondered how the boys were getting along with Ann Marie as he drove home.

12 A TIME TO WANDER

Now that Alice had dogs on the property, she wanted to look around the property. She could hear the dogs outside barking up a storm. Alice wondered if they had come across bears or squirrels. Alice knew that the dogs would need to learn what critters were safe on the property. Erik needed the dogs to get used to the property, learn the property lines, and be taught not to wander into the other property. Erik had a great sense about animals and had said that these dogs were exceptionally quick learners.

Mr. Alexander left extra early this morning to do surgeries scheduled at the hospital. It was nice not having to explain how she was feeling this morning. Valerie was always early checking her vitals. Today was the first day that Alice had been able to shower and dress independently. It was quite an accomplishment. She was feeling stronger every day. After breakfast, Alice strolled out to the stables, where she found Erik tending to the horses. She knew the routine, so she started feeding and brushing the horses.

"Erik, will you be taking the dogs out to teach them our property line today?" he smiled at her. "Yes, I'll take them out on leash the first few times. Why do you ask? Would you like to join us today?" Alice was so excited she almost yelled it out but held herself together, "yes, that would be fabulous." As Erik prepared the dogs for the walk, Alice followed behind quietly while Erik instructed the dogs. Alice wanted to give each one names, but Erik explained that they already had names and it would be difficult to change them and maybe even confuse them. So Alpha, Beta, Commander, Delta, and Eddie would have to stay as their names. Alpha was the lead dog, and Beta looked very strong. Commander was big, broad, and very impatient with the other dogs. Delta was young but very obedient. Eddie was the smallest of all and full of energy and joy.

Alice was taking in all the sounds and smells. She felt like she could feel the colors on her face. There was a slight breeze that seemed to carry the fragrances of every flower. She couldn't remember the names of the flowers, but she could tell that she knew them before. A familiar smell was so sweet and tasted like honey on her taste buds. Some purple flowers smelled like fruit, and the sweetness made her taste buds go crazy. The yellow flowers seemed to bring warmth to her face; the smell was like the sun, warm and pleasant. Alice closed her eyes for a moment to take in the fragrances. She could hear the bees humming around the flowers, and the butterflies fluttering sounded like thunderous wings. Alice could hear birds in the distance bickering, maybe over a nesting area. She was enjoying the smells, the sounds, and the warmth. She felt so at peace out here in the meadow.

Alice listened carefully and could hear the water in the creek. It was gentle but powerful. It was soothing and rhythmic yet a little scary. She even thought, she may have heard a fish jump. Alice could almost see the fish. It was a silver fish but with rainbow colors. It sparkled as it jumped from the water. Alice laughed, "I have quite an imagination," she thought. Suddenly she could hear the dogs again and realized she had been daydreaming for a moment. She had fallen behind and needed to be at least close enough that she would be within a reasonable distance of protection if the bears appeared.

Alice had only been awake for a couple of weeks and started to feel exhausted. They had hiked for some time, and she needed to sit down. She looked up to see where the dogs were, but suddenly everything went black. Erik heard a sound and turned to look when he saw Alice on the ground. He rushed to her side. He carried her back to the main house.

A Mother's Broken Promise

When Valerie saw them, she ran out to meet them. She had the wheelchair ready as Erik neared. Valerie reached for Alice's arm to take her pulse. She was asking Erik what had happened when Alice opened her eyes. "What happened?" she asked. Erik responded, "I'm not sure. I heard a noise and turned to find you on the ground." "I was looking for the dogs, and everything went black," Alice explained. "Erik, where are the dogs?" "Mrs. Alexander, you are my priority. I left them out in the meadow. I will go round them up." Alice smiled and said, "I hope they are all okay."

Erik headed back for the dogs and was pleasantly surprised to see that they were just hanging around. They seemed to be waiting for him. He called out to them as he approached, and they came running. They had been frolicking and seemed to be enjoying the freedom. Erik decided to take them all off-leash to see what would happen. All the dogs immediately circled him and sat at attention. He smiled and whistled then the dogs began to run in the meadow. Erik gave a double whistle, and the dogs returned to him. Erik knew that they were very fortunate to have these dogs. He ran them along the creek and instructed them not to cross. He trained with them for a couple of hours before heading in.

Erik headed in to check on Alice. When he arrived, he encountered a furious boss. Mr. Alexander was waiting for Erik to enter the house, and he let into him like a bear after honey.

Mr. Alexander was yelling at Erik, but all Erik was interested in was finding out how Mrs. Alexander was doing. Mr. Alexander was in a rage, "What were you thinking? Why would you allow her to go with you? When you decided that she was going with you, you should have watched her closely. Why in the world would you have allowed her to go anyway? I don't know if I can ever trust you again, Erik! What am I supposed to do with you? You have been with me for such a long time, and I do not know if I can trust you!" He patiently waited until he was no longer being yelled at to ask how she was. "How is Mrs. Alexander doing?"

Alice was resting in her room. She was dreaming of playing with those two beautiful little boys. She was in a meadow with beautiful flowers all around her. The colors were so vibrant and full of life. The two little boys were running and laughing. She saw the flowers almost move out of their path as they ran. The flowers seemed to be alive. The butterflies on the flowers flew up and surrounded the boys as the boys ran. Alice attempted to catch up with them, but they just kept running. Suddenly the butterflies started to lift the boys higher and higher. Alice tried to jump and bring them down, but they floated away with the butterflies. She awoke in a panic. Her heart was thumping out of her chest. She suddenly felt like she was going to cry. Tears welled up, but she fought the urge and gathered her thoughts. She was alone in her room. She reached for a glass of water that was sitting on her nightstand. As she drank, tears ran down her face. She started to cry. Then she heard the men at a distance talking. She buried her face in her pillow and cried.

She prayed, "Lord God, answer me if You are out there. Why do I dream of these two little boys? What does this dream mean? Did you take my boys away? I feel like I am someone else. Why did this happen to me? I do not remember the way I look. Why is my face so disfigured? How can my husband still love me? I need answers. Please answer me."

Suddenly she heard someone at her door. There was a soft and quiet knock. She did not want anyone coming in, so she pretended to be sleeping. She heard the door softly open. Valerie was quietly asking, "Mrs. Alexander, are you awake?" Alice was holding her breath, hoping that Valerie would go away. Valerie came around the bed and reached for Alice's arm to take her pulse when she noticed Alice's face. She reached over and wiped tears away.

Valerie was looking at Alice with such compassion. She brushed her hair away from her face. Valerie was so gentle and loving that Alice could longer hold things in. She started sobbing. Valerie leaned over and hugged her. "Mrs. Alexander, let it all out. You don't have to keep anything from me." Alice cried for quite some time, and when she felt like she could no longer cry, it started all over again.

It felt like a lifetime of tears had just emptied out of her. Alice smiled at Valerie, "Thank you for being here for me. I truly appreciate you. I feel better now. I need to know something." Valerie observed her as she continued. "How can you look at me? I see myself, and I do not know if I can continue to look in the mirror. I scare myself." Valerie held Alice's hand, "I see the beauty in you. You have a gentleness about you. I can see that you love deeply. You have a beautiful heart. There is a glow about you."

Alice asked, "I don't feel like I love my husband, so how can you say that?" Valerie smiled, "I can tell these things. I am an excellent judge of character." Alice smiled, "I don't even know if I used to go to church, do you?" "Yes, I do," Valerie answered, "would you like to go with me on Sunday?" Alice hesitated, "do you think Mr. Alexander will let me go?" Valerie smiled, "Is that a choice he should make for you?" "I don't think so, but I feel he may not want me to go." Alice quietly spoke as if he was within earshot. "I haven't gone anywhere since I awoke," she added. Valerie nodded in agreement, "where would you like to go?" "I would like to go shopping. I do not like any of the clothes in my closet." "Well, let us see how you feel in the next couple of days, and we can plan to go out for a little trip. We do not want you to be overexerted." Valerie hoped that this would lift Alice's spirits.

Alice immediately started to make plans. She started to think about the colors that she would like to wear. Suddenly, Alice remembered her scarring. She looked at Valerie, "maybe I'm not ready to go out in public yet. I do not want people staring at me. I may scare little children." Suddenly she was overtaken by grief, and tears rolled down her face. Valerie understood that she needed healing from the trauma, but she is unsure how to approach it. She had been doing physical therapy with Alice, but she did not feel qualified for the trauma healing sessions. "Alice, would you like to speak to someone about trauma healing? Maybe even a pastor would help." "I do not even know what church I may have attended before. I will ask Mr. Alexander at dinner time."

Suddenly Alice heard the commotion and discussion between Jack and Erik. She sat up and yelled for them, "Hello! Hello! I'm awake, and I do not want anyone blamed for my decision. Hello! Can you hear me?" the men heard her calling out and came running. "Are you okay?" they spoke in unison. Alice smiled, "I don't want Erik blamed for my decisions. I chose to go along; he would not have been able to stop me even if he had wanted to put up an argument." She paused, then continued, "I'm doing well now, and that's all that matters, right?" she smiled, hoping that they would give in. The men looked at each other and smiled. They nodded in agreement, and they both agreed to never speak of this again.

Jack rushed over to his wife and hoped to help her lay back, but Alice had other plans. Alice looked at him, "I am doing fine. I want to join you all for dinner." Mr. Alexander knew it was no use to try to argue. He nodded and said, "may I help you get ready?" Alice shyly answered, "Valerie can give me a hand. I would rather be alone for just a minute." Valerie re-

entered and asked, "What would you like to change into?"
"Have you asked if we can go shopping yet?" Alice asked.
"No, I haven't felt it was good timing." Valerie wasn't sure
that any day soon would be a good day after today's incident.
Alice knew what Valerie was thinking, "Today is a great day to
tell him that I am going shopping." "Are you sure? I mean,
after today's incident." Valerie stammered. Alice smiled with
confidence, "Today is perfect. I do not want to be coddled. I
am a grown woman and have needs too. Besides, I hate
everything in the closet."

As they entered the dining room, they looked at each other
and smiled. Alice began to speak, "Oh my! What is for
dinner? It sure smells so good!" Janie proudly said, "Chicken
fried steak, mashed taters, and corn! I thought you should
have some comfort food." Alice smiled and nodded with
appreciation. "You are going to have to teach me to cook. I
have no memories of ever cooking." As she sat next to Erik,
she gently touched his shoulder and smiled at the man who
carried her outdoors. Erik jumped up as she sat down and
pulled out her chair. "Mrs. Alexander, you gave me quite a
scare today." She smiled, "I am good now." He nodded and
knew it was best to drop the conversation. Mr. Alexander was
watching her closely. He wondered why she chose to sit next
to Erik instead of her usual spot. Alice turned and looked at
her husband, "Darling, I am going shopping at the end of the
week. I need clothes. I'm not sure if the clothes in my closet
truly fit my taste. I feel I am ready for an upgrade." He
watched his wife speak with a confidence he had not seen in
quite some time.

"Are you sure you can handle it? You did just have an
episode?" Mr. Alexander questioned. "I believe I am more
than ready. Besides, I do not like the clothes I have in the
closet. These clothes just do not feel like me. Please don't be

discouraged." She added as she noticed his facial expression of dissatisfaction. "I did the best I could after the fire and getting you back home." She responded, "I am not completely unhappy with the clothes. I just want to pick them out for myself. I appreciate you working so hard to find things you thought I would like. I just need to do it for myself; I want to feel these clothes belong to me. I want to feel like I am in my own skin." This time she did not even look at him for fear that he would be so hurt.

"I understand," Jack replied. "Would you at least let me take you?" "No. I want to start doing things by myself. I want to feel independent. IN ADDITION, I do not want you around if people look at me funny. I need to get stronger and do not want you to feel you have to protect me from everything. I have already been a huge burden on you and need to make life easier for us. You do not need to worry." Jack knew Alice was right. She needed to feel confident about herself and get stronger. He thought to himself, "Maybe I will get the wife I always wanted."

13 SHOPPING DAY

Alice arose bright and early. She was so excited about her shopping adventure that she hardly slept a wink. She and Valerie had made plans to leave early and have breakfast in a café nearby on the way into town. Janie had fixed such a lovely breakfast it seemed a shame to leave it. Nevertheless, they had already made plans and apologized to Janie. So, Erik and Janie sat down for breakfast with Mr. Alexander.

Alice and Valerie headed out in Valerie's car. It was a silver 2000 BMW convertible roadster. Valerie smiled at Alice and asked, "Are you ready?" "Oh yeah!" Alice said. The top was on since it was chilly outside, but it felt like they were flying. As they pulled up to the Open Doors Café, the ladies smiled at each other and took a deep breath. "Let's go see what kind of food we can enjoy." Valerie encouraged Alice. Alice just nodded her head, suddenly feeling herself doubt her decision. She thought, "Am I ready to go out in public. I haven't even looked in a mirror yet." Valerie noticed her hesitation, "We don't have to do this." "I'm ready." Alice interrupted.

As the ladies walked into the café, all eyes turned and looked at them. Alice held her head up and walked to a booth near the middle. The ladies sat down and started looking at the menu. Alice adjusted her scarf again to make sure she was adequately covered. Valerie smiled at her and whispered, "You look stunning. What do you see on the menu that you may want to try?" Alice was looking at the menu at all the options. It felt overwhelming that there were so many breakfast options. She was not sure she even knew what most of the items were. Then she noticed the blueberry pancakes. She smiled, "I will take the blueberry pancakes." Valerie nodded as if to say good choice. When the waitress came over, she looked at Alice. "You must be new in town; I have never seen you here before." Alice smiled, "I am new. My husband moved here over six months ago. We have the ranch outside of town." "My name is Carmen. I will be your server today, and I am happy to meet you. Welcome to the area! Since this is your first time, your meal is on the house. I will send the owner over to meet you. She loves to know all our neighbors." Alice smiled, "Thank you. I will take the blueberry pancakes today." Carmen smiled, "would you like the full meal or just pancakes?" "I am feeling hungry, so I will take the full meal. What comes with that?" "Well, you have options. Hash browns or country potatoes, two or three eggs, coffee, milk, or juice?" Alice smiled as she contemplated her options, "I will take hash browns, two poached eggs, and orange juice, please." "If this isn't enough for you, we have killer biscuits and gravy. You just let me know." Alice suddenly realized that she had just ordered for herself and knew what some of these things were. As Valerie placed her order, Alice wondered if she would recall anything else.

Valerie and Alice sat enjoying their meal when the owner came up to them. "Valerie, it is so good to see you again. I have not seen you in such a long time. Who is this beautiful lady with you today?" Valerie made the introductions, "Alice, I want to introduce you to my sister, Mary. Mary, this is Alice. A good friend of mine. I have been helping her at the ranch." Mary smiled, "it is a pleasure to make your acquaintance. I hope we can become friends in the days to come." Alice smiled, "Mary, Valerie didn't tell me her sister owned the café. It is a pleasure to meet you." Alice smiled at Valerie. Mary excused herself, and the two continued chatting. They spoke about the shops they would go to and even started talking about where they could have lunch. Mary came to say goodbye before they left. As the two got into the car, Valerie apologized, "I'm sorry I didn't tell you it was my sister's place." Alice smiled, "I'm sure you have your reasons. It's okay. I forgave you immediately. Let's get moving and find some clothes I will enjoy wearing."

Alice was enjoying the drive from the country to the city. She was impressed with all the farms, ranches, and vineyards, and the colors were amazing! She noticed every fence that was up. There were white picket fences, metal fences, log fences, and even some made of rocks. She wondered why the fences were so different. She noticed some people had dogs and others didn't. She even thought she had seen some ostriches. As they left the country, the city started to appear. She noticed that life seemed to leave too. She saw the buildings and people rushing everywhere. It was not a life that she liked; maybe the shopping would take her mind off the loss of the vibrant living colors. She began to wonder where the other house was that burned down. Was it in the country or the city? Suddenly she had more questions. Then her thought went to Jack. She wondered where his office was and if he enjoyed what he did.

The roadster stopped, and Alice was jolted back to reality. She looked over at Valerie and smiled. "Well, are we here?" She asked. Valerie smiled and said, "Yes. Let's take the top down and experience the city in the open air." Valerie reached over her head and released the top from both sides. The top started to lift, and the sun shone brightly into the car. As they slowly proceeded into the city, Alice could feel the sun on her face. It felt wonderful, and she rested her head back and enjoyed the rays warming her face. As she opened her eyes, she saw the skyscrapers and was in awe of the height. "Are we going into one of those?" Alice pointed to the skyscrapers. Valerie laughed, "If you would like to." Alice was unsure if she wanted to, but a part of her did. She shook her head no, then yes. Finally, laughing, she said, "I have to!"

Valerie drove into a parking structure, and Alice was like a small child gazing with amazement at all the sights. Nothing was familiar to her. As they walked around the shopping centers, they chatted about the clothes and styles. Nothing was familiar to Alice yet. Alice looked at all the clothes and even tried some things on. She bought a few things, and nothing was like the clothes she had in the closet back at the house.

Time flew as they shopped. Alice suddenly noticed that she was starving, so they headed to an area with lots of restaurants. As they discussed what to eat, Alice saw a small shop. It looked like a dessert shop, but that is where she wanted to go. As they entered the shop, she could smell all the wonderful smells that tickled her palate. Valerie smiled and asked, "What are you in the mood for?" "I'm not sure; I don't remember what these names mean." Alice was feeling a little lost. Valerie reached over and touched her hand, "it's okay. Let's look at the displays and see if anything looks good." Alice walked closer to the displays. She saw brown things and other things that were very colorful. "I want that!" she pointed at the collection. The young lady behind the counter smiled, "Oh my goodness. You have chosen the house special, Heaven's Delight. It has chocolate, coconut, cashews, and almonds. This cake is an excellent choice." Alice felt so excited to dig into her dessert. Valerie had ordered some chocolate candies. Alice smiled and said, "Now, this is the way to eat a meal. Dessert first, then the main meal." Valerie was not sure she would enjoy her meal this way, but she was wrong! Valerie bit into her chocolates and let out a loud laugh. "Oh, my goodness! Alice, you are right! This is a much better way to eat a meal!" The two ladies laughed and giggled all afternoon.

They had asked Carmen what she recommended for lunch, and they were on their way to another small restaurant. Upon arrival, they looked for the owner, Charles. Charles seated them in a corner booth so they could see all that took place when people arrived. He did not even take their order; he just started bringing out different plates for them to share and try. As people arrived, they were seated in booths, and the servers spoke to them as if they knew each customer. They never took one order. They would bring plates out, and people would enjoy every morsel on their plates. No one went up to the cash register; they just left money on the table. Alice wondered, "how do they know how much to pay?" She finally called out to Charles, "Charles, do you have a moment?" As he came closer, he smiled at Alice, "How may I help you, my lovely Alice?" "How do people know how much to pay you? Why aren't they placing orders? How do you know what they want?" She was like a child with all her questions.

Charles explained, "Well, you see, Alice. The customers have been coming here for some time, and the team has all been here since I opened this place. Every day of the week, we offer a selection of four meals. Two are breakfast, and two are not. If the customer says they would like breakfast, they get the two meals or the same if they do not want breakfast. They then get the non-breakfast meals. They know that they will be happy with whatever the meals are. I have been here for over 30 years. I like to keep them on their toes or, shall I say, keep their tastes buds guessing. Every day is a different menu with no entrees replicated in a month. I have never had a complaint. In addition, they know that all the money I make in excess goes back into our youth. The inner-city kids get meals and a place to stay with the extra funds. I have even taught a few how to cook." Alice smiled, "What a great concept! I love that! Charles, I plan to come back again to see what else you have cooking. I live in the country, so I can't come too often, but I will be back!" Charles smiled and asked, "How far out do you live?" Valerie smiled at Alice and responded, "We live in a community about an hour and a half north of here. Perkins." "I'm not familiar with that part of the country." Charles walked away to take care of the kitchen.

Valerie noticed the time, "I can't believe it is now four. We better hurry out of the city before the traffic gets bad." The two ladies walked back to the parking structure. Alice said, "Thank you, Valerie, for such a wonderful day. I feel a little tired, but it is a good tired." Valerie asked, "Are you feeling strong enough to walk back to the car?" "Oh yes, I'm fine. I love the people we met today. The dessert was delicious, and Charles has such a great place. I would want to be able to help him somehow. Not sure if Jack would be interested, but I am." Alice felt weak as they reached the car, but she did not want Valerie to worry, so she did not say anything. As she slipped into her seat, she leaned back. "I think I may take a nap on the way home." "Valerie, thanks again for everything today." Alice closed her eyes and drifted off to sleep.

14 CHANGE IS IN THE AIR

Ann Marie had picked up the boys after school like most days, but today the boys were different. They both were chipper and talkative. Ann Marie drove home wondering what was going on. The boys were in the back talking about their day at school. Samuel had testing today, and he felt terrific about the Spelling test. Frankie was talking about a girl that was stung by bees at recess. He felt terrible for her, but he was happy that he was not the one that was stung. Frankie told Samuel that the girl had cried and had to go home early because her face got swollen, probably because of an allergic reaction. Frankie explained in detail how she was first crying, then her face turned red, then started swelling up all over. First her cheek, then her lips, then her eyes. Her mom had come to get her, and the class had to be quiet while Mrs. Jones took care of her.

As the car pulled up to the driveway, the boys noticed that their Auntie Rae's car was near the garage. They jumped out and ran inside before Ann Marie could even get out of the vehicle. The boys had not seen their Auntie Rae since the night of the party, and that was not a good day. The boys jumped on their aunt and hugged her. The boys pleasantly surprised Auntie Rae with their reaction. She had not seen them in this good of spirits in over two years. As she hugged the boys, she remembered her dear sister and the joy that she brought. "I have missed you so much and wanted to come and see if we could go to dinner?" "Daddy is not home yet, but he should be home soon," Samuel answered. "Auntie Rae, we have missed you so much!" The boys wanted to play a game with their aunt, but she was concerned about homework. "Today is Friday, and we never have homework for the weekend," Samuel said. "Alright, what would you like to play?" Auntie Rae asked. "Would you like to play Guess Me?" Frankie asked. "Sure, I would!" she responded.

Ann Marie headed towards the door to lock it, but she noticed something strange outside. She saw a man lurking outside. Ann Marie immediately closed the door, locked it, and grabbed her phone to call Seth. She dialed him; as she heard his voice, she whispered, "Are you almost home? A man is walking around looking suspicious." Seth's heart sank, "write down his description and keep an eye on him. I will call the police. Make sure to keep the boys inside with all the doors locked." "Rae is here with us. I will alert her without worrying the boys." Ann Marie hung up and walked toward everyone. She smiled at Rae and waved her over, "Rae would you like to help me get a snack for the boys?" Rae walked towards the kitchen, "boys, why don't you head upstairs and freshen up before a snack. I can come up if you want me to." She added. In unison, the boys said, "We are big enough to wash by ourselves. Auntie Rae, we are not babies!" They were laughing as they went upstairs.

Ann Marie immediately filled in Rae, and she headed to the window to see the man. There was no one in the side yard, so she walked to the front. As Rae looked out, she could see someone in dark clothes moving around the bushes. She wanted to run out there and confront the person, but she remembered the boys and did not want to add any trauma by this ordeal. Ann Marie joined her at the window. She had a pen and paper with some descriptions. She asked, "What does the person look like?" Rae answered, "I have not seen the face, but I'm guessing about six foot tall, weighs about 180 pounds." Ann Marie was writing everything she was hearing.

Rae noticed that the person was looking around the house. "Do you think this could be the city person taking readings?" Ann Marie looked but could not see if the person was wearing a uniform. The day was gloomy and overcast, so they could not see clearly. It felt like they had been watching this person for a long time before they saw the police arrive. The person was startled by the police and looked like he wanted to escape.

The two ladies watched from inside as the police stopped the car and called out to the person. They decided to keep the boys entertained so they would not see what was happening outside. The boys were in their rooms and almost finished changing clothes. They went into the bathroom together. "Why do you think Auntie Rae is here? She hasn't been here for a long time?" Frankie asked. Samuel smiled, "Maybe she just missed us. Let's finish up so we can play with her until daddy gets home." Frankie was not satisfied with the answer, "Do you think she knows something about mommy?" Samuel wondered the same thing, "I don't know, but she will tell us when daddy gets home if she does." "I hope daddy gets home real soon!" Frankie smiled.

The ladies were still looking out the window as the boys came down the stairs. "What are you looking at?" Frankie yelled. The ladies were shocked that the boys were already coming downstairs. "Oh, nothing. What would you like for a snack? Your dad said he will be some very soon." "Can we skip our snack and go straight to dinner?" Samuel asked. "Well, I think your dad may be tired and want to rest a little before going out," Rae answered. "Okay, I want some apples and peanut butter," Frankie said. "I don't want anything to eat." Samuel followed. Rae had not been paying attention and asked again, "What would you boys like to eat for a snack?" The boys looked at each other puzzled, "Auntie Rae, is everything okay?" Samuel asked. "Yes, why do you ask?" Rae did not realize she had asked the boys twice about eating. Samuel answered, "You asked us twice, Auntie Rae." She looked at them apologetically, "I'm sorry, boys. I guess I was thinking about something else. So, what did you say you wanted?"

Samuel did not answer but was watching her closely. Frankie repeated, "I want apples and peanut butter." "Okay, let's get the apples out of the refrigerator and peanut butter out of the pantry." Samuel was still watching her, and he did not move. Frankie ran to the pantry for the peanut butter. Rae turned and looked at Samuel. She knew he was on to her, "Samuel? Will you please get the apples?" Again, Samuel did not move, "Auntie Rae, can I talk to you alone?" "Ann Marie, can you help Frankie?" Rae did not take her eyes off her nephew.

They walked into the dining room, and she sat down. "Samuel, you know I don't want you to feel afraid or hurt, right?" "Yes." "I also know that your dad is always doing his best to keep you safe and happy." She continued, "Do you feel safe today?" "Yes." "Well, your dad wants you to stay safe in the house. Can you do that?" "Yes." "I do not want to overstep your dad's request, so I can't say anything until he gets home. Can you be okay with that until then?" "I want to know if this has to do with mommy." He pressed. "No, this doesn't have anything to do with your mom." She responded. "Does it have to do with you?" "No. I am fine. Don't worry about me." "Does it have to do with Frankie?" "No, honey, I do not want you to worry. Everything is fine." "Then why do you look worried?" "Your dad should be home any minute, and then he will tell you what you need to know." She attempted to reassure him, but he was not feeling easy about whatever was bothering her.

He argued, "I am big enough to take care of my little brother, so I am big enough to know what is going on." She smiled, "You are the best big brother in the world. No one else could have helped him during this time when he had been hurting so much. I could never comfort him when he cried. You were the only one that could get him to calm down. You are a kid that has lost part of his childhood. You are only nine. You should not have to be dealing with everything you have been. I am so proud of you! I want you to have as much of that childhood as you can. I want to be able to help more. Will you allow me to?" Samuel felt tears build up but fought them, "You can't take us away from daddy." "Oh gosh, that's not what I mean. I mean, I want to be able to come over more often and help here. I changed my work schedule so I can do that." Rae was smiling but feeling his pain. "Oh, okay. We would love to have you here more often. We have missed you so much, Auntie Rae."

Seth arrived outside. He ran to the front of the house where the police had someone they were questioning. Seth approached the officers. "What's going on here?" he asked. "Seth, this isn't what it looks like. This is a city employee checking out a gas leak. We have confirmed with the city, and his story checks out. He was trying not to alarm anyone, but evidently, your nanny saw him and called us." "Have you spoken to the ladies inside?" Seth asked. "No, we haven't. Daniel didn't want to alarm anyone since he didn't smell or detect gas." The officer continued, "I thought it was weird that he wouldn't have knocked on the door so that nothing was ignited inside. Unfortunately, we were on hold with the city, which delayed our investigation." "Daniel, we will allow you to head home." As Daniel walked away and got into his vehicle, they observed him. Jonathan was the officer who knew Seth, "I thought it was suspicious that he didn't knock on the door. I cannot arrest him for looking suspicious, but I will keep a close eye on this person. There is something about him that I am not fully trusting. We did run a check on him, but nothing came up."

Seth talked to the officers and then walked inside. "Hey boys, I'm home!" He nodded 'no' to the ladies as he hugged his boys. "Daddy, Auntie Rae wants us to go out to eat!" Frankie was so excited that he was screaming with excitement. "Daddy, can we go, please!" Seth smiled, "I think it is a great idea. We have not had dinner with your auntie in a long time. Ann Marie, would you like to join us?" She smiled shyly, "I am honored to be invited. Yes, I will come along." "Okay, where do we want to go?" Rae asked. "Can we go out for pizza?" Frankie chimed in. They all smiled and nodded in agreement. "We all fit in the van; shall we all go in the same car?" Seth asked. "Yes!" The kids yelled. The two ladies smiled and agreed.

They slipped out of the van as they arrived at The Pizza Parlor, and the boys ran to the door. They held the doors open for all to enter. They saw one table available when they entered and headed towards the table. Frankie stopped and stared. Everyone watched him, and he did not even blink. Seth asked, "Frankie, are you okay?" He did not answer or move. Samuel put his hand on his brother's shoulder, "Frankie, Frankie, what do you see?" Frankie answered, "I remember when mommy was here with us. We were here to celebrate my birthday. She had a huge cake that she shared with everyone in the place. She was wearing a purple dress and a white sweater. She was laughing because I got cake on her dress. She was so happy. She did not even get mad at me. She never got mad. She was always happy. I miss her so much. I cannot wait until we come back with her. This is the same table where we sat." He moved towards the table and pulled out his chair. He sat down quietly and smiled at the memory of this fun time with his mommy.

A Mother's Broken Promise

The waiter came and took the order. There was much laughter and conversation that night. It did feel like things were changing for them all.

15 THE VISITOR

Saturday mornings were usually lazy days. Today was no different. The boys got up early and went into Seth's room. They told him to stay in bed and they would make him breakfast. Seth was happy to see that his boys were looking so much better. As they left his room, his cell phone dinged with a text. It was his friend wanting to come by for a visit. He responded and explained that the boys were preparing him breakfast. They set a time for eleven for a visit.

The boys went downstairs as if not to awaken anyone, but they had already awakened their daddy. They tiptoed down the stairs. Smiling at each other, whispering, "Shall we make cereal or pancakes?" Frankie wanted to make pancakes, but Samuel said, "We would have to have daddy help. We could make the frozen ones in the toaster if you want?" Samuel remembered that they still had a few of the frozen ones leftover. Frankie's eyes lit up, "Yes. Let's make those. We can make some toast too. Should we have grape or apple juice?" "What about orange juice?" Samuel asked. Frankie smiled sheepishly, "What if we have all three?" They both nodded in approval.

Samuel headed to the refrigerator to get the pancakes and juices. Frankie headed to the pantry for bread. Frankie asked, "Can we make sausage? I love sausage with pancakes!" I can put them in the microwave. I think they are already cooked and just need warming up." The boys worked together to get breakfast finished. Frankie went to get the trays out of the pantry when he realized they had not used them in a long time. He asked, "Samuel, when is the last time we used these?" Samuel asked, "Used what?" "The trays," Frankie answered. "I don't remember; why?" Samuel answered.

"They are too high for me to reach them. I need your help."
Frankie called out. Samuel walked toward Frankie, "Oh, okay.
I can reach them." As he reached up to get them, he realized
they had not used them since their mommy was there, but he
did not tell Frankie.

The boys loaded up all the food onto the tray. They had a
glass of milk, orange juice, grape juice, and apple juice. They
heated the sausage, pancakes and made toast. They had even
washed grapes for their breakfast. They were climbing up the
stairs very carefully with all the food when Seth stepped out
of his room and took the tray. The boys jumped up onto
Seth's bed, and they sat down to enjoy the feast. They
chatted about the breakfast they had made and what they
wanted to do this weekend.

The boys wanted to see their aunt later in the afternoon. Seth
said, "Let me text her to see if she is off today or this
afternoon, but we don't want to wake her up if she is home
and sleeping, right?" The boys smiled and nodded their
heads. They enjoyed their breakfast and started to tell silly
stories.

Seth started, "Once there was a king with two little princes.
They were brave little princes. One day, a spider came to
bother them, but they jumped up and squashed it. They saw
that they had spider guts on their shoes, so they went to the
creek to clean them. They jumped into the creek and washed
the guts off by stomping in the water. When they came to the
king, the king asked the boys, "Why are your shoes wet?"
They answered, "We washed off the spider guts we had
gotten on our shoes." The king laughed, "That is a great way
to remove spider guts! Throughout my kingdom, let it be
known that this is the newest and best way to clean off spider
guts!" They all laughed at the silly story!

Samuel went next. "There was a little mouse that was so very hungry that he went up to the cat in the house. He asked the cat, "Would you lift me so I can see if there is any food on the table that I may eat?" The cat was not nice, so he said, "No way!" The mouse was hungry and sad, so he asked the dog, "Mr. Dog, sir, would you help me get some food?" The dog was very nice, "Yes, what do you want to eat?" he asked. The mouse was so hungry, "I would eat anything you can get for me." The dog went into the kitchen, and he came out with a huge sandwich. It had cheese, turkey, lettuce, tomatoes, and pickles. The mouse was so excited. The dog asked him, "Do you want the whole sandwich, or will you be willing to share it?" The mouse thought, "I will be happy to share it with you." The dog smiled, "I am also hungry, and I will cut it in half." The mouse thought about it and said, "You are much bigger than I so that you can have most of it. I just need a small piece for me." The dog began to cut it, stopped, and said, "Why not just share it. I can take a bite, and then you can take a bite." The two new friends shared the sandwich, and both were very happy. Their bellies were so full that they gave him the crumbs that remained when the cat came by and wanted a bite. They became friends and lived happily ever after.

Frankie was next. "A long time ago in a faraway land, there lived a princess who was taken away from her family. She was sad because she was missing her family. One day she saw a creek and went fishing; she caught the biggest fish she had ever caught, and it spoke to her. It said, "One day soon, beautiful princess, you will be going home to see your family." The princess jumped up and down with excitement and joy. Unfortunately, she forgot all about the fish, dropped it, and it swam away to find its own family. When the princess noticed that the fish was gone, she laughed and splashed in the water to say, "Goodbye, Mr. Fish. Have a good time with your family!" The fish jumped out of the water with a big splash saying, "Goodbye, princess! Have fun with your family!" The end.

After laughing and discussing the great stories they told, it was time to clean up. The boys each headed to their rooms for showers. Then, they decided to stay indoors and play in their bedrooms for the morning. They each had a special project to finish.

Jonathan, the police officer, came by the house. It was unusual for him to visit. Seth prepared himself for whatever Jonathan had to say. The boys were upstairs in their rooms playing.

Jonathan began, "Seth, I want you to know that I am your friend first, then an officer. I did more searching into Daniel, the city employee. It appears that Daniel is not his real name. He is new to the department, and the person that hired him did not do his due diligence with a complete background check. His real name is Ralph Edwards. He has warrants in a couple of states for assault on women. I just happened to see the fax come through last night. We have police officers arresting him as we speak. I wanted to be the first to come to make you aware. I am so happy that nothing happened here. You have been through so much already, and I know the boys do not need to have more trauma in their lives."

Seth sat in shock and silence. When he finally felt he could speak, "Does this guy have any connection to my beautiful Francie's having gone missing?" Jonathan continued, "No, we do not believe so. He just moved to this area a few months ago. We are checking to make sure of his whereabouts two years ago. We are still actively looking into your wife's disappearance." "When will you know where he was two years ago?" Seth asked. "We hope to have answers in a couple of weeks, if not sooner. How are your boys doing?" "They are doing a little better, but they have just started sleeping through the night. I do not want to see them go backward. Is there any way to keep this quiet and off the news? I do not want them to hear from anyone what just went down here. We don't watch television here so that they won't hear it at home."

Jonathan and Seth continued to speak of life, but Seth could not get his mind off this man. "Jonathan, can you do a drive-by every day for a few days? I don't want reporters or anyone else coming by the house." Jonathan nodded, "I am happy to come by personally to make sure no one comes around. But, Seth, why don't you and the boys get away for a few days?" "We have plans to get away, but it's not for a while." Seth was looking worried. Jonathan put his hand on his friend's shoulder, "Listen. I will contact you personally if any news comes across the airways. But, Seth, do not worry. The entire police station is actively working to solve this case. We want to bring Francie back to you." Seth's eyes shifted, "Boys, why don't you come to say hello to Jonathan. You boys remember my friend, right?"

Jonathan turned, "Samuel, Frankie. How are you doing? Sorry, it has been so long." The boys ran down the stairs. "Uncle Jonathan!" Frankie yelled. Samuel smiled and said, "Frankie, he is not our real uncle." Frankie laughed, "I know, but he is daddy's best friend, so he is my uncle!" Jonathan hugged the boys. "Wow! You boys have gotten so big! I was hoping we could get lunch. What do you think?" Frankie was the first to answer, "How about hot dogs?" Then, Samuel chimed in, "I want a cheeseburger. Can we get ice cream afterward?" Jonathan answered, "Whatever your dad will let you have." Seth laughed, "I guess I can be the bad guy. Well, we are ready so let's go!"

They headed out the door, and Seth made sure everything was locked and secure. They drove to the only burger place in town, The Burger Hut. When they entered, they saw a few people they knew from school. The boys ran to say hello. Seth and Jonathan grabbed a table and discussed what to put on the jukebox. They laughed about the songs; the oldies were the only choices. When the boys joined them, they had a special request. They wanted Elvis Presley's 'I'll remember you, Teddy Bear, Bridge over troubled water, and Always on my mind.' They knew that their mommy always used to play those songs. The boys always felt closer to her when they did things that mom loved to do.

The burgers, hotdogs, and fries arrived at the table. They disappeared faster than they appeared at the table. They were famished. The boys giggled the entire time as they ate. They were reminiscing about the last time their mommy had been there. Mommy loved grilled hotdogs, and so did Frankie. The owner would make special grilled hotdogs for mommy whenever they came to The Burger Hut. Samuel joked, "I think Andy loved mommy. He would always make her favorite stuff." Seth laughed, "Andy and mommy have been best friends since kindergarten. He does love her. He loves her like a sister." Frankie finished listening about someone else loving his mommy, so he changed the subject, "Can we order ice cream now?" Jonathan quickly caught on, "We can order anything you would like, young Frankie."

Frankie was so excited, "Can I have a banana split? I like what mommy likes!" As they raised their hands for the server to come over, Andy headed over. Frankie did not like this. "Can we get the same person that took our order earlier?" Andy joked with him, "What's the matter? Do I smell bad?"

Frankie was not feeling like being friendly, "No, I just want the other person." Andy smiled, "Okay, no problem. I just wanted to come over and tell you, our specials. Is that okay?" Frankie watched him carefully, "Okay, but" Seth interrupted, "Andy, we would love for you to take our dessert order." Frankie gave his daddy a quick look.

"Okay then, today's special is a banana split any way you want it," Andy said with a smile and carefully watched his young customer, Frankie. "What do you mean, any way you want it?" Andy answered, "Well, the normal split has strawberries, chocolate, and pineapple, but you can have it any way you like. I feel you may want pineapple, coconut, chocolate, and blueberries with whipped cream and no cherries on top. How did I do?" Frankie looked at him and asked, "How did you know what my mommy likes?" Andy smiled, "We have been best friends since kindergarten. We used to have ice cream every Saturday, right here in this place." Frankie smiled at Andy, "Yes, I want it just like mommy does." Andy finished taking everyone's order and left.

Andy returned with all the ice cream. He gave Frankie his first, "I give you yours first because you are my very best customer. Enjoy, young Frankie." As Andy walked away, Frankie asked, "Can you tell me stories about mommy when she was a kid?" Andy turned and smiled, "I would love to. What if you guys come back next Saturday, and I will make sure someone else is cooking so we can sit and tell stories." Frankie smiled, "Daddy, can we please?" Seth nodded his head, "Yes, of course. It would be fun to hear stories about Francie."

16 THE DREAM

Alice could hear the car sounds, and the car radio was quietly playing in the background. Alice could hear the sounds outside the car; the road was smooth but made a bumpy noise. Alice also listened to the cows in the distant mooing. The sound of a rooster crowing far away became more distant. Finally, Alice started to have everything go black and silent.

There was a stream, blue and rocky. Alice could see white caps cracking the water with a sharp sound. It was as loud as if a bucket of water poured onto Alice. Then she heard a beautiful sound. There was so much giggling. She looked around; she could not see where the giggling was coming from, but Alice spun round and round to find who was giggling; she fell into a meadow of daisies. The meadow was so alive. The daisies were moving as if they were breathing. Alice could smell the fragrance; it was as sweet as honey. She could hear the honeybees flying from flower to flower, making a buzzing sound. Suddenly she heard the giggling again. She turned towards the stream and saw three figures. It looked like someone big and two little ones. As the figures came into focus, she noticed a man and two little boys. They were running and giggling. She was watching the boys running toward the water and screaming with joy. As they ran, it was clear that they were going to jump into the stream As they neared the stream, Alice began to worry about the boys. She got up and started to run towards the boys. Suddenly Alice was flying towards the boys and flew over them. She saw them look up at her and yell out to her, but she could not understand what they were saying. The boys were waving and laughing. She saw their pink cheeks and faces glistened like the sun as she flew back towards them. They laughed as she flew by and continued to wave. She saw them run towards the stream and jump in. As she flew over them for the third time, she saw him. She stopped in midair and watched the man. He was smiling and laughing. His eyes sparkled, and his smile seemed to brighten the already sunny day. Alice could sense the love he had for his sons. She could feel the warmth of his love. It warmed her up as she watched him. He was tender and gentle with the boys. The sky suddenly filled up with balloons, which were red, white, blue, and yellow. She flew among the balloons and lost sight of the boys and the dad. She was frantically searching for them, but the balloons were around her. She tried to get below the balloons, but there were so many that she could not move. She awoke.

Alice opened her eyes and saw she was in the car. She looked at Valerie and smiled. "Are we almost home?" "We have a few more miles. Is everything okay?" Valerie asked. "I had a beautiful dream." Alice hesitated to finish her sentence. "What do you think dreams mean?" Valerie was tentative but finally answered, "I believe God speaks to us in our dreams." Valerie waited for Alice, but there was silence between them. Alice looked out into the world; she saw the beauty around her. She wondered to herself, 'God if you are out there. What are you telling me?' Alice sat silently, looking out the window. She saw every flower along the road, every cow, every horse, every critter, even the tiny bugs that flew past.

Valerie pulled up into the driveway as it was starting to get dark. Alice could hear the horses neighing, calling out to her. Suddenly, her eyes filled with tears. Alice was unsure why she was feeling so emotional, but the tears flowed out as if the gates were suddenly opened. Valerie put the car in park and looked over at Alice. "Are you okay?" Alice suddenly broke down uncontrollably and cried out. "I want to be normal again. I want my life back. I do not want to look like this anymore. I want to be beautiful and free again. Am I wrong to want this, Valerie?" Valerie reached over to comfort Alice, "You have every right to want your life back to normal. What has brought on all this emotion?" "I had a dream. It was so beautiful, and it felt so real. I want things to go back to normal. I want to be beautiful again." Valerie was thinking about how to respond, but Alice beat her to it. "I know that beauty is from within. I want more than that. I want to be happy again." Valerie smiled, "Alice, don't give up. You will have everything that is supposed to be yours, and I will help you! You can count on me. I believe God is talking to you loud and clear. So, pay attention to your dreams. Ask God to tell you what the dreams mean." "Valerie, do you think God talks to me?" Alice was not sure. "He does. We are so busy with life that we do not listen to His voice during the day. At night, He can speak to us through our dreams. The bible calls them night visions. Sometimes, we hear Him during waking hours but think it is our conscience or intuition. He is that voice in our thoughts telling us to do the right thing. Encouraging us when we are ready to give up. He loves you, Alice." Alice smiled at Valerie. She was starting to feel much better. The ladies had been in the car for over thirty minutes. They stopped to get all the bags out of the trunk as they exited the vehicle.

As the ladies entered the house through the back door with arms full of bags, Jack entered through the front door. "Wow! You know how to shop!" Jack smiled. "We had a fun-filled day. I am so excited about my new clothes. We had breakfast and then headed into the city for shopping. Our breakfast was delicious, but Janie, it did not compare to yours. Janie, I brought a small gift for you. I just wanted to show you how much I appreciate the delicious meals you prepare for us."

Alice handed Janie a small box that was gift-wrapped. Janie was so careful with the beautiful gold wrapping; she had never seen anything so beautiful. Janie's eyes filled with tears, "Oh, Mrs. Alexander. This bell is the most beautiful I have ever seen. Thank you so much for your kind thoughtfulness." Alice reached out and hugged Janie, "Please call me Alice. And you are so welcome."

Jack was smiling at the tender moment he was witnessing. He thought to himself, 'she is just as wonderful as she always was.' As he turned to leave the room, Alice called him, "Jack, I brought a small gift. I wasn't sure what you may need, but I saw this and hoped you would enjoy it." Jack reached for the gift bag. As he reached in, he felt something fuzzy. Jack pulled out a small stuffed dog. He smiled, "Thank you. I will take this to work, so I have something you have given me near me." "I thought you might want to get used to a stuffed pet first, so maybe someday we can have an indoor dog," Alice said jokingly. "Oh, I see. You are trying to break me in." Jack added teasingly.

"Where is Erik? I have something for him as well." Jack turned to face Alice, "Erik? He should be in soon. He called me when I was on my way home." Jack excused himself to freshen up before dinner. Alice headed to her room with the shopping bags. Valerie was right behind her with an arm full of bags. "Okay, what would you like to wear today for dinner?" Alice smiled, "I don't know. I bought so much that I cannot remember what I may like the most. Let's look and see what I should wear."

The ladies started pulling out clothes from the bags. There were skirts, skorts, pants, and shorts. They also pulled out dresses and blouses. She had even bought a couple of T-shirts to wear when she worked with the horses. Valerie held up a couple of her favorites, but Alice was not feeling like those things. Then she saw it, a dress. It was purple with a floral design. It had pink and yellow flowers that were faint but visible. The sleeves were mid-arm and not too tight. She said, "I think I am going with this dress. There is something about it. I felt so pretty when I put it on." The dress was a button-up on the front. It had many tiny little buttons, but Alice did not have to undo them all. Valerie smiled, "You look gorgeous! It complements your skin tone. The way your hair lays on your shoulders makes you even more attractive." Alice felt herself blush.

The ladies walked out of the bedroom, down the hall, into the dining room. Jack was the first to see them. "Wow! That dress looks great on you, darling." Erik was next to notice Alice, "Mrs. Alexander, you look marvelous! You were right; the clothes you had did not fit your personality. You look amazing." Alice blushed at all the attention she was getting. She had Erik's gift in her hands. "I got this small gift to show my gratitude for all you have done for me, Erik." "You didn't have to, Mrs. Alexander. It is my pleasure to have you in the stables." Alice handed him the gift. Erik opened the box. He could not believe his eyes, "Mrs. Alexander, this belt buckle is great. Thank you so much!" The belt buckle had his name with horses and dogs. It was something he did not have and had never received a gift from anyone before. He had no family, and this was most definitely his family.

"Well, shall we eat?" Alice blurted out, feeling that the moment was too intense. She headed to the table where Janie had a delicious-looking table set. There was a fresh veggie platter, baked chicken in lemon sauce, baked potatoes, and homemade freshly baked bread. It not only looked delicious but also smelled so good. Alice could not wait to dig in, but the others were having a conversation in the hallway. She called out, "Come and get it. I will eat it all if you don't come in." Alice could tell that something was going on as they entered the dining room. "Can we please pick up the conversation after dinner?" Everyone smiled at her and nodded. Alice announced, "I had such a beautiful day shopping and would like to finish the day out without any talk of trouble. Whatever it is, can wait for later, please."

As they sat down, the conversation and mood changed. Alice chatted about the sights and stores and could still feel her dream's peace, beauty, and reality. She would not share this dream with anyone, not even Valerie. Alice was feeling hopeful. "If there is a God. He is going to help me." She thought to herself.

When everyone had finished eating, Jack asked, "Alice, is it okay if we discuss what is on our minds?" Alice was not sure she wanted to hear, but in all fairness, she did ask everyone to wait until after dinner. "Yes, of course. It must be important if you were all discussing it when I walked away." "Erik has spotted the bears coming closer to the house and stables. We would feel much better if you would not go out without either Erik or Valerie." Alice's heart sank for two reasons: she felt some of her independence leaving, and the horses may be injured.

Alice answered, "How safe are the horses?" Erik replied, "I will be closing and locking up the gates so the bears can't enter the stables. The dogs will stay in the stables with the horses. I may stay there too for the next few nights. Mrs. Alexander, please do not worry about the horses; they will be safe. We are more worried about your safety. I would request that you call me when you want to come out so I can walk out with you. I hope this doesn't make you uncomfortable." Alice was thinking about the horses, "Is there a way that the bears can enter the stables?" "No, the gates we have are made of metal, and only a bulldozer would be able to break in." He answered. "What about the dogs? Will they be safe enough with you there?" Alice asked. "We will all be safe. I believe the bears should head back up into the mountain area soon. They may be looking for food and will not find any here. We keep everything bearproof." Erik reassured her.

"Well, when can I go see the horses? I heard them calling out to me when we arrived." Alice wanted to see how safe her horses would be. "I would prefer that you wait until tomorrow morning." Jack interrupted. "Erik, did you see the bears tonight?" Alice continued, "I can make it quick." Erik could see that she was determined, "What if you use the binoculars to look when I head out to close things up." "I suppose if that's the only way for tonight." Alice was very disappointed.

Erik headed out to the stables after he had gotten a couple of extra blankets for himself and the dogs. Alice went out onto the patio and used the binoculars to look around the property. There was quite a bit of lighting due to the full moon. She looked around the entire property and could not see any of the bears. Once she felt good about the arrangements, she headed into the house. Jack stood at the door, keeping an eye on his wife. He knew that she would not be able to rest knowing that the bears may be on the property. "I don't think they are out tonight. They may have headed to the neighboring property to the empty cabin." Alice nodded her head in agreement; but was saying a little prayer just in case. "God, if you are out there. Please take care of Erik, the dogs, and the horses. Thank you, Lord. Also, watch over our house as we sleep."

Alice headed to the bedroom to turn in for the night. She hoped to have more dreams like the one she had in the car on the drive home.

17 STORY TIME

The week flew by for Seth, but it dragged on for the boys. They were looking forward to the stories. They had agreed that 2 pm was a good time for a late lunch. So, they piled in the truck, and the boys could hardly hold in the excitement. Instead, the boys giggled with joy as they drove up to The Burger Hut.

Andy greeted the boys at the door. "Come on in. I took the liberty of ordering special meals that your mom used to like when she was little. I hope that's okay?" He was following the boys as they headed to their favorite spot. It was the booth that was closest to the jukebox. So, they could see everyone in the place. After they sat down, Andy smiled, "Did your mom ever tell you the secret of this booth?" The boys looked at each other and nodded no. Andy went on, "When I bought this place, I made sure I didn't change anything. Look under the table, right here in this area." The boys scrambled under the table to look and see what they would see. To their surprise, they saw a message 'Francie loves this booth.' They popped their heads up and asked, "Daddy, did you see what mommy wrote?" Seth smiled, "No, I never have seen it. Let me look." "What was mommy doing writing under the table?" Samuel asked. "Well, she used to be so funny," Andy said. Frankie corrected him, "You mean; she is so funny." "Yes, of course! That is exactly what I mean. She was funny when she was little and still is."

"What else can you tell us?" Frankie asked. Andy smiled, "Well, did you know that your mom was a tomboy?" The boys nodded no. Andy continued, "She was about six years old when she first got on a horse. We used to be neighbors, and she would always come over on her horse. Francie was always trying to get me to ride with her, but I was too afraid of horses, so I did not. One day she convinced me to get on with her, and she would make sure I did not fall off. Therefore, I climbed onto the fence, and she came close to me. When I got on, she said, 'hold on tight.' She took off so fast that I thought I would fall off. I never did, but she laughed so hard because I was screaming so loud. She got her horse to jump over a fence with me holding on for dear life. When her dad, your grandpa, saw what she was doing. He got so mad at her and yelled for her to get me down. She did not listen and took off towards the meadows. When we hit the open field, she made her horse go faster. She was laughing so loud that she did not hear me fall off. Suddenly, she must have realized what had happened, and she came back to me. She jumped off her horse and came to see if I was okay. I was crying, and she put her arm around me then said, 'why are you crying. Did you break something?' When I said no, she said, 'get up, wimp. My horse is going to get in trouble if you keep crying.' I looked at her and asked her, 'your horse?' She laughed, 'yes! I cannot get in trouble; I am my daddy's favorite girl! His little princess!' She was his favorite. It looks like our meal is coming."

The boys were laughing at their mommy when she was a kid. Finally, the food came, and the server put everything in the middle of the table. Andy began, "When your mom was little, she loved grilled cheese, macaroni and cheese, cheesy fries, and broccoli cheese soup. What do you think?" "I thought mommy liked corndogs when she was little?" Frankie asked. Andy laughed, "She did, but that was when she was a teenager." "Oh, okay." Frankie was laughing. "I love grilled cheese just like mommy." Samuel shared. Frankie added, "I love mac and cheese!" Seth smiled, "I do love her broccoli cheese soup." "Well, you will have to try the cheesy fries if you have never had them before," Andy added. Andy helped

Frankie serve a little of everything while Samuel helped himself.

The boys were enjoying their meal when Andy started with another story. "I remember during the summer of our tenth birthday. Francie wanted a new puppy, but her dad did not want another dog. They already had four, and he did not want another mouth to feed. Francie always wanted to bring home stray dogs. She had found a puppy that had been run over, and she did not want to allow it to die. Francie snuck the puppy into the garage. She bandaged up the puppy and prayed that God would heal it and not allow it to die. A couple of days later, her dad heard a puppy crying. He looked around the garage and found it. He knew immediately which one of the children would do this. He picked up the box that the puppy was in and carried it into the house." "Who has a puppy in the garage?" he asked. Francie came running downstairs, "She is mine! Please do not take her away. I love her!" She cried out. "I found her on the road. A car hit her. I know she is going to be okay." "We will have to take this puppy to the vet and make sure she will be okay." He was unhappy about the puppy, but he saw how cute the puppy was and how much it meant to his little princess, and he could not break her heart. He told her that 'she was to care for it.' He did not want her mother to have the burden of a new puppy. Francie was so happy she promised that she would take good care of it. Francie took her puppy upstairs to her room, made a bed, and named her puppy Princess Buddee. Francie had wrapped the puppy in yellow bandages, and the next day Francie and her dad went to the vet. When the vet saw who was walking through her door, she shook her head and laughed.

"Francie, who are you rescuing today." Francie answered, "This is Princess Buddee. I found her on the road. She was bleeding, and I bandaged her up. I prayed, and I know she is okay." The vet led them to a room where she checked the puppy. It appeared that she was going to be okay. The vet said, "Francie, I would suggest you give this puppy to me so I can take care of her." "No, she's mine. I already told Princess Buddee that I will give her a good home." The vet continued, "This puppy is so tiny. She needs to be bottle-fed. Her injuries will heal, but she is not the kind of dog that you should have around other animals. This puppy is a pit bull terrier." "I can do that. She is a good puppy. I will teach her to be friendly and loving to other animals." Francie was not going to give up her puppy. Francie's dad asked, "Doctor, do you think this puppy could be dangerous?" Francie interjected, "I prayed for this puppy, and God gave her to me. She is going to be a good dog when she grows up. God told me." Francie's dad put his hand on her head, "Francie, if you heard this from God, we would keep her." "Francie got to keep her dog. She used to go everywhere with her dog. The dog would walk her to school and then go home. Then she was waiting for her across the street from the school to walk home with her. Well, with us, we always walked home together." The boys listened to the story of their mommy. They looked at their daddy, "Did you know Princess Buddee?" they asked. "No, she died before I met your mommy," Seth answered.

Andy said, "I have one more story for you. This one is going to surprise you." The boys sat quietly, eagerly listening. Andy continued, "Francie was thirteen. It was the summer before high school. She wanted to train to run a marathon. It was not easy to convince her not to when she decided to do something. I tried to tell her that it would be too hard and take too much time. She and Princess Buddee ran out in the meadows when a bear suddenly appeared. She stopped in her tracks and was silent for a little bit. Princess Buddee was barking at the bear, and Francie held on tight to her so she would not run and attack the bear. Francie remembered that she was not supposed to run away from a bear. She froze for a moment and was not sure what she should do.

Then Francie started yelling at it. She said, "Go away from me. I command you to leave!" She waved her arms and started jumping up and down. The bear looked at her and suddenly ran away from her. When she got home and told her dad, he made her stop running through the meadows. When she told me the story, I could not believe her at first. She told me that she remembered how God had protected Daniel when he was thrown into the lion's den and how David had fought a lion and a bear. She thought, 'if God protected them, he will protect me.' She told me that she was terrified at first, but then Francie felt so brave she knew nothing could hurt her. Your mommy is the bravest person I know."

The boys wanted to hear more about their mommy, but it was now dark outside, and they needed to head home. Andy invited the boys to come back soon. Frankie said, "Daddy, I like Mr. Andy," as they left, "and I liked the stories he told us about mommy. Do you think we can come back soon?" Seth answered, "We can try. We are usually busy, but we just need to plan it and make a date." The boys were exhausted from the day's adventures. They had both fallen asleep on the way home. Seth carried them both in his arms and up the stairs to bed. He kissed them goodnight as he tucked them in and went straight into his room. Seth flopped on his bed, exhausted. He closed his eyes and drifted off to sleep.

Seth dreamt of his bride, the love of his life. She was young, in her twenties, and so full of life. Francie was laughing, pregnant, radiant, and she seemed to glow. It was a yellow or golden glow around her entire body. When she laughed, it sounded thunderous. He was standing in a parking lot. She was twirling in the grassy area. He heard a sound and turned, there was a car coming at him, and he ran to get out of the way. He saw the car racing towards his bride. Seth screamed out for Francie to move but saw Francie freeze and look straight at him. He saw her open her mouth but could not hear any sound. The noise was deafening. He awoke in a sweat. He jumped out of bed and checked on the boys. They were sound asleep, and they looked so peaceful. He got a drink of water and crawled back into bed. He fell sound asleep again.

18 THE BEAR ENCOUNTER

The meadow was bright, glowing yellow, and full of flowers. Alice heard a noise and turned to see a bear rushing at her. Everything seemed to go into slow motion. Alice could hear her heart thumping very rapidly. She stood her ground and yelled at the bear. She made herself as big as she could by waving her arms and jumping up and down. Alice screamed as loud as she could. The bear stopped and looked at her. It reared up on its hind legs and made a growling roar that made her feel like her hair was blown backward, just like in a cartoon. Alice did not move a muscle. She decided that she needed to scream again. As suddenly as she saw the bear charging at her, it disappeared. Alice turned around, looking to see if it was behind her but saw nothing. The meadow suddenly was so quiet that she could hear the bumblebees humming. Alice turned again but could not figure out where the bear had gone. She looked up but could only see a bald eagle soaring high. Then she heard the eagle's call, and it seemed to speak to her. "Don't be afraid; you are safe." She was not scared but in awe of the bear disappearing and the eagle's appearance. She turned her eyes and saw the flowers radiating with blue, purple, and yellow colors.

Alice awoke early and hurried to get ready for her day. As she showered, she thought about her dream. 'I wonder what this all means,' she thought to herself. 'I had been in the meadow when I encountered the bear.' She continued to think about what things could mean. Finally, Alice finished her shower, got dressed, and hurried out of her room.

She entered the kitchen to the beautiful aroma of Janie cooking breakfast. "Janie, good morning! What are we going to have today?" Janie turned and smiled, "Oh no! My cooking must not be what it used to be if you can't smell what I'm cooking." Alice laughed, "Of course, I know! The turkey bacon smells delicious, and the pancakes smell sweet as honey." They both laughed.

Jack entered the kitchen, "What's all the laughter about?" Janie laughed, "Oh, Mrs. Alexander made me think I was losing my cooking skills." Jack looked confused. Alice added, "Janie, you know I was just teasing you. You sure know how to dish it back, though." "Well, it looks like everyone got a great night's sleep. Has Erik come in yet?" Jack asked. Janie answered, "No, I have not seen him yet."

Jack reached for the house intercom, "Erik? Are you at the stables?" Jack waited for a response, then tried again, "Erik? Where are you?" Jack then picked up his cell phone and dialed Erik, "Erik, how you doing? Where are you? Call me back as soon as you get this message." Jack was looking worried. "I am going to head out to the stables. I will be right back." Alice went to her room to get the binoculars. She watched Jack walk out to the stables. She could see that the stables still looked closed up. Alice could tell that Jack was looking around, a little worried. She could not hear him but thought he was most likely calling out to Erik. As Jack arrived at the stables, Alice saw Erik emerge. Alice felt a huge relief and said to Janie, "I see Erik. He looks exhausted. Must have overslept." She continued to watch through the binoculars until both the men headed back and were safely inside. Alice could see that they were discussing whatever happened last night, but she could not understand what they were saying. She knew by their faces that it was not a good conversation.

Alice greeted the men at the entryway. She was watching them closely, but they did not give anything away. "Erik, we were worried about you. How are you this morning?" Erik replied, "I am so sorry. I had a late night and overslept. The dogs overslept too." "Come on in and let us have some breakfast. We want to hear all about the night over breakfast." Alice encouraged him.

As they all sat down, Erik began his tale. "It must have been about midnight when the dogs woke me with snarling. They could hear or sense something outside. The horses were upset too. I got up to investigate but could not hear anything. I did not want to open the gates, so I went out the hidden door. I had a flashlight but could not see or hear anything. The dogs and horses were very riled up. Suddenly I heard snorting at the back of the stables. I made some noise to scare away whatever was back there, but it continued to snort. I was being careful not to startle whatever it was. I knocked on the stable walls and whistled as I walked to the back. I finally heard something run off into the darkness. I kept making noise as I walked to the back. I did have my gun with me, so I was not too scared. I let off a round and heard whatever it was, run away faster. When I got to the back, I could see some digging. I guess that it may have been a raccoon or badger. The tracks it made were too small for a bear. I walked around the grounds for about an hour but never saw or heard anything. That's when I headed back into the stables. I stayed up for a few hours and probably fell back asleep about four this morning."

Alice was eating her breakfast as she listened very attentively. "Erik, do you think it could have been a small or young bear?" Erik looked at her, "I don't believe so. The tracks were different; I had never seen these before. Whatever it was, it ran away when it heard me. I believe we are safe, and the animals are safe too." Alice did not believe him due to the concerned look on his face. She continued, "What do you think it was?" Erik looked at her and tried to sound optimistic, "I don't believe we need to worry about what it was because I don't think it'll come back. I am going to place some traps just in case." Alice jumped in, "Won't the dogs be injured if they come across the traps?" Erik replied, "Mrs. Alexander, I will keep the dogs away from the traps." Alice was offended, "Oh, so we are back to Mrs. Alexander?" Erik smiled, "I'm sorry, Alice, please forgive me. I am just trying to keep you safe first, then the animals."

"I forgive you, Erik. I understand. However, I am also concerned for you, the horses, and the dogs." Alice attempted to smile. "Janie, thank you for a delicious breakfast, but I better work on those traps. Alice, please stay indoors. I would feel better and less stressed if I knew you were staying in today." Erik smiled a concerned smile. "Erik, I promise to stay inside this morning, but I would like for you to take me out this afternoon so I can love on my dogs and horses." Erik shrugged his shoulders and nodded his head yes.

Jack watched and listened very carefully, but it was time for him to interject. "Alice, I need to put my foot down on this. I do not want you to go out today until we figure out what creature lurks around the property. Would you please stay indoors today?" Alice responded, "Look, I'm not a child. I know you both are worried about me, but I will be fine. What is the worst thing that can happen? The bear mauls me, and I have a few more scars? Besides, I promise to make sure that Erik is near me and takes me out." Jack argued, but Alice continued, "I am not afraid. I am concerned about the animals and need to be around them for my sake. I'll be careful." Jack knew he would not win this argument.

"I will stay home today to make sure you're fine." Alice was shocked, "What? You do not need to do that. Valerie will make sure I keep my promise. Right, Valerie?" Valerie had been extremely quiet this entire time but turned to face them all, "I do not want to be in the middle of this situation, but I will make sure Mrs. Alexander is not out of my presence. This whole bear thing or other creature really scares me. Mr. Alexander, you have my word." Jack shook his head, "Okay, I am feeling outnumbered. I will go to work but want to have you all update me with any news." Everyone nodded in agreement.

Jack headed out of the house with his briefcase when he heard something around the back of the house. He stopped in his tracks and turned around slowly. He fiddled around with the keys and pushed the emergency button, which started the horn on the car honking. Jack suddenly saw a huge brown bear rear up. Jack did not move a muscle. His mind was racing, 'What should I do? Should I try to run inside?' Suddenly he noticed Erik running out at the sound of the horn and stopped in his tracks. Erik held the doorknob in his hand and pulled the door shut. He did not want anyone else running outside. Jack spoke up first, "Should we start yelling?" Erik answered, "Let's wait a minute and see what he does first. If he looks like he advances toward us, we will, but for now, let's see if he runs away due to the honking." The men stood in silence. Finally, the bear lowered his body on all fours, turned, and ran away towards the meadow.

All three women were standing with their faces plastered against the windows. They were in shock and silent.

The men watched silently as the bear ran away. They both knew it had not been a lengthy encounter, but it seemed to be hours that they had stood in silence. Erik was the first to speak. "Well, now we know for certain. This bear is very comfortable coming near the house. We need to get Wildlife Assistance to come out today. They will need to capture this one and relocate it." As they turned towards the house, they saw the women looking out the window in shock. Erik smiled, waved at them, and half-jokingly said, "I think Mrs. Alexander will stay inside now. Hopefully, she will see the importance and possible danger." Mr. Alexander said, "I'm not sure I should leave you here alone with the women." Erik smiled at him, "Well, I better check the stables." "Erik, I will come with you. Let me call the office." The men headed into the house.

Alice spoke first, "That was a huge bear! How are we going to keep our pets safe?" Erik looked at Mr. Alexander, "The horses and dogs are not pets. They should be fine. I will not let them out of the stables until Wildlife Assistance comes and traps the bear. They should be able to get here today. I need to make that call; if you will, please excuse me." Jack was on his cell calling the office, "Hello Brittany. It is Dr. Alexander; I will not be in today. Please reschedule my patients and let them know I have a bear on my property that I need to deal with. Thank you. Have a good day. I will see you tomorrow."

Alice could hear Erik on the phone too. "Hello. This is Erik at the Alexander's Stables. We have a bear that is on the property and needs immediate assistance. (There was a silent moment) Yes, we will make sure to stay clear of it. It was just by our back door to the house, so it will need to be relocated. (Silence as he listened to Wildlife Assistance.) No, we have not shot at it. If it is the same bear from last night, I shot into the air to scare it away. Yes, we will be waiting for you. Thank you. We will see you soon."

Alice was looking out the window towards the meadow using her binoculars. "Why do you think the bear is so close to the house?" Jack came up behind her, "I am not sure, but it will be relocated. When bears get this close to homes, it is best to take them higher into the mountain." "This bear will find its way back, won't it?" Alice asked. "The goal is to get it far enough that it won't, but there is always a possibility. When they are caught, it does traumatize them, so hopefully, they don't return." Jack wanted to be as honest with his wife as possible. Alice continued, "What if that is a mama bear trying to find food for its babies?" Jack smiled, "Alice, you think of everything, don't you? If it is a mama with cubs, Wildlife Assistance will take the whole family away as one unit. They wouldn't separate families." "Okay, good. That makes me feel better." She answered. Alice closed her eyes and let herself daydream.

Jack asked her, "What are you thinking about?" Alice opened her eyes, "Oh, I was picturing the meadow. I think the meadow is so beautiful this time of year." Jack looked at her puzzled, "What do you mean?" Alice realized what she had said, "Oh, I was just imagining the meadow in full bloom with wildflowers." Jack responded, "Well, you must have quite the imagination. I can't picture that at all." Alice turned to look at him, quite surprised, "You mean, you can't picture wildflowers and bees buzzing?" "No. I cannot. I don't think I ever could." Jack stated. "That's odd, don't you think?" Alice asked. "I think it's odd that you can. I think that is what makes you unique. If only I could have an imagination like that, I would probably paint or write or something." Jack was smiling at his wife. "Have I ever painted?" Alice asked. "No, never," Jack answered. "I think I would like to start," Alice stated. "I have heard that it is very healing for people to paint. Don't be surprised if your imagination makes you think or feel that things you imagine are real." Jack responded. "Alice, Erik, and I will go out to the stables. Please stay indoors."

The men headed out to the stables to look around and take care of the animals.

Alice started to think about the dreams she was having. She could not shake the little boys; she felt so close to them. Alice continued to look for the bear, hoping to see if the mama bear had cubs. She could no longer see the bear but continued to search the meadow. She started to remember the meadow in her dream. In her dream, the meadow was full of daisies. She closed her eyes and began to see the boys and their dad. Alice flew over them but stopped above them. Suddenly she could smell the flowers and the fragrance and hear the bees humming. Alice suddenly heard the boys giggling, and she smiled. She wanted to continue remembering this dream, but she could hear Valerie speaking behind her.

Alice smiled at Valerie as she pictured all the details of her dreams. She wondered if she had dreamt the bear dream because this would happen this morning. Maybe she would see the boys soon if this were the case. Alice closed her eyes and saw the vibrant colors in the meadow. The daisies were so bright and yellow; the blue of the Butterfly Weed seemed to ripple like water. Suddenly, she heard Valerie in the distance, "Alice, a penny for your thoughts. Do you want to share?" Alice smiled and carefully thought about what she would share with her friend, Valerie. "This morning, I dreamed about a bear in the meadow. Do you think I dreamt this because of the events today?" "Possibly. Would you mind sharing the details of the dream?" Valerie asked.

"Okay," Alice continued, "The meadow was bright, glowing yellow, and full of flowers. I heard a noise and turned to see a bear rushing at me. Everything seemed to go into slow motion. I could hear my heart thumping very rapidly. I stood my ground and yelled at the bear. I made myself as big as possible by waving my arms and jumping up and down. I screamed as loud as possible. The bear stopped and looked at me. It reared up on its hind legs and made a growling roar that made me feel like my hair was blowing backward, just like in a cartoon. I did not move a muscle. I then decided that I needed to scream again. As suddenly as I saw the bear charging at me, it disappeared. I turned around to look and see if it was behind me, but I did not see anything. The meadow was suddenly so quiet that I could hear the bumblebees humming. I turned again but could not figure out where the bear had gone. Then I looked up for some reason but could only see an eagle soaring high. Then I heard the eagle's call. It seemed to speak to me. "Don't be afraid; you are safe." I was not scared but in awe of the bear disappearing and the eagle's appearance. I turned my eyes and saw the flowers radiating blue, purple, and yellow colors. Then I woke up."

Valerie had her eyes closed. She had been praying while she heard the dream. Valerie opened her eyes and looked at Alice. "I hear the Lord saying that this dream is a warning dream. You are in a meadow, which represents a peaceful and beautiful place you would go to enjoy and rest; this is you. The bear represents a demon that will come to attack, but it disappears. The Lord is taking care of you. Then you see the Bald eagle, which is royalty, and it tells you that you are safe and not to fear. Then you see the beauty of the meadow again. You also hear the bumblebees humming, which represents angels ascending and descending. I feel the Lord is promising you peace and happiness. You just need to seek Him. He says you are royalty, which tells me you already know the Lord. In the dream, you had no fear, so you need not be fearful." Alice looked at Valerie, "I want to know more about God. Can you get me a bible? As I read more, I feel that I will discover who He is and thus discover myself. In addition, I want to try to paint. Can we go shopping for supplies?"

Valerie could see the light entering Alice. "I would be happy to get a Bible for you. Would you like to borrow mine until we can get out and buy you one?" Alice smiled, "I would love it if we could read together. Would that be okay?" Valerie was getting excited, "I would love to do a Bible study with you, Alice." "Do you think Janie would like to join us?" Alice asked. "We should invite her to join us, but we do not want her to feel pressured. I have never really shared my faith with her." Valerie answered. Alice turned and called out for Janie, "Janie, are you available for a few minutes?" Janie came from the kitchen, "Alice, are you in need of something?" Alice smiled, "Yes, I would love to invite you to join us for a Bible study if you would like." Janie's face lit up, "Alice, I am honored to be invited. I would love to join you. I was praying while we watched the bear outside. I asked the Lord to send him away. I believe He answered my prayer." "I am just so blessed to have the two of you watching over me." Alice was feeling so happy.

19 THE DREAMERS

The boys awoke early with the sun shining right on their faces. They both came running out of their rooms, so excited to share their dreams with their dad. "Daddy, daddy," cried Frankie. He burst into his daddy's room. "Daddy, daddy. Look, the sun is shining! It is time to get up! I must talk to you." Seth was aroused from a deep sleep. "What's going on?" He asked. Frankie jumped on his daddy's bed; Samuel was close behind him but stayed on the side. "I had a great dream!" Frankie excitedly yelled. Samuel added, "Me too!" "Frankie, may I go first this time? Daddy, may I jump in with you too?" Seth responded first, "Yes, of course. Come on, get up." Frankie was in deep thought, "I might forget my dream if I wait for you to share first." Samuel put his arm around his little brother, "Can you please wait for me to go first?" Frankie nodded, "Okay, but first can I say a small part so daddy can help me remember my dream?" Samuel agreed, "Okay, that's a good idea." Frankie looked at his daddy, "Daddy, just say cabin to me, and I should remember my dream."

Samuel looked at his brother, a little amazed. "I dreamed about the cabin too." He continued, "We went to the cabin, and there we found gold. The treasure was in a hiding place, but we just knew where to find it. There was a floorboard that creaked, and when we looked to fix it, we saw more gold. The creek was full of water, and something sparkled in the creek. When we went to check it out, we saw many fish. They were very colorful. I saw blue, purple, yellow, red, and white fish. When we threw out our fishing lines, we caught so many that we decided to share with the neighbors across the creek. We had so much fun! We were laughing so much." Seth smiled, "You know it is almost time for us to go to the cabin. Frankie, would you like to share your dream about the cabin? We can talk about the dreams after we hear all the dreams."

Frankie smiled, "We were driving to the cabin in a big blue car. It went so fast that I thought we were floating. We sang songs all the way there. When we got to the cabin, I saw the creek, and I could see the fish jumping. We hurried up and got out our fishing poles. When we went fishing, the fish just jumped into our arms. They all looked like rainbows. They were all different colors. They were very colorful. So beautiful. I had one in my hands, and I said, 'mommy would love to eat this one.' So, I put it in my pocket, and we kept on fishing. When it got dark, we finally went inside the cabin. Daddy, you turned all the lights on, and we brought in all the fish. We put them in the freezer to take them home, but we ate a few. The one I had put in my pocket was no longer in my pocket. I found a gold nugget in my pocket. Daddy, you laughed and said that I had found the golden fish. When it was bedtime, we went to sleep, and when we woke up." Frankie stopped telling his dream. He sat very quietly for a while. Frankie looked at this daddy, then at Samuel. Smiling, he continued, "When we woke up, mommy was in the kitchen sitting at the table. She had made pancakes and sausage and was waiting for us to wake up. She said, 'I was finally able to come home.' I was so happy that I jumped on her lap and kissed her. Daddy, you, and Samuel were hugging her. She was sandwiched between us all. That was a good dream!" Seth was smiling but shaking his head. "Those both are excellent dreams. What do you boys think they mean?"

Samuel started, "I think that because we both dreamed about the cabin. We are going to see things that make us happier. I think the fish is good food and there were so many in both dreams that we are going to have a lot of fun and food to eat.

We both found gold which I think means richness or happiness. We need some more happiness in our lives, Daddy. Frankie, what do you think?"

"I only think one thing. We are going to get mommy back. She is our gold. The rainbow is God's promise to us. That's all!" Frankie did not need more explanations.

Seth smiled at his boys, "You boys are good at interpreting dreams. Mommy taught you very well. I agree with both of you. I believe there is something we will find at the cabin that will bring us so much happiness. These dreams could mean that we will be rounding the corner on healing. Both of you dreamed of eating lots of fish, which are very colorful. I agree that it seems like promises. God promises to take care of us always, so he is feeding us and showing us that there will be happier days ahead. Frankie, I know that you think mommy will be there but do not be disappointed if she is not there. No one has been to the cabin in a very long time. It will be dusty, so we will need to clean it when we get there. Let's agree not to get our hopes up too high, okay?"

Frankie looked at his daddy right in his face, "We are getting Mommy back at the cabin. God promised me!" Samuel knew that he would not change his mind when his little brother said something. "Frankie, I believe you. Let's be happy! We are going to find our gold. We both dreamed it, so it must be true."

Seth was unsure he wanted to share his dream since the mood seemed to change. "How about I share my dream later. We should get some breakfast. Shall we make something or go out?" Samuel was the first, "Can we ask Auntie Rae if she can come with us or come over? I want to tell her our dreams." Seth answered, "I would like it to stay just the three of us. I hope that's okay?" Frankie replied, "I want Auntie

Rae to come too. It is always just the three of us. I miss Auntie Rae. Can we see if she is off today?" Seth nodded his head reluctantly, "Well, let's call her to see if she is up or home? Samuel, do you want to call her?"

Samuel reached for his daddy's cell phone. The phone was ringing. Samuel looked at his daddy and knew that his daddy wanted more time alone with them. He did not know what to do, but he knew his little brother needed to see Auntie Rae, but he wanted to help daddy too. Then he heard her voice, and she asked, 'Seth, are you there? Hello?' Samuel answered, "Auntie Rae, it's Samuel. We just wanted to see if you wanted to come over for breakfast. Daddy, Frankie, and I are going to make the works. All you must do is come and eat." "Are you sure I cannot bring something? What time do you want me to come over?" Rae was asking. "If you give us an hour, we can be showered and make breakfast," Samuel added. Samuel felt his heart breaking, torn between what he and Frankie wanted and what daddy wanted. Finally, he spoke quietly, "Auntie Rae, I love you so much."

Tears started rolling down his face. "Goodbye and see you soon." He spoke. He gave his daddy the cell phone, and Seth knew his boy was older than he indeed was. Seth put his arm around Samuel and hugged him. "I love you, son! Now, let us get ready, so we are not too stinky when Auntie Rae arrives. We better hurry too so she doesn't get here and tries to make breakfast." Frankie yelled as he ran up the stairs, "Last one out of the shower has to eat rotten eggs!" They were all laughing as they raced upstairs.

The boys knew the routine of showering. Samuel was always first, but Frankie would get his clothes and brush his teeth while his brother showered. Samuel stripped his clothes off and jumped in the shower. He let out a scream, "The water is too cold!" Frankie was laughing as he brushed his teeth.

Frankie went out to get his clothes ready. Frankie continued to laugh as if someone were tickling him. As Samuel finished his shower, he asked, "Frankie do you want me to leave the shower on so you can jump in?" "Yes, please!" Frankie said between laughter. Samuel stepped out of the shower and wrapped himself with his towel. Frankie was ready and jumped in, "Samuel, this water is warm! Thank you for leaving it on." Frankie continued to laugh all through his shower. Samuel sang 'Row, Row, Row your boat' as he brushed his teeth and combed his hair. When he finished, he went into his room to get dressed. Frankie finished showering and got dressed when he heard his brother singing 'the song.'

Samuel did not even realize which he was singing. "I love you in the morning. I love you in the afternoon. I love you in the evening. I love you every day. I will always love you my sweet baby boy." Frankie joined in, "I love you in the morning. I love you in the afternoon. I love you in the evening. I love you every day. I will always love you my sweet baby boy." Seth heard the boys singing and came out of his room dancing and singing, "I love you in the morning. I love you in the afternoon. I love you in the evening. I love you every day. I will always love you my sweet baby boy." Frankie started laughing again. He did not see his daddy dance very often. The boys started dancing like their daddy and worked their way downstairs into the kitchen. Seth interrupted the singing, "Are we making the works today?" "Yes!" The boys sang out in unison. Seth asked, "Do we want to continue singing or put some music on?" "Let's do both!" Frankie sang. Samuel headed to the radio and turned it on. All three cracked up laughing when they heard the song that came on, 'Hound Dog' by Elvis Presley.

They worked in the kitchen like a fine-tuned machine. They each knew where to find the food and who was doing what.

Seth always did the stove things, and the boys always got out the ingredients. Today, they would feast. They had taken out the bacon and sausage. Samuel was getting all the pancake ingredients ready. Frankie was in charge of fruit, jelly, and syrup. The boys were busy preparing when the doorbell rang. Frankie jumped out of his seat and ran to open the door. Seth was right behind him. Seth unlocked the deadbolt and turned off the alarm.

Auntie Rae had an arm full of groceries. "Good morning, Auntie Rae! Come on in." Frankie grabbed one of the bags. Rae smiled at Seth, "I thought I would bring lunch since you're making breakfast." Seth smiled and hugged his wife's older sister. "I'm glad you're here. We are almost ready to eat." Samuel greeted his aunt, "I'm happy you could come. What do you have in the bags? I told you we had everything we needed." Rae smiled at her nephew, "Look at you so grown up. I thought I would bring a few things for lunch. It'll be a project for us." Rae grabbed the few things out of the bags that needed to be refrigerated. "Looks like you guys have been busy this morning. It smells delicious! Can't wait to dig in." Frankie had set the table and was finishing placing the napkins down. Seth was placing all the food on the table.

Rae asked, "Where do you want me to sit?" Frankie pulled out the chair next to himself. "This is for you." Samuel added, "First we will eat, then we want to share some dreams with you." Rae smiled, "Sounds like a plan." Seth reached for Frankie and Samuel's hands, "Let's say grace." They all held hands like old times. Seth looked at Rae, "Would you like to say grace today?" Rae smiled, "I am honored. Abba, Father in Heaven. We thank you for this food. Bless the hands who made it. Nourish us daily with Yeshua, the Bread of Life. In Jesus Name." They all said, "Amen."

Rae started the conversation with her week. She had been working seventy hours a week. She smiled as she told the story, "I was at work and had a round in the ER. A young woman arrived by ambulance from a car accident. The doctor was shouting instructions, then suddenly he stopped. He had tears in his eyes. He said, 'I can't work on this girl.' We all looked at him, shocked to hear him say that. Then he said, 'This is my daughter.' We all looked at him, and our hearts sunk. We did not have another doctor available; everyone else was already in surgery. I looked at him and said, 'You must. We do not have another doctor available. You are the only one that can do this surgery.' He started to cry, 'Someone, please call me wife. Let her know that our daughter is here.' One of the nurses ran out to make the call. The doctor prepared for surgery. He had his little girl's life in his hands. With every stitch he made, he cried. Another doctor walked in when we finished the surgery, but he was too late. The girl was going to be okay. That was the hardest day of all. When a father sees his child hurting and does not have time to cry or heal himself, he must step up and get the job done." Rae looked at Seth, "I am so sorry that the family hasn't been more helpful. I am here now and want to do all I can or all you will allow me to do. When the doctor had to operate on his daughter, it made me think of you. I can't imagine how hard it has been for you." Rae reached over and put her arm around Frankie, "I am so happy you invited me to come over. So, what has been going on here at the Laurel house?"

Samuel and Frankie looked at each other and smiled. Samuel spoke up first, "We invited you over because we wanted to tell you our dreams, we had last night." Rae smiled, "Oh, please tell me. The suspense is making me even more curious."

Samuel began, "We went to the cabin, and there we found gold. The treasure was in a hiding place, but we just knew where to find it. There was a creaky floorboard, and when we looked to see how we could fix it, we saw more gold. The creek was full of water, and something sparkled in the creek. When we went to check it out, we saw many fish. They were very colorful. I saw blue, purple, yellow, red, and white fish. When we threw out our fishing lines, we caught so many that we decided to share with the neighbors across the creek. We were having so much fun! We were laughing so much. Auntie Rae, when I woke up, I felt so much joy." Rae responded, "That sounds like a fun dream. Do you want me to tell you what I think?" Samuel answered, "Do you want to wait until after Frankie tells you his? You can if you really want to?" "I would love to share right now, if that's okay?" She was looking at Frankie. Frankie nodded, "Sure! It is okay with me.

Rae began, "The cabin speaks of a place of rest and coming together to get closer to each other. Gold speaks of wealth and blessings. The creek is a boundary; however, this boundary also has many fish, which can represent food. They were very colorful, we could talk about each color, but I will say that these seem like promises, to keep it short. The neighbor may also need some comfort or food. You said that you were having so much fun, laughing and joyous. I feel that when you go to the cabin, you will get some long-needed rest and healing. Maybe in your healing, you will help the neighbor. How did I do?" Samuel smiled, "I like that interpretation. It makes me happy."

Frankie smiled and began, "My dream is really busy, so pay attention and keep up with me. We were driving to the cabin in a big blue car. It went so fast that I thought we were floating. We sang songs all the way there. When we got to the cabin, I saw the creek, and I could see the fish jumping.

We hurried up and got our fishing poles out. We headed to the creek. When we went fishing, the fish just jumped into our arms. They all looked like rainbows. They had all the different colors on them. They were very colorful. I had one in my hands, and I said, 'mommy would love to eat this one.' Therefore, I put it in my pocket, and we kept on fishing. When it got dark, we finally went inside the cabin. Daddy turned all the lights on, and we brought in all the fish. We put them in the freezer so we could take them home, but we ate a few. The one I had put in my pocket was no longer in my pocket. I found a gold nugget in my pocket. Daddy laughed and said that I had found the golden fish. When it was bedtime, we went to sleep, and when we woke up." Frankie stopped speaking; he sat very quietly for a while. He looked at his aunt and continued, "When we woke up, mommy was in the kitchen sitting at the table. She had made pancakes and sausage and was waiting for us to wake up. She said, 'I was finally able to come home.' I was so happy that I jumped on her lap and kissed her. Daddy and Samuel were hugging her. Mommy was sandwiched between us all. That was a good dream!"

"Wow!" Rae was in awe of the dream. "Frankie, you are right! That is a busy dream. It is very interesting that you both dreamt about the cabin. The dreams are similar but different." Rae was looking at Seth, "What are your dreams like?" Seth answered, "I might share later. Go ahead and interpret Frankie's dream." Rae continued, "So the cabin will be a place of rest for you, but you dream the drive there in the big blue car. The big blue car represents your ministry or mission, Frankie. I feel that Holy Spirit or God is the blue car. Who was driving?" Frankie answered, "I don't remember, but I guess it must have been daddy. Because I am a kid!" Rae smiled, "Okay, that's okay. Frankie, you are on a mission because you find the fish that turns into gold. The fish jumped into your arms; this can mean that something is coming back. You put the special fish in your pocket, which is your heart, and you were saving it for your mommy. Your mommy is always in your heart. The gold nugget speaks of purity, and you are so pure in your love for mommy and Yeshua. The freezer also represents the heart where you are storing more fish or food. You also dreamt of your mommy, who could represent her or Holy Spirit, and she made food for you. Feeding you or nourishing you. God is telling you that He is taking care of you." Frankie interrupted, "I want to know, is mommy going to be there?" Rae looked at Frankie, "I do not know. God will need to tell you that. You need to pray and ask Him. Besides, that was an excellent dream. You boys are dreamers, just like your mommy. I think your daddy is a dreamer too." Rae was now looking at Seth. "Would you like to share your dream?" Seth was looking down, "No, I am not ready."

Frankie got up and ran to his daddy, then threw his arms around him, "it's okay, daddy. You do not have to share your dream. Sometimes, dreams are just for us." Seth was in awe of his little one, "How did you get so smart, little one?" Frankie started giggling as if someone was tickling him. Everyone started laughing. They laughed for a long time before Samuel spoke, "Auntie Rae, I was just thinking. What if the neighbor has some information about mommy? Maybe that's why we go the neighbors' across the creek in my dream." Rae answered him, "Dreams are sometimes like parables. Yeshua used to teach in parables. When we dream, we need to ask God what it means. We learn to interpret dreams with God's help, but the meaning may be different than what we want it to be."

Frankie looked over at his aunt, "I have visions of mommy. Sometimes Samuel and daddy see or smell what I am seeing.

What about that?" Rae was feeling uncomfortable, not wanting to smash her nephews' hopes. "Dreams are sometimes called night visions. So daytime visions are the same. We still must ask God what He is telling us." "Do you believe in ghosts?" Frankie asked. Samuel interrupted, "The visions we have are not ghosts. Mommy is alive." Frankie was annoyed, "I didn't say mommy was a ghost. I am just wondering if Auntie Rae believes in ghosts." Rae answered, "I do not believe in ghosts. I know that when people say they see a ghost, what they are seeing is a demon. They are seers." The boys' eyes opened wide. Seth was nodding no. Rae continued tentatively, "You believe in Yeshua, right?" The boys nodded yes, and she continued, "Demons are spirits, not ghosts. Holy Spirit is God's Spirit." Seth interrupted, "I think that is enough talk about this subject. Shall we clean up and go outside?"

Everyone got up and started clearing the table. Frankie asked, "Auntie Rae, what are we having for lunch?" "I thought maybe burgers and dogs would be fun to have for our picnic outside." "Yeah, that sounds like fun!" Frankie answered. Samuel added, "We haven't grilled burgers and dogs in a long time. But first, we need to clean the grill." Seth said, "Why don't we enjoy the sun for a couple of hours before we talk about cleaning the grill."

The boys ran outside, and Buddy, their shepherd mix, was waiting for them. Seth watched them race around the yard with Buddy. They had not played like this in a very long time. Seth knew in his heart that healing was finally beginning. Rae stood by Seth, "You are doing a great job. They are great kids. So much like you and Francie. I see you both in each one of them." Seth turned to look at Rae. He had never really looked at her. Francie was so full of life that everyone else was in her shadow. Rae had kind eyes. Her face showed the stress of her job and missing her sister. She was the only one that never blamed Seth. He knew he could trust her, but he was not ready to share. "Thanks, Rae. I appreciate you coming over today. I must be honest; I did not want you here today. I wanted to spend time with my boys. We rarely have a great day like today. I was selfish and wanted it for myself. But I must admit, I am glad you're here." Rae smiled at him, "Whenever you need to talk, I'll be here. If you need me to spend time with the boys so you can have private time, I can do that too." Seth smiled, "Thanks, I appreciate that. I want to spend every minute I can with them. I don't need alone time."

Rae answered, "Whatever you need. Francie is my little sister and always will be. You know I see you like my brother, not a brother-in-law." Seth smiled, "I can't believe how fast my boys are growing up. They are just too mature for their age. They have been through a lot these past two years. I don't want them to be let down if their dreams don't come to pass like they are expecting." Rae smiled at Seth, "It is a good thing that they are talking about their dreams. Keep encouraging them. There is nothing like the faith of a child. I wish we could all have that kind of faith."

Suddenly, they noticed that the boys and dog had stopped running around. The boys were sitting in the garden, and Buddy was right next to them. Seth laughed, "Come on. Let's try out your childlike faith." They walked in silence towards the garden. Seth drew in a deep breath as they approached the garden. Rae was confused; the garden was not in bloom, yet she smelled roses. Seth said, "Welcome to our world. Boys, do you see mommy?" The boys nodded yes. Rae stood right behind the boys. Her eyes opened wide as she saw her sister. Frankie laughed, "You see, mommy, don't you, Auntie Rae?" "Yes, I do," Rae said with tears running down her face.

Samuel asked, "Do you smell her roses?" "I do," Rae whispered. They had been in the presence for about fifteen minutes before Rae spoke, "I believe the Lord is telling you that your mommy is okay. The smell of the roses, I believe, represents His presence." When the vision went away, Rae began to cry. She kept apologizing because she could not stop crying. Frankie and Samuel giggled. The boys were filled with so much joy that it became contagious. Everyone was laughing, and Buddy was barking and jumping.

Rae asked, "How long has this been going?" Frankie answered first, "For a long time." Samuel said, "I started seeing and smelling things since the party." Seth added, "It hasn't been too long for me." Rae asked, "Is this the only place this happens?" Frankie laughed, "No! Sometimes we see and smell her inside too. Sometimes at school." Rae added, "God has been visiting you for a long time. He has been comforting you. I am so happy!"

Frankie asked, "Is it lunchtime yet?" Everyone laughed. "No, but we can start getting ready," Seth said. Everyone worked together to clean the grill and prepare for lunch. It was a great day at the Laurel's home.

20 A TIME FOR AN ADVENTURE

It had been a couple of weeks since the bear issue. All was safe again, and Alice was tired of feeling cooped up. After breakfast, she spent a little time with Valerie doing her physical therapy. Alice had not yet started painting, so she grabbed her paint kit and headed out the door. She set up her things on the patio. She sat and looked around to see if anything inspired her to paint.

She looked around, but there was not too much color. She looked out at the stables and decided to try to paint horses. She softly spoke to herself, "Hmm, what color should my horses be?" She heard a whisper. She turned her head to see who had answered her. She did not see anyone. Puzzled, she asked again, "What color should my horses be?" She heard a quiet voice, "Big black one." She looked around again and saw no one. "Okay, I will paint a big black one."

She opened her brush kit and looked at the different brushes. She had no idea where to start. Her eyes kept going to a medium-size one, so she picked it up. She opened the paints and dipped her brush into the black. Suddenly, it felt like someone was holding her hand and helping her paint. She watched as her hand made smooth strokes. She thought to herself, 'I feel like I have painted before.' She felt so much peace as she painted. To her surprise, the horse looked like a horse. As she painted, she just knew which brushes she needed for the different parts of the horse. She also seemed to know how to mix the colors on the palate. She was almost done with the painting of the horse when she started to feel lethargic. She cleaned the brushes and closed the paints. She decided to leave the artwork outside. As she walked back into the house, she felt so dizzy that she knelt so she would not fall. She called out, "Valerie! Janie!"

She opened her eyes to see the two women kneeling next to her. "What happened?" Alice asked. "We heard you call us and came running out. You appeared to have fainted. Your vitals are fine. How do you feel?" "I feel great! I remember a sudden feeling of being tired or lethargic. I was walking toward the door when I felt dizzy, and that's all I remember." Janie asked, "Is it possible that you over-exerted yourself?" Alice answered, "I don't think so. Physical therapy was easy this morning, and it wasn't that much work to bring my art stuff out." Valerie said, "I do not think it was over-exertion either. How did you feel while you painted?" Alice smiled, "I felt good. It felt like someone was guiding my hand with every stroke. The painting looks great." The women walked over to the painting. They were so amazed at how beautiful her first piece of artwork was. Janie said, "Wow, Alice! This painting is beautiful. I think you either have painted before, or God helped you." Valerie nodded in agreement, "This is fantastic! Look at the detail of the horse. You captured every muscle, every strand of hair, and the mane looks real. I am not an art expert, but this is great!" Alice smiled, "I think you're right. God was guiding my hand."

"Can we please not mention this to Mr. Alexander? I do not want him to worry. I think this is a God thing." Alice stated. "I agree," Valerie said. "Janie?" Alice asked. "Mums the word," Janie answered. "Shall we go inside and have some refreshments?" Janie asked. The women walked inside in awe. They were each having a moment of taking in what they had just witnessed.

Janie headed to the kitchen and brought out some lemonade and cookies. "At first, I thought I should keep it healthy but decided we should have a fun day instead." Alice smiled, "That's a great idea! Besides, it's our celebration of my first painting." Valerie added, "These cookies look delicious!

What kind are they?" "White chocolate macadamia nut," Janie answered. "Oh, my goodness! These are delicious! Janie, you know how to spoil us. Thank you!" Alice said. Valerie added, "These tastes heavenly."

Valerie surprised the women, "I know I don't share too much, but I feel that we are becoming terrific friends. May I share a dream I had last night? It will be good practice for us to help each other interpret dreams and learn to hear what God is telling us." "Yes!" the women answered in unison. Valerie smiled and started, "I don't remember too much about the dream but recall these few details. In my dream, I was a giant. I saw myself walking through meadows and mountains, but I did not have far to walk because I was so big. I do remember that the meadows were in full bloom. So many different vibrant colors, almost as if they were alive and moved. The mountains were easy to climb."

Alice shyly said, "Well, I think you are small in stature but a giant in the Spirit. We recently studied Mark 9, which talked about Jesus' transfiguration. So maybe you are going through a transformation?" Janie replied, "That's good, Alice. Yes, we did a study about the top of the mountain where some disciples saw Jesus' transfiguration. Could this also be a look at the colors in heaven?" Valerie smiled, "Yes, excellent ladies. Things seemed very easy, so I feel God says that some things will come easily. Would anyone else want to share a dream?"

Janie volunteered, "I usually dream about food. In this dream, I was at a party in a mansion. I saw that there were only a few of us there. The host gave me a goblet that was silver. The design on the goblet was the most beautiful thing I had ever seen. The instruction was not to share our drink with anyone else. We then sat down to eat, and the food was so delicious. We each received a meal created specifically for us. Flavors that I can't even explain." Alice was unsure but attempted, "I feel God is telling you that you are so important to Him that He is serving you the best food and drink at a feast." Valerie smiled, "Excellent, Alice. I also feel that the Lord is setting the table in front of your enemies, just like in Psalm 23. The meal was created with you in mind, and the Lord knows everything about you, even what you will enjoy most and the smallest details of your life."

Alice was not feeling sure about sharing but decided to trust the ladies. "I had this dream some time ago. If you can help me get some clarity, I would love that! There was a stream, blue and rocky. I could see white caps cracking the water with a sharp sound. It was as loud as if a bucket of water poured onto me. Then I heard a beautiful sound. There was so much giggling. I looked around but could not see where the giggling was coming from. As I spun round and round to find who was giggling, suddenly I was in a meadow of daisies. The meadow was so alive. The daisies were moving as if they were breathing. I could smell the fragrance; it was as sweet as honey. I could hear the honeybees flying from flower to flower, making a buzzing sound. Suddenly I heard the giggling again. I turned towards the stream and saw three figures. It looked like someone big and two little ones. As the figures came into focus, I noticed a man and two little boys. They were running and giggling. I was watching the boys running toward the water and screaming with joy. As they ran, it was clear that they were going to jump into the stream. As they neared the stream, I began to worry about the boys. I got up and started to run towards the boys. Suddenly I was flying towards the boys and flew over them. I saw them look up at me and yell out, but I could not understand what they said. The boys were waving and laughing as I flew back towards them. I could see their pink cheeks, and the sweat on their foreheads glistened in the sun. They laughed as I flew by and continued to wave. I saw them run towards the stream and jump in. As I flew over them for the third time, I saw him. I stopped in midair and watched the man. He was smiling and laughing. His eyes sparkled, and his smile seemed to brighten the already sunny day. I could sense the love he had for his sons. I could feel the warmth of his love. It warmed me up as I watched him. He was tender and gentle with the boys. The sky suddenly filled up with balloons, which were red, white, blue, and yellow. I was flying among the balloons and lost sight of the boys and the dad. I was frantically searching for them, but the balloons were all around me. I tried to get below the balloons, but there were so many that I could not move. I woke up feeling terrified. During most of the dream, I had so much peace."

Janie was crying, "That is such a beautiful dream, Alice. I could see everything that was happening as you spoke. I felt the peace, the love, and then your fear. Do not be afraid. Everything is going to be okay. I do not know how I know this, but I feel or sense this. I do not know how to interpret that dream. It was beautiful."

Valerie smiled, "It is a beautiful dream. I also see so much hope. I will highlight a few things then we can talk about them. But first, did you feel these were the same boys you dreamed of?" Alice answered, "Yes, but I have never seen the man in my dreams. This dream was the first time I saw his face so clearly. It is not Mr. Alexander." Valerie put her hand on Alice's hand, "Remember, dreams are parables. The stream usually represents the outpouring of the Holy Spirit or the Word and a place of refreshing. You saw that the stream was blue and rocky. Blue is usually the color of the Holy Spirit, and Jesus is our Rock. I feel the meadow with flowers represent you giving praise to Christ. His fragrance can be the smell of flowers. The giggling or laughter, especially from

children, can cover a heavy heart because it brings rejoicing—
so much joy. You saw three people. Three is the number of
the Godhead – Father, Son, which is Christ Jesus and the Holy
Spirit. You also saw the Father who loves these two boys.
Two is the number of you and God. A relationship is what
God wants with you. Flying can mean rising out of the flesh
and into the Spirit, breaking physical laws. Balloons can
represent a celebration, childlike faith, freedom, and filled
with Holy Spirit; do not be afraid of floating like the balloons.
You get lost in the balloons, so get lost in Holy Spirit. I think
this dream has two meanings. One is speaking about God and
your relationship with him. Now, because I know that you
feel these are your boys. Children are our promises from God.
I hear the Lord saying that you need to trust Him, and He will
give you the desires of your heart. You are His child, and He
loves you so much. Everything is always in His timing. Trust in
Him. Remember, Jesus is always interceding for you. Those
are the prayers I believe the balloons represent."

Alice smiled and spoke after a few moments of soaking up the
interpretation. "Can I say something that is going to sound
crazy?" The women looked at her and nodded their heads in
approval. "There is no judgment from us, Alice," Valerie
whispered. Alice continued, "I don't feel that this is really my
home. I believe the man and boys I dream of are my real
family. I think that God is telling me that I will see them again.
I flew over them three times. I heard them laughing and felt
their love. I do not know why, but it just seems that I do not
belong here. I still do not have any feelings toward Mr.
Alexander. I feel he is a stranger to me. He did not even
know I could paint. That is so weird to me." Alice stopped
before continuing, "I don't know why but I feel locked up. My
brain is healing, and I feel like I am remembering things and
feel that I do not belong here." Janie reassured Alice, "I do
not know why you feel like that, but I know that Mr.

Alexander spent every moment he could caring for you. He seems to love you very much. I will stand with you if things get difficult. I trust you. I believe in you too." Valerie added, "Alice, you know I will help in any way I can. Let's make sure God leads us in anything we do." Alice shook her head, "Yes, I only want to do what is right."

"I want to go out to the meadow to paint. I feel that it is a place of rest for me. I know Mr. Alexander would be angry if I went out alone. Would either of you like to join me?" Alice asked. Janie answered first, "I have so much to do today. It is the day I clean everything. I would love to join you sometime. May I have a rain check?" "Yes! Of course." Alice answered. She looked at Valerie, "What do you say?" "You know, I have never painted, so I would love to try." Valerie was getting excited.

The women gathered all the paint gear, and Valerie grabbed a couple of chairs out of the garage. "Well, I think we have what we need. Oh yeah, let me grab a couple of hats to wear." Valerie headed back into the house and the hallway." Alice started laughing when Valerie remerged, "What kind of hats are those?" Valerie smiled, "They are gardening hats. Which one would you like to wear?" Alice continued to laugh as she reached for the pink one with flowers. "Who picked out these hats? She asked. Valerie was feeling a little embarrassed, "I did. I thought we needed hats that gave us character." Alice teased her, "Well, you accomplished that for sure."

The women walked out towards the meadow. They chatted about the interpretation of dreams. "Why do you think we sometimes have nightmares?" Alice asked. Valerie smiled, "Well, sometimes we have nightmares that are not always nightmares. They can be a warning from God. Some nightmares, the enemy is attacking us because we have open doors." Alice looked at her, puzzled, "What are open doors?" "We may be in sin or never asked God to forgive us for some things in our lives. The devil can then attack us and give us nightmares." Valerie responded. "Hmm, that's interesting. I wonder what kind of dreams Erik is dreaming of. And Mr. Alexander? Do you think animals dream?" "Oh, yes! I have seen and heard dogs dreaming. Sometimes they bark or whimper in their sleep. I like to imagine that they are playing in meadows full of life." Both women laughed as they imagined the meadow full of dogs running around, chasing balls and each other.

"This looks like a good spot to set up." Alice was smiling as she turned to look around. She could see the mountains, the creek, the neighbor's cabin, and the stables. Valerie also looked around, "It does look like a great place. We will be smack in the middle of everything. I forgot to let Erik know that we would be out here. I wonder if he will let the horses out today. They have not been out in a long time. Ever since the bear issue. You think I should call him?" "No, he will see us if he lets the horses out. It would be fun to see them running around us."

The women were busy setting up the art easels and preparing for the painting adventure. They both were taking out some paint and placing it on their palettes. They then stood and looked around, looking for something to inspire them. Alice spoke first, "I found my inspiration." She sat down to paint. Valerie was still looking around when she saw something or someone coming toward them. "Alice, do you see that?" She was pointing toward the mountains. Alice turned and looked, "No, I can't see anything." Valerie kept looking, "I see something or someone coming toward us." Alice searched the mountain edge, "I am not seeing anything." "Maybe it's just my imagination." She answered. "I think I'll paint the mountain range." She secretly wanted to keep her eyes on whatever it was that she could see in the distance.

Valerie glanced back, "Wow, Alice, that looks beautiful!" Alice let out a little giggle, "I must be honest. I feel like someone is guiding my hands." Valerie laughed, "Mine just looks like a blob of paint. Tell me your secret." Alice turned to face Valerie, "Just say, God, paint with me. Sometimes, I feel like my eyes are closed, but I know they are not. I feel a gentle guiding of my hands." "Okay, I will try that. Lord, guide my hands; this is your painting." Valerie looked towards the mountain range. "I see a man. He is carrying a small pack. Looks like a hiker." Alice looked towards the mountain range. "I don't see anyone. I think that's what you are supposed to paint." Valerie took her paintbrush and dipped it into the paint. Suddenly she felt like someone had grabbed her hand and guided every stroke. The blob was now looking like something beautiful.

The women sat for hours painting. Neither woman spoke for quite some time. Alice was busy finishing her masterpiece when she turned to look at Valerie. "Oh my, that is beautiful." She spoke softly as if not to interrupt her friend. Valerie looked up from her painting, "It does look good." Valerie looked over at Alice, "I am so amazed at the beautiful things God does. I have never painted before. I feel so much at peace." Alice was smiling, "Look! I think it's Erik!" She was pointing towards the mountains. They could hear the dogs barking. "Let's walk towards him. I feel like I need to move anyway." Valerie and Alice washed their paintbrushes.

The women started walking toward Erik and the dogs. When the dogs noticed them, they rushed towards the women. Alice was laughing as she suddenly started running towards the dogs. Valerie hollered, "Alice, be careful!" Alice did not look back; she just kept running. Suddenly she stopped, she screamed, "Noooo!" Erik started to run. Valerie started running to Alice.

Alice fell to her knees. She was crying and reaching out to pick up a puppy. She gently picked up the puppy, cradled it, and sobbed. "Who did this to you? You poor little baby." Valerie was the first to get to Alice. "Oh my! Alice, may I see him and see if we can save him?" She was reaching out to hold the puppy. "We are out in the middle of nowhere. Our neighbors are not at the cabin. Where could this puppy have come from?" The dogs were the next to arrive. They were growling and barking at the women. "No! Sit!" Alice commanded them. The dogs settled down a bit, but they were still not happy. Erik finally arrived. He looked at the women, "This isn't a puppy. I mean, it's a wolf pup." The women looked at each other in disbelief. Valerie asked, "Do you think the mother is nearby?" "It must be somewhere nearby. I am not sure why it would have been left injured. Mother wolves are very caring. This pup may have wandered off and mauled by something." Erik said. Alice asked, "We can take it and nurse it back to life, right?" "I don't think so. It would be dangerous for our dogs." Erik did not want to get involved with wolves. Valerie asked, "Should we take it to the vet?" Erik responded, "I don't think the vet wants to deal with a wolf either." Alice interrupted, "I can't just leave a puppy here to die. What if his parents don't find him in time to save him?" Erik was trying to be practical, "This isn't our problem. This is nature's way of keeping the numbers down." Alice looked at him, shocked, "That is not true! If God put this pup in our path, we are to save it. I will not leave him here to die." Erik felt like a heel, "We can't play God to every animal." Alice was now getting angry, "I am not playing God! We have been given hearts for a reason, and my heart is telling me that I cannot allow this beautiful little critter to die. If God wants it to die, it will under my care." Valerie looked at Alice, "I can't tell what's wrong with this pup. We will need to take it to the vet." Erik shook his head, "You have quite a strong spirit, Mrs. Alexander. I won't argue with you but know that the vet may not want to handle this wild animal." Alice looked at him, "I will keep that under consideration. The vet will deal with me if they don't want to care for a cub." Erik laughed, "Yes, I can see that, Alice. You are a force to be reckoned with."

Erik helped the women carry all their things back to the house. Alice had the wolf pup in her arms. "What should I call you?" She paused and looked around, "I will call you Alpha. You will grow up to be strong and a leader. You will teach us the beauty of wolves. You will teach us how to love." The dogs had calmed down, sensing that Alice would keep and care for the wolf pup.

They heard Janie calling them in for lunch as they arrived at the house. "Alice, do you want to have lunch first, then head to the vet's?" Valerie asked. "No, I want to care for this pup first." Alice was holding the pup as if it were a human baby. Valerie headed into the house to speak to Janie. Alice smiled at Erik, "You know that I love animals. I want to see this pup heal. I will do whatever it takes to see this pup become a full-grown wolf." Erik responded, "You know that wolves are not pets. They are wild animals and will act like wild animals." "I will teach him. He is a gift. I wanted a puppy, and now I have a wild one." Erik shook his head, "Alice, you are something else. What do you think Mr. Alexander will say about a wild animal?" Alice smiled, "He won't fight me. I believe he has a kind heart and will understand that this is a living animal that needs a mother and love." Erik responded, "I hope so for your sake."

Valerie came out of the house with two lunch bags. "Janie made us a lunch to go. We need to make sure that you eat on time and keep up your strength. Erik, Janie, has your lunch ready inside." "Thank you, Valerie. I will be in shortly. I just need to take care of the dogs." Erik smiled and walked away.

Valerie and Alice got into the car. They put the pup into a carrier that they used for the dogs. They ate their lunch on the way to the vet. "I wish I had kept the puppy in my arms," Alice said. "It is safer in the carrier. Besides, we needed to eat and had to have our hands available. What do you think Mr. Alexander will say?" Alice was unsure, but she knew what she planned to say, "I will just tell him since he didn't get me a puppy, God provided." The women laughed and thanked God for the blessing.

They heard the pup stir and whimper as they arrived at the vet's office. Alice hurried to get Alpha out of the carrier as they got out of the car. Dr. Ben Cruz was a tall, gentle man. When he saw the women walk in, he asked, "What do you ladies have today?" Alice's eyes lit up, "We found Alpha in the meadow by my house. We want to have you check him out and see what's wrong with this pup." Dr. Cruz walked over to see, "Do you know you have a wolf pup in your arms?" Alice smiled, "Yes, I am well aware." Dr. Cruz smiled, "Please call me Ben. To whom do I have the pleasure of speaking?" Alice smiled shyly, "I am Alice Alexander. I live up the road at the Alexander stables." "Oh, well, it is a pleasure to meet you, Mrs. Alexander. Let me take Alpha and see what he has been up to." Alice handed him over, "Please call me Alice."

As the doctor examined Alpha, he spoke, "I do not see any broken bones. He looks a bit dehydrated. He looks healthy other than some small cuts. What are your plans for this wolf pup, Alice?" Alice answered, "Well, if he is healthy. I plan to give him a home and raise him like a beloved puppy." Ben looked at Alice, "Wild animals do not normally become tame just because humans raise them. They will behave like wild animals. What do Erik and Mr. Alexander have to say?" "Erik is not excited, and Mr. Alexander has not heard about Alpha yet. How old do you think he is?" Ben answered, "He looks to be about five weeks old, maybe six. What do you know about wolves?" "Nothing, but I am willing to learn how to raise one," Alice answered. "I will tell you what. If, at any time, you are not able to care for Alpha. I want you to bring him back to me. I will put him in the hands of a wildlife refuge. You realize that your husband may not allow you to keep him for the sake of the other animals." Ben hoped that Alice would reconsider but could tell she had her heart set on keeping Alpha. Alice answered, "I will be able to raise and love him just like a real puppy." "How much do we owe you, Dr. Ben?" Valerie asked. "Nothing. This one is on the house. I try to help landowners every time they bring in injured wild animals. That's my part in caring for the Lord's creatures."

Alice smiled, "Thank you. I appreciate you looking at Alpha. Thank you also for caring for the wild animals. I know this encourages people to try to save them instead of leaving them to die." Ben smiled, "Yes. We must do what we can. I admire your willingness to become a mother to this wolf pup. I can tell he already loves you. Look at the way he is nestled into your arms. You have already imprinted on him. Make sure to call if I can help in any way. Make sure to use a blender for his food for now. They normally eat regurgitated food at this age." Alice smiled and giggled, "Should I chew up his food for him?" Ben laughed, "Yes! Highly recommend that!" Valerie shook her head, "You two are getting gross! Alice, let's head home and get this little one situated." Alice followed Valerie out the door, "Thanks again, Ben."

The women were excited about this puppy. Alice spoke to Alpha, "I will be a good mommy to you. I promise to do all I can to make you happy." She was tickling his belly. Valerie asked, "What if Mr. Alexander says you can't keep him?" "I will just have to convince him. That's all." Valerie asked, "How do you think you will feel if you have to give him away to a wildlife refuge?" "I do not even want to think about that because I think I may cry at the thought." Valerie felt a little fear, "Well, you better get ready. It looks like Mr. Alexander is home early." Alice smiled at her, "Lord, give me strength, courage, and wisdom when speaking to him."

As they entered the house, Mr. Alexander greeted them at the door. "What have you been up to today?" Alice smiled, "I found a pup out in the meadow when we were painting. We are just getting back from the vet. He said that the pup is healthy." "What kind of dog is he?" Jack asked. Alice smiled, "It is a wolf pup." Jack backed away, "What?" Alice answered, "Remember I asked for a puppy, but you didn't get me one. I believe God gave me Alpha." Mr. Alexander looked at Valerie, "What were you thinking? We can't have a wild animal on the grounds." Valerie attempted to answer, but Alice stopped her. "Why are you blaming Valerie? I am an adult, and I chose to bring the pup to the vet. I chose to keep this pup. I found him. It is my choice." Jack looked back at his wife, "I'm sorry. I expect the people here to care for you to make wise decisions." Alice was furious, "Do you think I am not able to make decisions myself? I can and do every day. No one here is to blame. If you really want to have a conversation with anyone, it should be God. Ask Him why He put this pup in my life?" Jack was frustrated, "God? Really? How am I supposed to ask God questions? What makes you think God put this animal in your life? We live near the mountains. Do you think God put the bear here a few weeks ago?" Alice answered, "Yes, He did! I had a dream about a bear, and then it happened. He disappeared in my dream, and the bear left without hurting anyone. Alpha is my puppy. I will raise him." Jack was putting his foot down. "I demand you give him away. What are you going to do?" Alice was angry, "I am not a child. I am keeping him, and there is nothing you can do to make me change my mind."

Alice walked away from him and into her room. She grabbed a pillow, laid it on the floor, placed Alpha on the pillow, and sat on the floor beside him. "Don't worry, Alpha. I would rather move away than give you up. I know you are a gift from above." Alice heard a knock on the door, "Yes?" Jack said, "Listen, can I come in and talk?" Alice responded, "I have nothing more to say." Jack knocked again, "May I come in?" Alice hesitated, "Okay. But I do not want to argue."

Jack opened the door and smiled, "I see Alpha already has a bed. I am sorry. Please forgive me for not listening to you. I heard a wolf and panicked." Alice was surprised at the immediate change of heart, "What made you change your mind?" "I talked to Valerie, and she explained how happy you were to see that he was okay and how worried you were when you first found him. I know what a loving heart you have and should have been more sensitive to your feelings." Alice smiled, realizing that he did know her heart. "I am glad that you understand. Alpha is a good pup. I will raise him and train him like a regular dog." Jack continued, "I would like for you to promise me that if at any time, Alpha becomes aggressive with the other animals, you will consider what's best for them all." Alice nodded her head, "I will keep it all in mind. I do not believe that will be a problem."

Jack came over and knelt beside them; he reached out to pet Alpha. "He sure is a cute little guy." "Dr. Ben thinks he is only about five weeks old. He said I should chew his food up before giving it to him." She laughed as Jack looked at her trying to take it in. "I don't think he has eaten in a couple of days, so I need to feed him some meat." Jack looked at his wife, "You are not serious about chewing up raw meat?" Alice laughed, "I am just teasing you! Alpha does need to be fed.

Do you want to help?" "Sure, I can chew things for him," Jack responded sarcastically. They laughed as they got up and walked to the kitchen.

"Janie, what do we have for Alpha?" Jack asked. Alice smiled, "Do we have a good cut of meat?" Janie turned, "I think we have fillet mignon." Jack quickly answered, "Spare no expense on this pup!" Alice went to the refrigerator to see what she could find. Janie explained, "The only meat we have was for tonight's dinner. I have six steaks." "Well, he can eat mine now and the extra steak in a few hours." Alice asked, "When can we get more meat for him?" Janie answered, "All I must do is ask the grocer to bring me some. How much shall I order?" "I will need to feed him five times a day. He is a growing puppy and needs a lot of food. Once he gets older, I read that he will even enjoy fruit." Alice felt overjoyed that everyone was being helpful. "After he gets his strength back, I want to walk him around the property, so he knows where he is allowed to go. Wolves are supposed to be super intelligent. I also want to get him many toys. He needs to feel comfortable around the other dogs and horses."

Alice put the meat in the blender and added a little water. As she watched her new puppy eat, she felt a sense of belonging. Finally, Alice would have her own puppy to train and love. She was smiling as she imagined going to paint in the meadow and having Alpha romp around the meadow.

21 THE CABIN

It was finally time to head to the cabin. Seth had worked overtime to complete all his projects, but it was ten o'clock. They would not be leaving tonight. Seth arrived and saw that all the lights were still on. The boys greeted him at the door. "Daddy, can we go tonight?" Frankie asked. Samuel smiled, "No, Frankie. It's too far for us to go tonight. Daddy needs to sleep."

Rae had taken over so Ann Marie could head home. "I was beginning to worry," Rae said. Seth smiled, "Thank you for coming over to relieve Ann Marie. What time do you work tonight?" Rae responded, "I don't work until three am." Seth asked, "Do you want to crash here, so you don't have to waste time driving home?" Rae shook her head, "That would be a great idea. I can sleep here on the couch if that's okay?" Seth smiled, "Why wouldn't you just sleep in the guest room?" Rae was feeling bad, "I didn't want you to have to clean the room before you leave." Seth said, "Don't be silly! Get a good night's sleep before your shift. You are welcome to sleep here anytime. You know the password to get in. besides, this is a much closer drive to work than from your folks." Rae smiled, "Okay. I will stay here tonight and consider the other nights that I work." Seth added, "There are extra blankets in the closet if you need them."

"Okay, boys, off to sleep We are going to get up at five. We want to be on our way by six." The boys raced up the stairs, "Last one to bed has to eat worms!" Frankie laughed. Seth was right behind them, "Hey, that's not fair. I am always the last one in bed." Frankie laughed even harder. Samuel laughed, "Daddy, you don't really have to eat worms. You know Frankie is just teasing you." As they reached the top of the stairs, Seth caught up to them. He grabbed them both and carried them to their rooms. He dropped Samuel off first, then Frankie.

"Frankie, if I eat a worm tomorrow, I think you better join me." Frankie laughed, "No way! I'm going to be the first one in bed." Frankie raced into his room to change into his pajamas, then ran into the bathroom to brush his teeth. Samuel was not in a big hurry. He took his time changing into his pajamas. Frankie finished brushing, so Seth joined him in the room to tuck him in. "Do you want me to read you a bedtime story?" Frankie answered before Seth finished his question, "Nope. Not tonight, daddy. I want to sleep right away so I can wake up on time. I do not want us to be late. Mommy is waiting." Seth swallowed, "You know, not all dreams come true exactly the way we dream them." "I know, daddy. This dream is going to be true. I dreamt it three times exactly the same way." Frankie stated with confidence and faith. "Okay, I just want us to have a great time at the cabin. Promise me that we will have a great time no matter what happens. Okay?" Frankie closed his eyes, "I promise, daddy. No matter what, we are going to have a great time." Seth sat on Frankie's bed, "Okay, say your prayers so I can go check on Samuel."

Frankie knelt by his bed, "Our Father who art in heaven. Hallowed be thy name. Thy Kingdom come; thy will be done. On earth as it is in heaven. Bring my mommy home, Jesus. Bring her home at the cabin just like my dreams. Amen." Seth added, "Jesus, help us have a great time at the cabin. Amen." Seth tucked in his youngest son. As he tucked him in, he whispered, "I love you forever." Frankie smiled, "I like you for always." Frankie giggled, "Good night, daddy." Seth kissed his baby boy.

Samuel came out of the bathroom as Seth came out of Frankie's room. He picked up Samuel. "Why are you getting so big?" Samuel answered, "I'm a big kid now, daddy." Seth smiled at Samuel, "You are never going to get too big for me to carry." Samuel giggled, "What if I am as big as you?" Seth said, "I will use a crane or something." They laughed as they entered Samuel's room. "Are you packed for tomorrow?" Seth asked as he noticed something boxed up. "I have something special, but no one can see it yet," Samuel answered. Seth sat on Samuel's bed, "What do you think Frankie is hoping will happen?" Samuel smiled, "We both believe that mommy is coming to the cabin. We have been talking about it for a long time." Seth felt very sad, "What if mommy doesn't come to the cabin? What then?" Samuel looked at his dad, very confused, "Don't you want mommy to come there?" Seth felt horrible for questioning his son, "Of course I do, but what if she can't come?" Samuel insisted, "She will, daddy! We just have to believe!" Seth could see that he was not going to be able to get through. "I believe!" Seth said, trying his best to smile. Samuel knelt beside his bed, "Dear Jesus, give my daddy the faith to believe what you have told Frankie and me. Thank you, Jesus, for helping mommy find her way to the cabin. On earth like it is in heaven. Amen." Seth tucked his son in, kissed him, and said, "Good night, my sweet boy."

Seth closed Samuel's bedroom door behind him. In tears, he prayed, "Lord, please don't disappoint my boys. Give me the faith of a child. To be able to believe the promises you have given them and me. I am asking this mostly for their sakes but for mine too. I know you are a big, big God. I know what we are asking is not beyond what you can do. Your Word says on earth as it is in heaven. Help me to have that childlike faith that says you will never disappoint. Thank you, Jesus, for protecting us always."

Seth brushed his teeth and headed to bed. As soon as he laid his head down, he started dreaming. He was driving up to the cabin; the road was clear, without traffic or construction. The cabin was glowing. It looked like the sun was shining through it. When Seth walked to the door, he could hear voices. He reached for the doorknob, but there was none. Seth looked at the door, and it seemed to be on hinges; all he had to do was push on the door. It opened, and inside he saw a man sitting at a desk. He was looking at a gigantic book. He did not even look up but said, "Come on in, son. I have been waiting for you. Seth entered and asked, "What are you doing in my cabin?" The man laughed a big thunderous laugh. He said, "This is my cabin. I allow you to use it any time you want. You have not been here for quite some time. Why not?" Seth was not sure how to answer, "I am not sure what you mean." The man spoke again, "Why haven't you come to visit me?" Seth was feeling weak, "Are You, God?" The man responded, "Who do you think I am?" "I know You are God," Seth replied. God laughed. "Son, what do you want?" Without hesitation, Seth answered, "I want the mother of my sons back home." God asked, "Do you want this more than Me?" Seth stopped in his tracks, "My boys miss their mommy so much. I miss her so much too. We can't go on without You, Lord." "Do you believe I can do this for you?" Seth spoke before God finished speaking, "Yes! With all my heart, I believe You can." God said, "Do you believe I want to?" Seth answered, "I want to believe You want to, but my mind isn't sure." God asked, "Can you get your mind, heart, and body in one place of belief?" Seth answered, "I can with Your help. Your Word says I can do all things through Christ who strengthens me." Seth heard these final words, "I AM Who I AM." Seth awoke, sat up, and looked around. He expected to see the Lord in his room.

Seth could hear Rae getting ready to leave. He got up and went downstairs. Rae saw him, "I am so sorry if I woke you." Seth answered, "No, I woke from a dream, then heard you after a few minutes." Rae looked at him, "Are you okay?" Seth answered, "Yes, I am. I am going to get some water. Do you want anything?" Rae answered, "No, I am on the way out. I need to be at work in 15 minutes. Are you sure you're, okay?" Seth asked, "Yes, why?" Rae looked puzzled, "You look like you're glowing." Seth laughed, "Really? I woke up from a dream where I was talking to God." Rae smiled, "I think it was more than a dream. I'm sorry, I wish we could talk, but I must run." Seth answered, "Have a fantastic day! I know we will." Rae looked at him, not sure what he meant by that but smiled, "I will. You guys, be safe. Call me before you arrive and lose cell service." Seth reassured her, "We will. Don't forget to set the alarm when you arrive and leave." "Okay." Rae hurried out the door.

Seth grabbed a glass of water and headed back to bed. He laid his head down and began to dream again. He was in a ballroom. There were many people there. Most he did not know, but he saw a few of his old high school friends. He started to look around and see if Francie was somewhere nearby. He greeted all the people as he walked by. Seth decided to look in the kitchen. When he entered the kitchen, he saw an enormous stove. He saw that ten people were cooking, and everyone had on white chef hats and jackets. They were busy cooking the meal for that night. Seth turned and walked out of the kitchen, but he was in the dining room instead of the ballroom. He walked over to the table, and there was a place setting for everyone. Seth looked for his name. When he found it, he saw that Francie was to sit next to him. Seth sat down and waited. He waited for a long time. When people finally started to enter, he scanned the room for Francie. Most of the guests were seated, and he could not see Francie. As the final guest made their way to their seats, the door attendants began to close the doors. Seth could see the doors closing in slow motion. Suddenly, as they were within an inch of closing, a woman in a white dress entered. She walked like royalty, with smooth long strides, authority, and confidence. Her hair was loose and over her shoulders. Finally, Seth could see her face; she was smiling and glowing. The entire room had turned to watch her enter. There before him was Francie. Her eyes were sparkling, and she was radiant. She walked directly to her seat and smiled, "Is this seat taken?" Seth had stood up and pulled the chair out for her, "Please, have a seat here. You won't regret sitting here." "Please accept my apologies for taking so long to arrive. I had so much to do." Francie winked at him. Seth responded, "I would have waited forever. I'm glad you made it."

Seth opened his eyes to the sound of the alarm. He needed to get ready for the trip, so he got out of bed and showered. Seth could not shake his dreams as he finalized the checklist and marked off everything already packed and in the car. He headed upstairs to wake the boys. Samuel was already awake and getting dressed. He headed to Frankie's room; he could hear Frankie talking as he neared the door. He listened at the door and then opened it. Frankie was talking in his sleep and started laughing. Seth was gentle in waking his youngest son. He knelt by the bed and began to sing. "Wake up, wake up my little sleepy head. The sun is rising, and the moon has disappeared. Wake up, wake up my little sleepy head." Frankie opened his eyes and laughed, "Daddy, I was talking to mommy. She told me it was time to wake up. She was singing the same song you sang to me." Seth smiled, "That's great! You mean to tell me that mommy beat me to wake you up?" Frankie laughed, "No! You did it at the same time! I love you, daddy!" Seth hugged his little boy, "I love you forever." Frankie responded, "I like you for always." Seth laughed, "Come on now. We should get moving so we can head to the cabin." Frankie asked, "Are we going to eat breakfast or get something later?" Seth had not thought about breakfast, "We can do whatever you and Samuel want to do. Come on now, jump out of bed." Frankie jumped up and out of bed.

"What do you want to do for breakfast, Samuel?" Frankie called out to his brother. Samuel answered, "What about some fruit, and we get a better breakfast on the way to the cabin?" Frankie agreed, "That sounds like a good idea." Seth agreed as well, "Okay, sounds great to me. Let's get moving. I will get breakfast fruit ready." Seth headed downstairs to get the fruit ready to take. He gave the house a quick check just in case he had forgotten something. The boys were coming downstairs with their backpacks. Seth smiled at the boys, "I believe I have everything we need." Samuel added, "Whatever we don't have, we can buy." They laughed because that was what Francie always said as they left on trips.

As the boys got into the car seats and buckled up, Seth set the alarm to the house. Buddy jumped onto the front seat and took the passenger seat. Seth buckled up and said, "Okay, we are finally off. Your Auntie Rae may come by and stay in the house on the days she works overtime and extra shifts." Frankie started a prayer, "Jesus around us, Jesus in front, Jesus on the sides, Jesus behind us, Jesus above us, and Jesus beneath us. Thank you for your protection." Seth was impressed; he had not heard that prayer since Francie had prayed on their last trip. "Frankie, you remembered it." Frankie replied, "Daddy, I always say it but quietly. Today it was time to say it out loud." Seth handed the boys the fruit packs he had made for them. "We can talk about where to stop for breakfast when the sun comes out. Sound like a plan?" The boys answered in unison, "Yes, sir!"

The drive was usually a long six hours. Seth turned on the music so they could sing along. Frankie says, "Daddy, the sun is out in the middle of singing to an oldie. I think it's time we talk about where to eat." Seth laughed, and without skipping a beat, he asked, "Frankie, what do you feel like eating?" "I want pigs in a blanket," Frankie answered. Samuel chimed in, "That sounds good to me too." Seth answered, "Okay, let's look for a café. If you see one or a sign shout it out." They continued to drive another half hour when Samuel shouted, "I see that there is one in the next town. It looks like the name is Ole Timer's Café." "Good catch Samuel." Seth was glad his son had seen the sign because he had missed it. When they got into town, that was the first eatery they saw.

The boys jumped out as soon as the car was in park and headed to the doggy park so Buddy could finally relieve himself. After getting Buddy back in the car, they ran to the door and waited on Seth to catch up. Before they entered the café, they looked back at the car, as Buddy sat watching them hoping to get a doggie bag. As the boys entered, they looked for a corner booth. Frankie ran to the booth and jumped in. They all agreed that the booth was the best seat in the house. As they looked over the menu, the server came over. "Good morning, gentlemen. My name is Sunnie. Do you have any questions about the menu?" Frankie was the first, "Do you have pigs in a blanket?" Sunnie smiled, "Yes, we do. So, you get two pigs wrapped up feeling cozy. Would you also like some fences to keep them on your plate?" Samuel asked, "What are fences?" Sunnie smiled, "Well, they are hash browns in this part of the country." Frankie laughed, "I need the fences to keep my pigs in!" Samuel added, "Me too. Please." Sunnie asked, "Anything else for you two young men?" Samuel answered, "I would like some milk, please. Frankie, how about you?" Frankie replied, "Not me, I would like to have a milkshake." Sunnie glanced over at Seth, and he nodded yes. "Would you like that milkshake from a brown cow, a white cow, or a pink cow?" Sunnie was having fun with Frankie, "I want a brown and pink cow, please." Sunnie smiled, "Young man, you sure know how to order well." Frankie giggled. Sunnie looked at Seth, "What may I get you?" Seth asked, "Does the lumberjack special come with biscuits and gravy?" Sunnie answered, "If you want it, I can get it." Seth replied, "That would be great. I will also take a shake like Frankie's. Thank you."

Frankie grinned from ear to ear, "Mommy always says that ice cream fixes any upset tummy." Seth leaned over to his son, "Frankie, do you have an upset tummy?" "No, daddy, I am having ice cream, so I don't get an upset tummy." Frankie giggled. "Oh, I see. You are taking preventative measures. Smart!"

They decided to watch people and see if they could make up stories about the people that arrived. Frankie was always making up the best stories. A woman and man walked in and sat near the door. Frankie began, "See the woman in red and the man in blue. I think they have a white car. They want people to think they are Americans because they look like they are from a different country. I think the woman is a spy and the man is a doctor. Look at his hands; they do not shake when he holds his hand up. They are sitting by the door to make a quick getaway." Sunnie happened to be walking by and overheard the story. She added, "I saw diamonds in the woman's purse. The man smells like a gold mine." They all laughed as she giggled.

Samuel was next. He noticed a young man in the booth next to them, so he spoke very softly. "I saw the man with eyes behind his head. When he took off his cowboy hat, his eyes looked right at me. When I saw his eyes, he hurried up and put his cowboy hat back on. I heard his thoughts, and he thought, 'what if I run into the back and start cooking all the food.' Then he thought, 'I better not because I am so hungry, I might eat it all. Especially the pigs in the blanket that are fenced in.' They all laughed. They continued to make up stories until their food arrived. As Sunnie brought their plates, she was oinking. The people in the café turned to look and see what was going on. When they saw that she was serving the only two kids in the café, they all joined in, "Oink, oink. Oink, oink." The entire café was in laughter. Frankie was saving one of his piglets for Buddy. He never forgot to save him a treat.

Hours later, they arrived at the cabin. Frankie and Samuel looked at the creek and wanted to go fishing. Seth convinced them that the creek would still be there after unpacking the car as they carried everything into the cabin. Seth saw that the cabin was not dirty as he had expected.

As he walked to turn on the refrigerator, he saw the note.

> 'Seth, I know I was the only one that was privy to your trip. I came up a couple of days ago and cleaned the place for you. I wanted you to have a great trip and not worry about cleaning when you arrive. I spoke to the neighbor at the stables. He said that they had captured a bear and relocated it. They do not expect to have any other issues. I also figured you would forget to call me, so I had a landline put in. The number is (555) 555-4321. Please call me to let me know you have arrived. I promise not to bother you after you call. I just wanted to make sure there was a working phone in case of any problems. Have a great vacation. Get some rest, relaxation, and use the time to be restored. Love you all and see you soon.
>
> Rae'

Seth told the boys, "Well, looks like Auntie Rae came up here and cleaned for us. She thought of everything. It looks like she even put ice cream in the refrigerator for us." The boys laughed, "Yay! I love her!" "Okay, since Auntie Rae got everything done, we can go to the creek." The boys again yelled, "I love Auntie Rae!"

They grabbed their fishing poles and headed out to the creek, which was full of water but still safe. They cast in the poles and waited. Suddenly Samuel screamed, "I got one!" Just as he spoke those words, they all started catching fish. Suddenly, the fish started jumping. Buddy was so excited that he barked at the fish. Frankie screamed with joy, "I caught another one!" Then Samuel started laughing, "This is like our dreams." The fish jumped right into Frankie's arms when he finished saying that. "Look what jumped in my arms!"

Frankie screamed. They had caught so many fish that they had to carry some in their arms and shirts. "We will have to freeze a bunch of these." Samuel knew that the dreams were coming true as he spoke these words. Frankie added, "We can give some to the neighbors." Seth had tears streaming down his cheeks, "Yes, maybe we can go tomorrow after breakfast."

"Daddy, can we fish again tomorrow?" Frankie asked. Seth was smiling, "Yes, of course, we can." Samuel added, "We can take some fish for Auntie Rae since she cleaned the cabin for us. And just because she is my favorite aunt." Seth agreed that it was a good idea. He added, "I guess we can have a fish fry tonight. How does that sound?" Again, the boys were smiling, "Can we do it outside?" "We will have to build a campfire." Seth had barely finished his sentence when the boys cheered. "Yay!"

The grill was clean and ready to be used. Seth decided to fry five fish. The boys were famished, and all five fish disappeared as soon they were off the grill. One of the treats that Rae had left was ingredients for S'mores. The boys sat around the fire and ate S'mores. The conversation was about the fish they caught and fishing tomorrow. Buddy was having a good time too. He must enjoy fish and marshmallows. He was quick to steal them from Frankie before getting them off the stick. Frankie and Samuel laughed so much that Seth knew 'this was part of the healing they had needed for a long time.' The night was ending; the campfire had taken too many logs to count. It was midnight, and even though they did not have a schedule to keep, they needed to get some rest.

22 THE MEETING

Alice awoke, and like most days, she was feeling so happy. Alpha was a couple of weeks older and quite rambunctious. He jumped up and ran to her as she got off the bed. She sat on the floor and played with her puppy for a little bit. "Okay, we need to shower. Come on, Alpha; let's get cleaned up for our day." She looked in her closet and saw the clothes she wanted to wear. It was a spring dress with flowers and a bow on the back. She picked out some purple tights and then headed to the shower. Alpha was right at her heels. He knew that after she showered, he would eat. Once Alice came out of the shower, Alpha waited at the door for her to finish getting dressed.

Alice was singing as she came down the hall to the kitchen. "Good morning, Janie. Did you have a good night's rest?" Alice had her head in the refrigerator when she heard Jack coming in. "Good morning, Alice." He greeted Alpha with a pat on the head, "Hey boy, did you sleep well?" Alpha whimpered, and Alice looked back at him, "What's wrong with my baby?" Alpha wagged his tail. "Good morning, Jack. Do you have a busy day ahead?" Jack smiled, "No, just the regular busy schedule. How about you?" Alice was getting the meat out to chop into tiny pieces for Alpha. "Not super busy, just our usual." She answered. Jack turned to look at her, "What does that entail?" Alice looked at Alpha, "We like to go and play with the dogs, greet and work with the horses, and if there is time, we like to play in the meadow by the creek." Jack laughed, "That is busier than I am." Alice laughed as she prepared Alpha's breakfast. Alpha was sitting, waiting patiently as the others entered for breakfast.

Erik entered the kitchen, "Good morning. Janie, breakfast smells delicious as always. How is everyone this morning?" Valerie entered the kitchen as Erik finished speaking. "Good morning. It looks like I am the last to arrive. Alpha, how are you today?" Alpha loved Valerie; he immediately reacted to her and licked her hand. "I love you too, Alpha." The women were the only ones that Alpha would lick.

As everyone sat for breakfast, Alpha ate in his designated area. His food bowl was near the door. The people were laughing when Alpha heard something in the distance. His ears perked up, and he listened intently. Alice noticed his behavior and walked over to him. "What's the matter, baby? What do you hear?" Erik answered, "I believe our neighbors arrived last night." Alice smiled, "Oh really? That explains Alpha's whimpering last night. He acted as if he wanted to go out, but I was not about to let him out. He has good hearing. Isn't the cabin about a mile away from the house?" Erik nodded, "Yes, at least a mile. I believe it was the housekeeper; that was there a few days ago. She said the owners were coming out for about a week." Alice laughed, "Well, I guess Alpha wants to say hello." Jack interrupted, "I don't think the neighbors want to meet a wolf. You need to make sure to stay clear of them. Okay?" Alice acknowledged his concerns, "You are probably right. He is a puppy, though. He wouldn't hurt anyone." Jack gave her a stern look, "Most people don't like wolves. They know that they are dangerous wild animals. So, make sure to stay away from them." "I will." Alice knew she would not even try.

Jack headed off to work, and Erik was in a hurry to get to the dogs and horses. Valerie wanted Alice to do her physical therapy first thing. Alice responded, "I need to take Alpha out for his potty break before doing anything else. So, we will only be gone for a few minutes." Valerie looked at her, "Alice, I know what a few minutes mean. Please be back in fifteen. Okay?" Alice laughed, "I will try."

"Come on, Alpha," Alice called as she headed out of the house. It was only 6:30 am, and Alice did not feel like therapy this early. Alpha took the lead as they walked toward the stables. He was always eager to greet the pack of dogs. As they arrived at the stables, Alpha let out a howl. The dogs started barking, and they knew the baby had arrived. They all greeted each other in love and talked in a language only dogs understand. Alice felt happy knowing that the dogs had accepted him as their family.

She headed to the horses to see what she could do to help Erik. Erik asked, "Would you like to feed them today?" Alice went straight to her job. She was filling their buckets with grain. Erik was busy with the straw. "Can I give them their apples today?" Erik smiled, "Alice, you always want to give those treats. Of course, you can." After feeding the horses their grain, she headed to the back to grab a few apples to slice. Alpha was at her heels, following her wherever she went. Alpha chose Alice over the animals. She spoke to Alpha, "Do you want a slice of apple too?" As she sliced the apples, she gave Alpha one. Alice sat on the floor and allowed him to nibble on the slice as she held it. She giggled as she watched him. Erik could hear her laughing. He smiled; Alice appeared so much happier with her pup. He thought to himself, 'Even if this pup is a wolf, he will protect her as he gets older. She will be able to gain her independence.'

As Alice came out of the storage room, she had a bowl full of quartered apples. Alice greeted each horse by name and fed them apples. Erik watched as she would speak with each one, rub their chins, and stroke their manes. The horses loved her. They sensed her gentle spirit. Alice suddenly sat down laughing; she played with Alpha and rubbed his belly, "Are you, my baby? I love my horses too. I love all my animals. You are so spoiled little one." She was laughing as she played with her puppy. He jumped all over her, kissing her and nipping at her. Erik smiled; he knew wolves use their mouths like humans use their hands.

After they finished with the horses, Alice asked, "Will the horses be in the meadow today?" Erik smiled, "Alice, I think you sensed my thoughts. I want to let them out for a run, maybe about ten." Alice was excited, "That's perfect! I usually feed Alpha around that time. I will just pack up a lunch for him, and he can eat in the meadow. Then, I want to paint with the horses around me." Erik shook his head, "You are so funny. You want to get the feeling of being out in the wild. Horses and wolves around you!" Alice was laughing, "Yes! I want Alpha to feel what it is like to have nature happening around him. I do not just want him to think he is a regular dog. I want to take him on nature hikes sometime soon." Erik asked, "You will allow me to come along, won't you?" Alice smiled, "Of course. At least for the first year. I am getting stronger every day." Erik smiled, "Yes, you are Alice. I am proud of you." Alice winked at him, "I will be able to do everything on my own soon." They both nodded in agreement.

It was time for Alice to head back to the house for physical therapy. "Come on, boy." She called out to Alpha. Alpha raced towards her, so she began to jog. Jogging felt good; she focused on taking deep breaths. They ran all the way back to the house. Valerie was waiting for her when she entered, "That was longer than 15 minutes." Alice laughed, "I am sorry. I should have just told you I wouldn't be back for a couple of hours." Valerie smiled, "I know you too well, Alice. In order of importance: Alpha, dogs, horses, and then finally therapy. Thanks a lot!" Valerie and Alice laughed.

"At ten, I am headed to the meadow to paint. I also want Alpha to eat outside with the horses. The horses will be romping around in the meadow at that time. Do you ladies want to come along?" Janie spoke first, "That seems too dangerous for me. I will feel like I am in the Wild West. Do you think we will see cowboys and Indians?" She laughed. "If we get lucky!" Alice giggled. Valerie added, "If we get lucky, maybe the horses will be tame enough to catch and ride." They all laughed even louder. "We are quite a mess, aren't we?" Alice asked.

The women continued to joke and laugh while Alice worked on her physical therapy. "I know you saw me jogging. I do feel so much stronger. I didn't even get out of breath." Valerie smiled, "You are much stronger, Alice. Before long, you won't even need my help for anything." Alice got very sad, "You will always be around for me, right?" Valerie smiled and reassured her, "Alice, you have a friend for life. If I can no longer be of use, why would your husband want to pay me to hang out?" Alice asked, "Do you normally live in this area?" Valerie smiled, "No, my family is from this area, but I used to live in the city. When I got this job, it was as a live-in nurse. So, I moved here. I will always visit you regardless of where I live. Besides, you can come to visit me too." Alice laughed, "You will have to live in the country because that is the best place for Alpha. He is always going to be with me." Valerie nodded in agreement, "I will just have to buy something in the country."

Alice headed to the kitchen to pack Alpha's meal when they finished therapy. She was chopping up his steak when Erik entered the kitchen. "I am ready to let the horses out, Alice. Did you want to be in the meadow before I do?" Alice responded, "Yes, I am almost finished. Alpha and the ladies will be out in a few minutes." Erik headed out to the stables.

The ladies gathered all the paint equipment and headed out to the meadow. Alpha enjoyed his trips to the meadow and followed close behind.

The women headed to their usual spot. They were setting up the art easels and chairs when the horses came running out. The horses ran past the women. Alpha whimpered as he saw the horses running. The horses finally stopped running and settled down to graze on the grasses. Alice served Alpha his mid-morning meal. Finally, the women were ready to paint. They sat in a circle with their backs to each other. They had perfect seats to the beauty of the landscape. Mountains, the creek, and the beautiful colors of the meadow with the horses grazing. Erik walked up to them and asked, "Does anyone want to hike to the mountain's edge?" Alice's eyes brightened up, "Alpha and I will come." She rinsed out her brushes and left Valerie and Janie painting.

Alpha was running up ahead of Alice and Erik. Alice asked, "Did you come out here for me?" Erik laughed, "Yes, I must admit I did. You looked so happy this morning. I thought I would add more happiness for you." Alice drew in a deep breath, "I love the smell of the pines. It makes me feel like I have even more freedom in my life." Erik responded, "Before you know it, you and Alpha will be taking trips out here on your own." "I can imagine that!" Alice said. This was the first time she had gone this far.

Samuel and Frankie were just waking up. They could smell bacon cooking, so they hurried out of their room. Seth was in the small kitchen area, "Come and get it. Sorry, no fish for breakfast, but we can have some later if you boys want." Frankie said, "Oh no! I thought we would eat fish at every meal." Samuel laughed, "Daddy, he is just teasing you. You know we love bacon." Seth smiled at the boys, "You guys always keep me on my toes. Have a seat, and we will eat, then head out to fish or hike. Whichever you want to do." Frankie answered, "I would like to hike first, then fish in our creek again. I am still waiting for the rainbow fish." Seth answered, "Okay. Samuel, is that a good plan for you?" Samuel replied, "Yes, daddy. The hike sounds like fun. Who knows what we will see? Maybe we will see wolves, bears, and wild horses." They laughed and talked as they ate their breakfast.

"Make sure to put on some comfortable shoes for the hike." Seth was talking to both the boys. "We have our hiking boots; should we wear them?" Frankie asked. "Sure, if they are comfortable," Seth replied. They headed north from the cabin. Seth gave them instructions as they walked, "We are walking north. Look at where the sun is. If you ever get lost, you must look for the sun and the moss. The moss usually grows on the north side, but sometimes it will grow on all sides. Look at where the creek is as we hike. Right now, it is on our left side." As they hiked, Frankie kept looking toward the creek. "Daddy, will we cross the creek?" "Probably not today on our hike. I want to make sure you get comfortable with where the creek is. We can cross the creek on a different day. You see the fallen tree?" Samuel replied, "That is a good bridge for us when we decide to take the neighbors some fish." Seth laughed, "Yes, it could be a good bridge. We have a bridge on the south side of the property. It leads to the area where our neighbors have the stables." It was almost ten o'clock. "Can we go higher into the mountains?" Frankie asked. "We can continue up for about an hour if you don't get too tired. I have water in my pack if you get thirsty." "Can I have some now?" Frankie asked. Seth took his pack off; he was pulling out some water when they heard the commotion in the meadow.

"Looks like we get to see wild horses after all," Samuel said. The boys watched the horses run around. "I wonder if we can ride them," Frankie asked. "I don't believe they are tame horses," Seth answered. "I heard that they rescue wild horses. Not sure they have any intention of riding them." "Daddy, why do they have to rescue wild horses? If they are supposed to be wild, why rescue them?" Samuel looked at Frankie, "I think some people wanted to kill them, so people rescue them." Seth smiled, "That's right, son. Not everyone wants to allow horses to roam wild on their property." Frankie was looking sad. Seth added, "These horses were rescued so they would live. We should be happy for them." "So, our neighbors are good people for horses?" Frankie asked. Seth replied, "Yes, son. Mommy always wanted to rescue horses. We just didn't have enough room." They watched the horses for a while.

The Laurel's headed up the mountain for about thirty minutes, then headed back down. "Let's cross over the creek when it narrows." Samuel wanted to cross the water. Seth reluctantly agreed. "Okay. We need to be careful, so we don't slip on rocks." As they looked for a good spot to cross, Frankie asked, "Why are the rocks so big here?" Samuel answered, "That's how they broke when they rolled down the mountain." Seth laughed. They came across a shallow area. "Let's cross over here." Seth was leading. Samuel was behind Frankie, "Daddy, can I jump over the rocks?" "Sure, it is warming up. The sun will dry you up fast." Both boys started jumping. Seth laughed as he watched them jump across the creek. "Shall we head back down the mountain?" "Can we go a little further up?" Samuel asked. "You guys are not too tired?" Seth asked. "Nope. I just woke up so I can go for a long time." Frankie answered.

Seth began to teach again, "We crossed the creek, so our cabin is now on the right side of the creek just like the creek is on our right side." Seth pointed out the different flowers alongside the creek. He pointed to the woodpecker in the tree. "Do you see the woodpecker?" Frankie could not see him, "I can only hear him. I can't see him." Samuel said, "Look, Frankie. Above the branch, that looks like it has flowers. Frankie searched the trees, "Oh, I see him now. He is such a cute daddy. He has a crown on his head." They all laughed. "Alright, boys, let's head back down." Seth was following the boys. Samuel was leading the group.

Suddenly they heard voices. "Samuel, stop," Seth instructed. He caught up with the boys and stood in front of them. He became the leader of his group. "Stay close to me." He instructed the boys, "Let's keep quiet for a moment." They saw a man and woman with a puppy come into view. Seth shouted a greeting, "How are you doing today?" Erik looked up and greeted them, "Hello. You must be our neighbors. We are from the Alexander stables." Alice was trying to hide her face. "Hi, I'm Frankie. This is my brother Samuel." Samuel reached over and grabbed his little brother. Seth noticed the pup, "Is that a wolf pup?" Erik answered, "Yes. He is a good boy. He will not bite hard, but he is a puppy, so he may nip." Seth asked, "Is he safe around my boys?" Erik answered, "I think so. He is accustomed to humans. He is perfect when we take him to the vet."

Seth whispered to the boys, "I want you boys to be careful. Samuel looks like you do get to see a wolf too." Samuel laughed, "He sure is cute." Alpha ran up to the boys and sniffed them. Erik spoke, "If you kneel, he will get more comfortable with you." The boys looked at Seth. He nodded his head as he also knelt with the boys, "He sure is cute." Frankie giggled as Alpha licked his face. "I think we taste good to him." Samuel laughed. Alpha was pleased to meet the boys. They played together as Erik and Seth visited. Alice had stayed away, but Buddy ran up to her and loved on her.

Erik was explaining the bear situation. "I don't think we should have any other issues, but we can't guarantee that." Seth asked, referring to Alice, "Why isn't she coming any closer." Erik answered calmly, "She was in a fire and is uncomfortable around people." Seth apologized, "I'm sorry. I did not mean to pry. It just felt uncomfortable because of my boys. Buddy seems to love her." Buddy was licking Alice's hand and rubbing on her. The boys were laughing at Alpha. Erik responded, "Alpha acts like he knows your boys too. He must sense the gentle spirits."

"Well, we best get out of your way. We were just headed back for fishing." Erik asked, "Fishing? In our creek?" Seth smiled, "Yes. We caught a bunch." Erik looked so surprised, "In our creek? I have never seen any fish. I walk by it every day." Seth was laughing, "I guess we had a miracle happen. We must have caught twenty. They were jumping so high that some jumped into Frankie's arms." Erik could not believe what he was hearing. "Where exactly did you fish?" "West of our cabin. You are kidding, right?" Seth asked. Erik shook his head, "I haven't seen any fish for years." Seth smiled, "I believe we experienced a miracle. An answer to prayers and dreams. Well, we better get going, boys. Erik and Alice, it was a pleasure meeting you both."

Seth held on to both the boys' shoulders as he hustled them off. Frankie looked back, "I want to play with Alpha again. Bye, Alpha!" Alpha seemed to understand the boys were leaving. He started to chase them; then Alice called out to him. "Alpha, come!" Frankie and Samuel stopped in their tracks. They turned and looked at Alice. She was facing the opposite direction, and Alpha turned to chase his mommy.

The boys stood watching Alice walk away. Seth called to them, but they refused to move. "Daddy, look at her. She sounds like mommy." Seth knelt beside them, "Listen, you haven't heard mommy's voice in over two years. Of course, she sounds like mommy. She has a beautiful voice. That is Mrs. Alexander. She didn't even come to see you."

They decided to get across the creek when they found a shallow area as they walked down the mountain. They came across a spot and jumped across the creek. The boys were laughing as they jumped. Seth started to think about what Erik had said about the fish. He searched for fish but saw none. Finally, Seth asked the boys, "Are you sure you want to fish today?" Frankie smiled, "Yes! Today I think we will see the rainbow-colored ones." Samuel added, "We need to give Mrs. Alexander some fresh fish." Seth smiled, "Okay, sounds like a plan. Let's get to the cabin and get our poles."

When the boys saw the cabin, it became a foot race. "Last one to the cabin has to eat worms," Frankie yelled. The race was on. Seth was running behind the boys, encouraging them. "I am going to win." He shouted. Samuel ran next to his little brother, "I will beat you." Frankie was laughing and running as fast as he could. "Nobody is going to beat me." Seth laughed harder and said, "I don't want to eat worms." "Big fat squishy ones." Samuel hollered. "Yuck! Yucky!" Frankie laughed. They kept running to the cabin, and Seth was the last one there.

As they got the fishing poles, Frankie reminded his daddy. "You know who the last one was and what you need to do." Samuel smiled at his daddy, "A big fat squishy one, daddy." Seth teased the boys, "I think I would rather eat a fuzzy one. Maybe a skinny one. I know; I will eat one of the earthworms we use for fishing." Frankie was laughing, "No, daddy! The fish will be hungry. Not an earthworm." The debate continued for a few minutes. Then as they headed toward the creek, Samuel shouted, "Look, daddy! The creek is silver. I think that's the rainbow fish." As they continued to walk, they noticed that the fish were starting to jump. So, they walked faster but did no run with the poles in their hands.

The fish seemed to flood the creek. They threw in the lines and pulled fish out every time. They laughed as they saw that the fish did look like rainbows. Once again, they had about twenty fish. Frankie reminded Samuel that they wanted to catch some for Mrs. Alexander. Suddenly, they heard Buddy start to bark at something or someone. They looked around and saw Alpha across the creek. Alpha was far ahead of Erik and Alice. Frankie yelled, "Erik, come see the fish."

Alpha got very excited when he saw the fish jumping. Frankie started screaming with joy when he saw a fish jump out beside Alpha. Alpha jumped up and down beside the fish. He was barking and whimpering. When Erik and Alice arrived, they were shocked at the number of fish in the creek. "Oh my!" Alice shouted. They did not have any fishing poles or nets. Frankie and Samuel were giggling so hard that they were getting hoarse. They kept filling the coolers they had, and the coolers were busting out. Alice kept her face covered but was laughing softly. She did not want her face to get sore from the laughter and stretching of her facial muscles.

Suddenly the fish disappeared. They were completely gone. Seth yelled across the creek, "Erik, we have more fish than we can eat. Would you like to have some fish for tonight?" Erik looked at Alice, "Do you want some for tonight?" "I don't know what Janie has planned, but I would love to have some." Alice was smiling. Erik came closer to the creek, "We would love to have some. I'll cross over on the path and come get a few." "Alice, why not join us for an hour or so? We would love to visit with you." Alice shook her head and had Erik answer, "She will take a rain check. She needs to get home and rest for a few hours." Erik made his way over to get the fish.

Seth asked, "So Erik, do you believe in miracles?" Erik answered, "I do now. I am telling you; I had not seen fish in this creek for quite some time. You and the boys must be bringing some favor with you." Seth laughed, "Let me give you the phone number here so Alice can call to schedule the raincheck." Erik smiled, "it's okay. I will be the one to bring her over, so I will let you know when she is strong enough to visit." Seth asked, "Is this a way to say that she won't be coming to visit." Erik explained, "No, that's not what I mean. She is just getting back on her feet, and it has been a long day. She has been out since 6:30 this morning. Stables, meadow, painting, and then a hike. Plus, she cares for her pup." Seth continued, "Let her know the kids would love to show her how to fish. They are terrific kids. They are good at cheering up others." Erik grabbed the fish, "I will make sure she gets over here in the next couple of days. Erik walked away, "Thank you for the fish. You boys are the best fishermen I have ever met."

Alice was busy with Alpha. She had picked up his fish and tried to hold it without dropping it as it wiggled in her hands. Alice waved at the boys and turned, and she walked away with Alpha.

The boys were still by the creek. Frankie started screaming, "Daddy! Daddy! Daddy, look what happened!" He was holding a fish. "It jumped into my arms. Then it opened its mouth and spit this out." Frankie was holding a gold nugget. "This fish did it." He said as he held up the fish. Seth was in shock. He did not know what to say or do. Samuel was the first to speak, "Our dreams are coming true. Not exactly like we dreamed, but we have been seeing some of the things happening. Daddy, this is the best place ever." Samuel said and started crying. Frankie walked over to his brother and hugged him. "Don't cry, Samuel. God is watching over us." Seth reached out and took the fish from Frankie. He was examining the fish. It was purple with blue and yellow. Seth said, "I think we need to put him back in the creek. What do you guys think?" Frankie answered first, "Yes! I think so too." Seth walked to the edge of the creek. "God, if this is you. I am waiting for all our dreams to come true." Seth said as he placed the fish gently back in the water.

We better get inside and put some of these in the freezer. We will need to have another fish fry. Frankie took his daddy's hand and put the gold nugget in his hand. Seth smiled at Frankie, "We will keep this in a safe place. When we get back home, we will need to see a jeweler. Have him tell us what it is worth." Frankie smiled, "I don't care how much, daddy. I just want mommy back." Seth heard Samuel say, "Mommy is closer than we know." Seth looked at his son, confused by these words. "What do you mean, Samuel?" Samuel looked at him, confused, "What do you mean, daddy?" Seth asked, "What did you mean when you said mommy is closer than we know?" Frankie and Samuel looked at each other, "Daddy, I didn't say that." Frankie added, "He said that we don't need the money." Seth was perplexed. He knew what he had heard, but neither one of the boys heard what he had heard. Seth put it in the back of his mind until he could have some time alone with God.

Frankie and Samuel were discussing the fishing adventure. They were so excited to see the fish jumping again. Seth was surprised that they did not even discuss the gold nugget that the fish had spit out. They discussed whether they would have more fishing experiences like the last two. Then Frankie remembered Alpha. "Daddy, Alpha is really a wolf?" Seth smiled, "Yes, he looks like a wolf pup. Maybe when Alice comes over to visit you, ask her all about him." Samuel stated, "I think Alice is very shy. She was hiding behind the trees when we met her on the mountain. Alice also did not say too much. I could see that she is a very special person. I felt like I have known her for a long time." Seth looked at his son, "What do you mean by that?" "I don't know. I just feel like I love her." Samuel said. Frankie laughed, "How can you love someone you don't know? She didn't even talk to us." Samuel answered, "Maybe I just feel sorry for her. Something is wrong with her." Frankie smiled, "I think she sounds like mommy. Maybe that's why Samuel?" Seth asked, "She didn't talk to us. How do you know how she sounds?" Frankie laughed, "I don't know, but it is funny to me."

"Do we want to eat fish now or later?" Seth was trying to change the subject. "This will be a late lunch, so we will need to have dinner later than normal. Is that okay?" Samuel and Frankie laughed. "We will be eating fish every day for a long time, won't we?" Frankie asked. Samuel smiled, "Yes. We don't have to eat it every day but can keep it in the freezer until we want some." Seth was getting the grill ready as he listened to his boys. Then the subject changed again. "I want to play with Alpha. I think he is the cutest puppy I have ever seen." Frankie was laughing. Samuel smiled, "Buddy is the cutest puppy. You just don't remember him because you were a baby when we got him." Buddy was sitting by Samuel, sleeping. "How much fish do you want to eat today? I cooked five yesterday." Samuel said, "I think you should make me two fish." Frankie added, "I want two too." Seth laughed, "Should we make two for Buddy?" "I think he is starving, daddy." Samuel was advocating for his pup. "Frankie, how many fish do I need to grill?" Frankie answered very quickly, "Eight! Two for everybody." Samuel was smiling, "Are they all the same color?" "Once we grill them, they will be," Seth replied. "What else should we have with the fish?" Frankie smiled, "I only want fish." Samuel asked, "What about lemon?" Seth asked, "Lemon and what else?" Frankie started laughing, "More fish?" They all laughed. "Okay, but this is the only time we will do this. We need to eat healthy and get our vegetables."

Across the creek, Erik and Alice were walking back to the house. They could see that Valerie and Janie had already taken in the art equipment. Alice asked, "Why do you think there was so many fish?" Erik did not know how to answer, "I am not sure, but it must be an anomaly or miracle. I haven't seen any fish in a couple of years." "I want to grill Alpha's fish." Alice was thinking about the fish jumping. Erik smiled, "You know that he would eat it raw if he were in the wild?" Alice laughed, "He is not in the wild." Erik responded, "Once we get the fish in the house, I will run back out to get the horses in."

Valerie greeted Erik and Alice at the door. "How are you feeling, Alice? You have had a full day." "I feel great! After I feed Alpha, I will lie down for a few minutes. I want to grill the fish he caught." Valerie was amazed, "Alpha caught a fish?" "Well, kind of, sort of. The fish were jumping, and one jumped out at him." Alice held up Alpha's fish. "Interesting. I have never seen that happen; I've heard of it but never witnessed it." Valerie was thinking about the event. Finally, Alice asked, "Valerie, would you sit with me when I lie down." Valerie looked over at Alice, "Are you okay?" Alice was in deep thought and just nodded her head. Alice cooked up the fish and added chopped carrots, which Alpha loved by gobbling it up so fast that Alice was afraid he would choke. Alice called him to the door, "Come on. Let's go potty."

Alice headed back in to rest. Janie entered from the kitchen, "I made a lunch for you, Alice. Would you like to have it in your room?" "Thank you, Janie. You are so thoughtful. Yes, I will eat it in my room." Alpha was right behind her and headed straight for his bed. He, too, had had a long day. Valerie knocked, "May I come in?" Alice smiled, "Yes, please." Valerie made herself comfortable on the loveseat.

Alice began, "Today was quite the adventure. After painting, as you know, I headed for a hike with Erik. We encountered the family next door. I was afraid to let the little boys see me. I was afraid they would be frightened of me. Alpha took to them immediately, was licking and loving them. It was so cute to see. Their dog came up to me and loved on me. He acted as if he knew me. It was the weirdest feeling I had. The boys looked so familiar to me, and their dad was so handsome. I felt attracted to him. I cannot explain it. I did not say a word to Erik, and I was afraid of what he would think. My spirit was jumping. Then as we were returning, Alpha ran ahead. He headed straight to where the family was fishing. I heard them laughing. It seemed so familiar. What do you think, Valerie?" Valerie was unsure how to answer, "All I can say is that you need to trust the Lord. He will show you all things. Maybe He will give you a dream and give you some answers. Maybe, you dreamt of this family. That could be why they seem so familiar." "They invited me to come over for a visit. Would you come with me?" Alice asked. Valerie smiled, "Yes, of course. I would be honored to come along." Alice added, "I think Erik wants to come along, but I don't want him to. I do not want to hurt his feelings. How do I ask him not to come along?"

Valerie offered, "Maybe we should go when he is super busy." "He is busiest early in the morning," Alice explained. She continued, "What if we go at eight or nine in the morning?" Valerie asked, "Do you think that's too early? The kids may be sleeping in." Alice responded, "Any other time, and I think

Erik will see us walking there." Valerie had a plan, "What if we drive there?" Alice smiled, "I like the way you are thinking." Alice smiled, "I think Alpha and I will take a little nap. Would you wake us up in an hour?" "I will. Have a good nap." As Valerie headed out the door, she heard Alice. "Come on, Alpha. You can take a nap with me." Alpha jumped up onto the bed. They snuggled up and fell sound asleep.

Alice walked through the meadow when she noticed that the boys were playing by the creek. The creek appeared to be full and swollen with water. Alice could hear them laughing and was filled with joy at the sound of children laughing. She began to laugh, and Alpha began to jump and bark. She was walking toward the boys and could hear their conversation. They talked about their mom, and they spoke of her as if she was lost. She heard one of the boys screams, 'mommy come home.' She ran towards them, but suddenly she could not move anymore. Suddenly she was in mud up to her knees. Alpha ran to the boys, jumped into the creek, and swam across to them. Alice could not move in the mud. The more she struggled to move, the more stuck she became. She heard herself scream. No one seemed to be around to hear her screams. She screamed again. She opened her eyes. She looked around the room, and Alpha was lying next to her. Alice hugged her puppy and thought to herself, 'why did I have this dream? Why can't I reach the boys?' She closed her eyes, trying to fall back asleep, but she lay wide awake. She tried not to think about the dream, but the more she tried not to, the more she seemed to think about it.

Valerie knocked gently on Alice's door. Alice spoke up, "I am awake. Please come in." Valerie opened the door and walked in. "Alice, I need to take your vitals. Is that okay?" Valerie asked. Alice smiled, "Yes, of course." As Valerie took her vitals, Alice asked, "What does being stuck in mud mean?" Valerie spoke softly, "Could mean lots of things, but most likely, I feel you are stuck and unable to move forward. So, the question would be, why are you stuck? Why can't you move?" Alice was in deep thought. When Valerie spoke, she startled Alice, "A penny for your thoughts." Alice smiled, "Just trying to figure out why I can't remember anything. Shouldn't I remember things by now?" Valerie answered, "Brain trauma is tricky. Any damage to the brain may take years, or suddenly your memories flood back. The brain is a sensitive organ yet resilient. Just be patient and let it happen as it happens." That was not the answer Alice was hoping for, but she would have to be satisfied for now. Valerie asked, "Are you ready to go to the porch to paint? I have everything set up outside." Alice smiled, "That would be a very healthy and healing thing. Will Janie be joining us?" "No, she said; she was going to work on dinner. She is excited about the fish you and Erik brought back." Valerie replied.

Seth, Frankie, and Samuel spent the rest of the day cleaning fish. It was a big job. The boys were learning how to gut fish. Frankie said, "I am glad that we don't fish every day." Samuel laughed, "What's the matter, little brother? You don't like the blood and guts?" Frankie answered, "No, it's not that. I do not like the smell. Besides, we could be playing if we had not caught so many fish." Seth felt sorry for his boys, "You don't have to help me. I can do this alone." Samuel spoke first, "Daddy, we are helping you because we love you." Frankie added, "Yeah, daddy. I was not trying to complain. I told you I am glad we do not catch fish every day." He laughed.

"I am really proud of you both." Seth continued, "You woke up early, hiked, and fished. You even made new friends. It's been a busy day." Samuel suddenly felt sad, "The only way it could have been better would be to have had mommy with us." Frankie just suddenly began to laugh, "She is with us. She is in our hearts, which will never make me sad again. Remember, our dreams are all coming true." Seth was filled with hope and a feeling of pride. His little one was healing, and the thought could get him through another day. Seth spoke in a whisper, "Who wants to go swimming?" Samuel lit up, "I want to!" Frankie screamed with joy, "Yay! Let's go!" Seth laughed, "Go get your swim trunks. I will finish up with these last few fish." The boys washed up and ran into the cabin. Seth quickly finished the fish and carried them in to freeze them. He left eight in the refrigerator for later.

As they walked to the creek, Seth glanced to see if he could see anyone at the Alexander's home. Frankie hollered, "Look, daddy. I can see silver over there." Seth explained, "I think that's where the water is shallow. Let's go look." Samuel giggled as they walked towards that area, "What if it's more fish?" Frankie answered, "I don't think we need to catch more today." Seth teased them both, "We don't come to the cabin too often, so maybe we should." Samuel knew his daddy was teasing them, "We should come more often. So, we don't have to take so many fish home." Frankie interrupted the teasing, "Look! The creek is full!"

Seth stood by the creek in disbelief. "Wow! I think this area is a good place to swim. Looks deep enough but also safe. Let me walk through it first, and then you can get in if it's safe." Seth stepped into the creek; as he stepped forward, he fell waist deep and Buddy started barking at the sudden change. He walked the area, and much to his surprise, it seemed to be a small hole for them to swim. He looked at the boys and said, "Come on in!" The boys ran and jumped in, and Buddy followed them in. They laughed and splashed for hours in the perfect swimming hole. Seth looked up, and to his surprise, the clouds looked like a smile. He pointed up, "Check it out, boys." Frankie laughed, "It looks like a smile."

Samuel said, "It is God smiling on us." They laughed, splashed, and played some more. Time was flying by so fast. Seth noticed that the sun was setting, "We should head back to the cabin. I just realized we haven't eaten since breakfast." "I'm not hungry, but I could eat some fish." Frankie laughed. Samuel was getting out first, "We forgot to bring towels. I guess we just need to shake off like Buddy does." Buddy and Samuel started shaking. "This works pretty well." Samuel was laughing. Seth helped Frankie out of the water, "You are almost too heavy for me to carry you." Frankie replied, "I am getting bigger. You are so strong, daddy; I think you will always be able to carry me." Seth laughed, "I will always be able to carry you. Even when I am an old man." They chuckled, and Samuel added, "Daddy, you are never getting old." They all shook and laughed. They walked to the cabin in silence—each in his own thoughts.

Frankie was talking with God. 'How many of my dreams are coming true? I know that not everything comes true right away. But you know I want mommy home. Bring her home, Jesus. Bring my mommy home. Please, Jesus, bring her home.'

Samuel was thinking about everything that was happening. 'The fish was a miracle. There were no fish in the swimming hole. How did they get there? It must be a miracle. What other miracles can we see while we are here? I feel like I'm supposed to pray for Mrs. Alexander the next time we see her. How do I know these things? I know I am bigger than Frankie is, but we both have dreams that are coming true. What are you showing us, God?'

Seth was looking at every minute of this trip. 'The ride here was easy, and they had a great breakfast with Sunnie. The fishing had been incredible; then there is the gold nugget and the swimming hole. So, what does this all mean? What more should we expect?'

"Daddy, dinner should not take too long. We already prepared the fish." Samuel was opening the cabin door. Frankie started laughing, "I guess we could eat some grass, so we get some greens in us." Seth laughed, "Not for me, thanks! I think I will skip the greens. We can eat healthy tomorrow." The boys cheered, "Yay!" Buddy headed to the water bowl. "Buddy, are you hungry?" Frankie asked. Samuel answered, "He is excited about the fish tonight!" Buddy started barking and seemed to agree.

The grill got started very quickly. The fish disappeared just as fast as the grill turned them out. Frankie asked, "Do the fish taste better than any other fish we have ever had?" Samuel agreed, "I think so too." Seth was surprised, "I believe you are both right. I had not noticed until just now when you asked. I think these are heaven's fish. They are delicious." After dinner, they decided to put a puzzle together, which kept them up until 11 pm.

Alice's house was bustling. The fish was the best anyone had ever tasted. Jack asked, "Where did you get the fish? What seasoning did you use, Janie?" Janie glanced at Alice, "They came from the creek. I didn't do anything special, just lemon." Jack asked Alice, "Did you go fishing?" Alice answered, "No, I didn't. The neighbors gave the fish to Erik." Jack turned to look at Erik, and Alice nodded no. "The neighbors were outside fishing when I walked back from my hike. I went to say hello. You know, just being neighborly." "I have never met them. I do not even know the family's name that owns the property. I heard they had owned it for a long time. Maybe I should go over and introduce myself. Possibly this weekend." Jack said.

Erik added, "Oh, well, I believe they are leaving soon. They said they were only here for a few days. I did not even catch their names. They seemed like a friendly bunch of guys." Jack turned to Alice, "Make sure to stay clear of them. We don't need some rowdy guys bothering you." Alice smiled, "Don't worry about my feelings. If anyone says anything offensive, I will start crying and make them feel bad." Valerie giggled, "Not all men are bothered by tears." Alice added, smiling, "Well, I would have to be rude right back."

After dinner, everyone retreated to their rooms. Alice took out her sketchpad. She began to sketch her encounter with the boys on the mountain. Alice paid attention to the detail of their eyes, cheeks, and hair. She also remembered every detail of the father's face, mannerisms, and hair. In addition, Alice remembered every tree, shrub, and plant around them. She looked at the finished sketch and shook her head in approval. "This is good." She put the sketchpad away. "Alpha let's get you another potty break and get to bed. Come on, baby." She headed out of the house as Alpha took care of business. Alice looked up and saw the most beautifully lit night sky; the moon was bright, and stars were shining. There were so many stars that there was hardly any space in the night sky. Alpha ran back to Alice, and they headed to bed.

23 TIME TO FISH

Alice awoke bright and early like always. Alpha was ready to go out. Alice put on a robe and headed out for a potty break for her little wolf. Alpha hurried through to the door as Alice opened the outside door. She could smell something pungent; she suddenly realized it was a skunk. She called to Alpha, "Come on, baby. Let's get inside." He came running at her call. "Come on, let's get showered and get that smell off us." She could still smell the awful smell. As she showered, she became self-conscience of her scars. She ran her fingers over her body and face. She wondered if the children were afraid of her. "I must look like a monster to children." As she spoke those words, she began to cry. Alpha heard her and ran into the shower to see if his mommy was okay. He was not afraid of water, so he jumped in and jumped on Alice. She sat down, hugged her puppy, and sobbed; he licked and kissed her face. Finally, she gathered herself and finished her shower. She even bathed Alpha since he would not get out.

Alice wrapped her towel around herself and stepped into her closet. She looked around to see what she felt like wearing. Alpha was right behind her. He was tugging at some pants. She looked at him, "Do you want me to wear these?" He seemed to answer by jumping up on her. Alice found a shirt that looked good with her pants. Next, Alpha grabbed her tennis shoes. Alice laughed, "I need to have you pick out my clothes more often. I think these are great for today."

"Good morning, Janie." Alice greeted everyone, "Good morning, Erik. Good morning, Valerie. Good morning, Jack." Breakfast was delicious as usual; Janie had prepared omelets. She also had a variety of fruit. The table was so colorful. Jack was in a hurry, "Janie, I am so sorry I can't sit down today. I have patients waiting on me, so Alice, please forgive me. I must rush out. I hope you all have a good day. I should be home earlier than normal today. Maybe by four." Alice waved at Jack, "Be careful out there. I smelled a skunk earlier this morning. Are you going to grab anything? Muffin?" Jack rushed out, "Sorry, I've got to run."

"Valerie, I would like to take Alpha for a checkup today. Can you drive us?" Alice smiled. Valerie responded, "It could be a good day for a driving lesson." Alice shook her head, "I don't know if I'm ready for that." Erik agreed, "I'm glad you are sensing your safe zone. You can attempt driving anytime. Don't push yourself." Alice smiled, "Thanks, Erik. I won't push the driving." They all chatted over the delicious breakfast. Valerie and Alice discussed the schedule for the day. "I think you should get your physical therapy done first today. Then if you want, we can head out to the vet. The vet's office opens early so we can get in and out." Alice added, "I may want to paint in the meadow later this afternoon. Does anyone want to join me?" Valerie answered, "I may want to. Anyone else?" Erik nodded, "Sorry, I have a busy day cleaning stalls today; it will probably take me all day. I am also looking at possibly shoeing a couple of the horses, so I will be stuck in the stables all day. I will not even have time to take the dogs out for their run today. I might try at dusk. Janie, don't count on me for dinner." Janie answered, "I can pack you something to eat if you go out at dusk." "That is a great idea, Janie. Thank you!" Erik laughed, "I think you are trying to fatten me up." Janie replied, "We can figure things out over lunch, Erik." Alice added, "Janie, we may not be back for lunch. We will call you if we run late." Alice continued, "Thank you for such a great breakfast and conversation. I better get my physical therapy out of the way." Alice turned to face Janie, "Would you package six muffins as a gift?" "I'd be happy to. I will have them ready when you head out."

Alice and Valerie headed to Alice's room for physical therapy. As they ran out of the kitchen, Alice spoke, "I bathed Alpha this morning." Valerie laughed, "I thought he smelled mighty fine." "I felt that I smelled like a skunk after taking him out early this morning. He just happened to join me and got lucky." Alpha, as always, was at Alice's heels. Erik called out, "Did I hear you say skunk?" Alice turned to face him, "Yes. It was quite stinky. I hope it's headed off the property by now." Erik responded, "Okay, thank you. I will keep an eye out for it."

Valerie and Alice worked hard on physical therapy. Alice seemed to struggle a little with the treatment today. "I feel a little weak today. I may have overdone it yesterday. The hike took a lot out of me." Alice said. Valerie smiled, "it's okay. Some days will be harder than others. How are you doing emotionally?" Alice knew she could not hide too much from Valerie, "I broke down in the shower today. I was afraid that children would be afraid of me. I want kids so bad, but I look awful." Valerie responded, "Your kids will know you are beautiful. You are not scary looking, Alice. You are so beautiful. Look inside; you will see." Alice smiled at her friend, "Thank you. I needed to hear that today." Valerie asked, "What time would you like to head out to the vet?" Alice answered, "Soon. I also want to swing by the store and pick up a few things." Valerie responded, "Okay. Let me put away all the equipment, and we can head out."

Janie handed Alice the muffins as she left. "Please say hello to Dr. Ben for me." Alice laughed, "I will. Thanks for the muffins. I promise to give you all the credit." Alpha enjoyed sitting in his mommy's arms on the drive. The two ladies were singing and dancing along to the radio. Dr. Ben seemed to know or smell their arrival and smiled at his front door. "Hello, Alpha. Good morning, Alice. Howdy Valerie. What gives me the honor of your presence today?" Alice answered, "Just want my boy checked out. He is eating and drinking well. Good bowel movements. He bathed just for you." Ben laughed, "I don't think you need me then. He sounds like he is doing great." "Sorry, I forgot to give you Janie's famous muffins. She sends her hellos." Ben laughed, "I was expecting these and anticipating them. I heard your car and knew you had something good for me. You always bring me the best treats."

Alice and Valerie laughed. "We will pass along the message to Janie." Alice teased. Dr. Ben examined Alpha. Dr. Ben said, "He sure seems to be very well acclimated to humans. You are doing a great job with him, Alice." "He is so intelligent. I give a command, and he learns it immediately. He makes me look good." Alice smiled. Ben handed Alpha back to Alice, "He doesn't have to try too hard. You look great." Alice blushed. "Well, I guess that ends our visit with you today. When would you like to see him again?" Ben responded, "He is about seven or eight weeks old. Maybe in three or four weeks. He is doing great. Wolf pups are not normally this easy to deal with." Alice answered, "Thank you, Ben. We will be back soon."

As Alice got into the car, she spoke, "I would like to go find a couple of gifts for the neighbor boys." Valerie smiled, "That sounds good. What do you think you would like to get?" Alice responded, "I am not sure what they would enjoy. I thought we could go and see what my spirit feels is right when I see it. Then, I will know it is the perfect gift." Valerie answered, "There is a store down the street where we might find something. They have an assortment of things. Shall we look there?" Alice smiled, "That sounds good to me."

They arrived at the neighborhood shop 'Radiant Things.' When Alice stepped into the shop, she felt her spirit jump.

She did not know what it meant, but she thought, 'I will find something for the boys.' As she strolled through the shop, she saw things that made her smile. Alice could hear the shop owner talking with Valerie. Alice saw a blue car; it seemed to call to her. She picked it up, and immediately she knew this was for the little one. Alice continued to walk around the shop. She was just about to give up when she saw the silver pen. It was silver with fish that appeared to be an array of colors. It was a kid's pen kit with a small notebook. She walked to the counter where Valerie was still talking to the owner. Valerie immediately made the introductions. Alice smiled and asked, "Could you wrap these gifts for me?" The owner smiled, "I would be happy to wrap them. Do you have a wrapping paper preference?" Alice responded, "They are both for young boys. Whatever you think is best." Valerie and the owner continued to visit while they waited on the gift-wrapping.

Seth had awakened, and the boys were sound asleep. He looked at the clock; they had all slept in. He got up, showered, and then started breakfast. The boys awoke with the smell of bacon. They came running into the kitchen. They looked at their dad and then looked around the cabin. Seth hesitated to ask, "What are you looking for?" Samuel looked disappointed, "I was hoping our dreams were coming true." Frankie smiled, "Don't look sad, Samuel. It could still happen. We still have five more days here. What? No fish for breakfast?" They all had a good laugh. Breakfast was fun. Seth had made omelets into faces.

Suddenly, there was a knock at the door. The boys looked at each other, quite surprised. Seth went to the door. "Good morning. I hope I am not intruding. I am Alice from next door. This is Valerie, my nurse, and friend." Alpha ran in to greet the boys. Seth was numb. He stammered, "I'm sorry, where are my manners. Please come in. I am Seth, and these are my boys, Frankie, and Samuel." The women entered. Valerie was so excited that she could hardly contain her excitement, "Good morning, young men. Who is Frankie, and who is Samuel?"

The boys raised their hands as Valerie mentioned their names. Alice smiled shyly, "I didn't mean to interrupt your breakfast. We can come back later." Seth replied, "Don't be silly. Please come in and join us. Would you like some breakfast?" Valerie answered, "We ate earlier this morning. Thank you for the offer." Seth came to sit down, "What about Alpha? Does he need to eat? He seems to be getting the breakfast off Frankie's face." Alice replied, "We can't stay long. He needs to eat his meal soon." Seth asked, "What does he normally eat?" Alice answered, "Raw steak." Seth laughed, "Perfect! That is how I like mine too. I can fix him one." Alice replied, "I don't want to make you feed him. That wasn't my intention." Seth got up from the table, "It is my pleasure to fix this little guy something to eat." Seth pulled out a steak and started to chop it up. Frankie asked, "Mrs. Alexander, why do you wear a scarf across your face." Seth attempted to stop his son but did not get the words out in time. "Frankie, we don't ask those questions." Alice answered quietly, "I was in an accident, and my body was burned severely. I wear the scarf to protect myself from the sun rays." Frankie said, "Does it still hurt? We are not in the sun right now." Valerie looked at Alice and answered, "It is uncomfortable, no pain. If the sun hits the scars, then they can change colors. Like a sunburn." Samuel had been paying close attention, "I dreamed that I was supposed to pray for you. Can I pray later?" Alice smiled and shook her head, "Yes, that would be very nice. Thank you." Seth placed a plate of chopped steak on the floor, and Alpha devoured it. Frankie laughed, "Poor baby. He was starving." Alice was watching the boys. Her heart filled with so much joy she thought she might cry.

Frankie noticed the bag that Alice had beside her. "What is in the bag?" Alice giggled and reached down, "I brought you and Samuel a gift. I hope you enjoy them." She handed them the appropriate gifts. Frankie was the first to speak, "This car is just like the one in my dream. Thank you, Mrs. Alexander." He ran up to her and hugged her. Alice was caught off guard but hugged him back. She took a deep breath in, and tears welled up. Samuel spoke next, "Thank you so much. This is like the dream I had about the fish. How did you know?" Alice was unsure how to respond, "I felt these would be good gifts. I hope you like them." The boys answered in unison, "I love it!" Alice smiled, "I'm so glad you do."

Seth was watching Alice's every move and mannerisms. "The boys thought that you should go fishing today." Alice looked at him puzzled, "I don't know if I have fished before. You see, when I had my accident, I lost all my memory." Frankie quickly responded, "We are great fishermen! We can teach you." Alice replied, "I think I would love to learn. You seemed to be having so much fun yesterday." Samuel added, "It is a lot of fun. Especially when there is so many fish." Seth asked, "Shall we head out to fish?" The boys jumped up and cleared their plates off the table. "Come on, Alpha. We are going to teach your mommy how to fish." Frankie said.

Seth was the first to the door. "I will get the poles ready and head to the creek. Samuel, can you get mommy's camping chair so Mrs. Alexander can use it." Samuel looked at his daddy, "Are you sure?" Frankie added, "That's mommy chair. You can use my chair, Mrs. Alexander." Seth instructed, "Samuel, get Frankie's chair." With that, they all headed out the door.

The boys were ready for the fishing adventure with Mrs. Alexander. Frankie gave instructions first, "You can take the hook and add a worm-like this." He demonstrated. When Alice hesitated to grab a worm, Samuel grabbed one and prepared her pole. "Here you go. Now all you have to do is swing the pole and let go of this button when you do." Alice followed instructions and waited. Frankie continued, "Now you have to wait until the fish bite. You cannot be nervous because the fish feel you. You need to be calm." Alice whispered, "Okay. I am calm." Samuel added, "Also, you don't want to talk too much because your voice will make the line vibrate. That might scare the fish away." Alice whispered again, "Okay. Calm and no talking." Frankie started giggling, "You look so funny, Mrs. Alexander. You look nervous." His giggling started everyone else laughing. Suddenly, Alice screamed, "I felt something pull the line."

Frankie went into teaching mode, "Yank the line. Pull it back hard." Alice followed instructions. Samuel added, "Now, turn the knob and start to reel in the fish." Alice's heart was thumping, her palms were sweating, and she felt a surge of energy running through her. Alice felt the fish fighting, and it was hard to turn the knob. The pole was wiggling back and forth. Alpha was barking excitedly. It seemed like it was a very long time, but the fish was finally close enough that she could see it. "Look, there it is!" Alice laughed. Seth had the net ready and netted the fish. Alice spoke first, "That was so fun and exciting." Frankie laughed, "It is always exciting! We always have so much fun!" Alice said, "I miss this." Seth looked at her, "Did you say you missed this?" Alice was confused, "I'm not sure. Maybe I remembered something. I don't know." Valerie reassured Alice, "it's okay, Alice. Do not push it. Just let things happen."

Alice started laughing, "I want to do it again." Seth helped her with hooking the worm. Alice was hoping that she would recall something else as she fished. Seth looked at Valerie, "Still haven't caught anything?" "No. I guess I must be doing something wrong." Valerie laughed. Samuel smiled, "No, the fish must not be very hungry today. Sometimes, they just don't bite." Frankie started laughing, "You caught another one." Alice screamed with joy, "Oh my goodness!" She reeled it in with all the excitement from the first. Alpha barked at every fish. Every time Alice cast her pole in, she caught a fish. Frankie laughed, "Today is your day, Mrs. Alexander. The fish keep biting for you." They fished for about an hour; then, it was lunchtime.

"Would you ladies like to join us for lunch? I can grill up some fish." Seth asked. Alice answered, "We would love to have lunch." Seth gathered up the gear and headed back to the cabin. Frankie came up to Mrs. Alexander and grabbed her hand. He smiled at her, "I am glad you came to fish. It was a good day." Alice smiled at him, "Yes, it is a perfect day. Thank you for inviting us." Valerie laughed, "It wasn't good fishing for us all, Alice. I don't know what I did wrong." Samuel comforted Valerie, "Sometimes the fish are very picky about the worms they eat."

Seth was in his world. He was walking faster than everyone else was, and he thought, 'The memory of having Francie fishing with us was so clear today. It felt like she was here with us. I could smell her all day. When I hooked the worms for Alice, it felt like I was doing it for Francie. She hated hooking them, couldn't stand the thought of the worm going to its death.' He chuckled to himself, 'Francie always screamed when she caught something, even when it was a weed. She could never stop talking, but the fish did not care. They would rather bite her bait and leave mine alone. Lord why is Francie so vibrant of a memory today. More than any other day. I must get myself together. I must help the boys work through whatever they will have to deal with after this week. Come on, Seth, focus. You have company.'

Seth turned backward and spoke to the group, "How hungry are you guys? Shall I make one fish for each or two?" Frankie answered first, "I want two. Buddy and Alpha each want two too." Alice answered, "I am hungry. I'll have two." Samuel replied, "Me too." Valerie answered, "I will just have one. Thank you." Frankie counted, "Daddy, you need to make thirteen fish." Seth saluted him, "Yes, sir."

Seth entered the cabin first and then joined everyone outside. "Let's clean the fish, and I'll get the grill going first." Valerie asked, "Can I get anything ready for sides?" Seth laughed, "Yes, please. We have been bad about eating veggies these last couple of days. We have salad inside." Samuel asked, "Shall I get the plates?" Seth answered, "That would be great, thank you. You can show Valerie around inside. Thanks, Samuel." Samuel replied, "You're welcome, daddy."

Seth cleaned the fish while Frankie visited with Alice. "How did you like fishing?" Frankie asked. Alice answered, "I enjoyed myself very much. I guess I would say I loved fishing." Frankie continued, "Are you going to stay for dinner too?" Alice replied, "I should be getting back home shortly after lunch. Jack, my husband will be home by four." Frankie continued, "If you want, he can come over too." Alice replied, "He works all day, so he doesn't like to visit people. He talks to people all day." Frankie responded, "Oh, I see. He is not nice, right?" Alice chuckled, "He is nice. He is a doctor. When he comes home, he is tired. He just likes to relax at home." Seth interrupted, "Frankie, I think that's enough questions about Mr. Alexander." Frankie said, "Okay, daddy. My mommy is a doctor, and she is coming home soon.

Samuel needs to pray for you today before you go home. Okay?" Alice smiled, "Yes, that would be wonderful. I have never had anyone pray for me." Frankie looked puzzled, "Never?" Alice smiled, "Not that I remember."

Lunch was ready, and everyone sat down outside at the picnic table. Seth had seasoned the fish with his special seasoning and lemon. Everyone enjoyed the lunch, and there was a lot of laughter about the fishing excursion. The pups enjoyed their fish and some carrots too.

The women were getting ready to leave when Samuel asked, "Mrs. Alexander, may I pray for you?" Alice smiled, "Oh, thank you for remembering; I had already forgotten." Samuel came over and sat next to Alice. He began praying, "Dear Jesus. You gave me a dream where I prayed for Mrs. Alexander. I ask that you help her to remember and heal her brain. Our Father in Heaven, Thy will be done on earth as it is in Heaven. In Jesus' name. Amen." He opened his eyes and said, "How do you feel?" Alice opened her eyes, "I feel terrific. I feel so light. I don't know if I can walk." Samuel gave her his hand, "Let me help you." Alice stood up and held on to Samuel. "Thank you for praying. Today I have a hope that I think I did not have before. You pray very well for such a young boy. Thank you again, Samuel."

They walked the women to the car, and the boys waved goodbye. They had enjoyed their day with Alice and Valerie. Frankie said, "I like Alice and Valerie. I feel like when Auntie Rae is with us. It feels good." Samuel responded, "Jesus showed me that she would remember real soon when I was praying for her. I can't wait to see what she remembers."

24 MEETING NUMBER THREE

Frankie woke up very early, and no one else was awake. He was so excited about his dream. He heard a voice say, 'Don't tell anyone yet.' He asked, 'should I go back to sleep?' He heard, 'Yes.' Frankie closed his eyes and continued to dream.

Samuel woke up with the sun shining on his face. Seth had already awakened and was in the shower. Samuel could hear his daddy in the shower. He looked over at Frankie and saw that he was sound asleep. Samuel went to his backpack and pulled out the special project he had been working on for weeks. He opened it and thought, 'I should have wrapped it, but I didn't have time. I am sure that it will be okay like this when the time comes.' Samuel heard his daddy finishing his shower and immediately put away the project.

Seth popped his head into the boys' room and whispered to Samuel, "Do you want to shower now or after breakfast?" Samuel whispered, "I will shower now, daddy." Samuel grabbed his towel and headed to the bathroom. Seth prepared for breakfast. He was feeling like muffins and looked to see what he had to make muffins. Seth decided to make wake-up muffins and looked through the pantry when he encountered a note from Rae.

> Seth,
> I know how much my sister loved to make you Wake-up Muffins. I thought it would be good to have her special recipe and ingredients ready for you if you were craving them. I hope you are having fun! Your-sister-in-love,
> Rae

Seth laughed. Rae was funny that way. She did not like the term in law, so she changed it up a little. He was grateful that she was looking out for him. He gathered all the ingredients and started baking. He also put some bacon on the grill. Rae did not know that Francie had a secret she did not share with anyone. She would put crumbled bacon on his muffins. No one else had them made like that. Suddenly he felt the love and thought that 'he would make some for Rae sometime just like Francie made them for him.' As soon as he finished that thought, he thought, 'no way.' He laughed to himself.

Frankie woke up from the smell of bacon. Frankie came into the kitchen, "Daddy, I am so hungry I can eat a bear." Seth smiled, "Perfect! I am making bear for breakfast." Frankie laughed, "Gross! I don't really want to eat bear, daddy!" Seth laughed, "Oh, come on now. Bear tastes so good." Frankie asked, "Where did you find the bear?" Seth continued to tease him, "I got up early, and there was a little bear outside asking if he could come in. I said yes, come on in. When he came in, I tricked him into getting into the oven. Nothing better than a bear who volunteers to jump into your oven?" Frankie laughed, "That's a good story, daddy. Thank you for making it up for me." Seth smiled at this little one, "What makes you think it's a made-up story?" Frankie took a deep breath in, "If that's a bear in the oven, it sure smells like muffins." Seth responded, "Frankie, you sure do have a good sense of smell." Frankie replied, "I get it from mommy." Seth agreed, "Yes. You most certainly do." Samuel was walking in about that time, "What do you get from mommy?" Frankie answered, "My sense of smell." Samuel added, "Me too. I can tell that we are having wake-up muffins." Seth laughed, "You boys are good. We haven't had them in a long time, but you still recognize them." "This is mommy's recipe. They are the best muffins ever." Frankie boasted. "You are right, Frankie. Well, are you hungry, Samuel? Frankie said he was so hungry he could eat a bear." Samuel laughed, "That's bad, Frankie. Bears are nice; why do you want to eat one?" Frankie made a silly face at his daddy and Samuel. "That's just what I said and not what I meant. Besides, daddy is the one that said he is cooking one." They all laughed. Today's breakfast menu was wake-up muffins, bacon, and eggs. Seth had everything ready before Frankie had time to shower. "You can shower after breakfast, Frankie. You don't want your eggs to get cold." Seth said. "That sounds good because I am super hungry this morning," Frankie answered.

Across the creek, breakfast happened at 6:30 am, like always. Alice had snuck out early before everyone was in the kitchen. She had left a note for Janie.

> Good morning, Janie.
> Alpha and I are out for an early morning walk. I won't be long. I should be back before everyone has finished breakfast.
> Do not worry,
> Alice.

Erik and Valerie walked into the kitchen about the same time. "Good morning." They all said it about the same time. Jack entered the kitchen, "Good morning, everyone. It looks like we all beat Alice this morning." Janie was unsure what to say, "Shall we all get started? Alice left a note and said she would be a little late for breakfast." Jack did not like the sound of the message, "What do you mean she left a note?" Janie handed the note to Jack. Jack looked at Erik, "Would you mind helping me search for Alice to make sure she is, okay?"

"Of course, I don't mind," Erik responded. The men headed out of the house. Valerie looked at Janie, "Do you know where she may have headed?" Janie responded, "I found this note when I came into the kitchen an hour ago."

As Erik opened the door, in ran Alpha with Alice right behind him. "Good morning! It is a beautiful day. Are we ready to eat?" Alice walked in as if nothing was wrong. Jack started in on her, "What were you thinking going out by yourself this morning?" Alice stood her ground, "I am perfectly able to take walks on my own. I will continue to do more and more by myself. Whether you like it or not. I am healing very well. Alpha is my protector, and he will continue to grow stronger. I am too." Jack threw his hands up, "Can someone help me out, please?" No one answered. They did not want to get in the middle of them.

Erik changed the subject, "How was your walk, Alice?" Alice smiled, "It was wonderful. It was so peaceful. Alpha barked at every bug that dared to get in my way." Alice looked at Jack, "Are you going to sit and join us for breakfast?" Jack was disappointed that no one took his side. "No, I am heading to work. I will just take some coffee." Janie got up, "I can put it in a thermos for you, Mr. Alexander." Jack responded, "Thank you, Janie. I appreciate that." Jack said his goodbyes and asked Erik, "Please join me outside." The men stepped outside. "Erik, I would like you to discourage my wife from walking by herself. I see that she trusts and respects you. Can you do that for me?" "Of course, I will try," Erik responded. With that, Jack got into his car and left.

Erik joined the women inside for breakfast. "I can't believe how peaceful it is outside early in the morning. I could concentrate and hear the answers I was looking for." Alice was at peace. Valerie asked, "May we inquire what answers you got?" "I heard God telling me that He would change this situation for me." Erik asked, "You believe that you hear God?" Alice smiled, "Yes, I know I do. I had a dream about the accident. I was downstairs and trying to make my way out of the cellar. The door cellar was locked on the outside. I could hear the fire burning above me. The sound was loud and thunderous, and I could hear the beams breaking and falling. I screamed, but no one could hear me. I did not see anyone else. Erik, I heard your voice calling out. I screamed as loud as possible, but you did not hear me. I asked God to please take me home, but I heard Him say that 'it is not your time.' I saw a huge man stand in front of me and kept the beams from falling on me. He said, "Do not give up. It will be over soon." Alice stopped and looked at everyone. "You think I'm crazy, don't you?" Valerie answered first, "No, I don't believe you're crazy." Erik added, "I did call out for you; it was too late when I saw the fire. I had been in the stables, and the horses went wild. They must have thought the fire would consume them. I called 911 as soon as I realized the house was on fire. What else do you remember about the dream or fire?"

Alice continued, "I was able to follow the man to the stairs. Then a beam came down and crashed against the stairs. I fell backward. That's all I remember." Erik continued, "The firemen were searching for you in the house when they heard your screams from downstairs. It took them a while to get to you. When I went into the house, I could not find you. I had to run out because of the flames. I am so sorry; I could not find you before you were injured."

Alice smiled at Erik, "it's okay. I do not blame you. There is nothing to forgive, and if there was, it is forgiven. It's time for you to forgive yourself." Erik was in tears, "I can't forget the image when the firemen brought you out. You were unconscientious and so burned. I was not sure it was you. I have felt so much guilt, and most days it is so hard to see you like this. Knowing that, I should have found you." Alice put her hand in his, "I am fine. Look at me. I am fine. This is nothing. God is promising to heal me. I believe He will." Erik asked, "How can you be so sure? If He loved you, how could He have allowed this to happen to you?" Alice smiled, "People have free will. He never forces us to do anything. He gently encourages us to choose differently, but we choose. I don't know what started the fire, but I know that God is real and a God of Truth and Love."

Erik looked at her, "I used to believe there was a God. My son died, my wife left me, and then the accident happened to you. Why would that happen to me?" Alice looked at Valerie for support, "I don't know. I just know that I will not stop believing. I believe in a better life with children and laughter." Valerie answered Erik, "I don't know why your son died. Your wife made a choice that affected you. You need to choose to forgive. Unforgiveness hurts you more than you can understand. Unforgiveness turns into bitterness and hardens your heart. Jesus died for every sin, every hurt, and every pain so you wouldn't have to suffer the consequences of all these things."

Erik was sobbing, and Janie was too. After a few moments of silence, Alice spoke, "I didn't mean to bring back this pain, Erik. But, since you feel horrible, would you like to pray and have these things cleansed from your heart?" Erik answered, "Maybe another time or day. I have so much to do today. I am sorry I broke down." Alice smiled, "You don't have to apologize. You are my friend, and I will help you when you are ready. Won't we, Valerie?" Valerie replied, "Erik, whenever you are ready to pray. We are all here for you." Erik excused himself from the table and headed out to get his work done.

Alice looked at Valerie and Janie, "I will go see the neighbors. When Samuel prayed for me, it cleared up my head. I want to see if they can pray more today. I am going to go alone." The women did not know what to say. Finally, Janie asked, "Are you sure, Alice? What if you remember more and need help?" Alice laughed, "If I remember more, I won't need any help. I will need to speak to Jack and get more answers." Valerie asked, "What time do you want to go over?" Alice responded, "Now." Janie asked, "Do you want to take something to eat?"

Alice asked, "What would you recommend?" Janie smiled, "How about some fruit? That's easy, and you don't have to worry about it being refrigerated or kept warm." Alice smiled, "That would be fantastic. Thank you, Janie, for the recommendation." Valerie asked, "Are you sure I can't walk you over? I don't have to stay." Alice smiled, "Alpha is coming with me, so you don't have to worry. I am sure they can bring me back if things get tough for me. I can also call you if I need help." Alice stood up and helped Janie pack some fruit.

Alice walked toward the neighbors with excitement. She could feel the energy that seemed to beam out of her. When she arrived at the creek, Alpha began to cross before her. He jumped from rock to rock. Alice followed his lead. Alpha began to bark as he approached the front door. Buddy came running, and the two greeted each other with love and kisses. Alice greeted Buddy too. He was delighted to see them. Buddy let out a whimper as he kissed Alice. Almost as if saying, 'I missed you.'

Samuel heard all the commotion and came to see why Buddy was barking. Samuel greeted Alice, "Good morning. How are you today? Please, come in. Frankie and daddy will be happy to see you." Alice responded, "Good morning, Samuel. It is good to see you today. I am glad you are all awake. I was afraid I would wake you up." Samuel asked, "May I help you with these?" Alice was pleasantly surprised at his little gentleman manners, "Thank you. They were starting to get heavy for me." Samuel grabbed the bag and reached for her hand. Alice smiled at him. It was so sweet that she felt joy fill her heart.

Samuel opened the door, "Look who is here for a visit." Frankie turned and almost fell out of his seat. He jumped up and ran to Alice, hugged her, and said, "I am so happy to see you!" Seth smiled, "Good morning! If you had called, we would have come over to walk you here. Please join us; we were just getting ready to eat." "Something smells so good. What is it?" Alice asked. Frankie chimed in, "It's Wake-up, muffins!" Alice laughed, "Well, I would love to wake up to these muffins."

They sat enjoying breakfast when Alice asked, "Who is the good cook?" Samuel answered, "It's my daddy. He and mommy used to cook together all the time. Mommy is the one that taught him to cook. He did not know anything about cooking before mommy. Right daddy?" Seth smiled, "Yes. You are right, Samuel." Alice smiled at the story. She looked at Samuel, "Samuel, I love your name. Does everyone call you Samuel? It is so formal for such a young man. May I call you Sammie?" Samuel got very serious, "Why?" Alice responded, "Well, I am not sure. I just feel like I am supposed to call you Sammie." Samuel answered, "Everyone calls me Samuel; only mommy calls me Sammie." Alice apologized, "I am so sorry. I did not mean to hurt your feelings. I am happy to call you Samuel." Alice continued, "Do you know the story of the prophet Samuel in the Bible?" Samuel was getting emotional, "That's why I am named Samuel."

Frankie quickly changed the subject when he saw his brother close to tears. "I had a cool dream. I dreamt of you." He said to Alice. Alice replied, "You did? Will you share your dream?" Frankie smiled, "I can only share a part of it. Jesus said I cannot share it all." Frankie continued, "My dream was like today. We were having breakfast when you came to the cabin. I heard Jesus tell me to pray for you, and I did. Then a miracle happened." Alice waited, but Frankie stopped sharing his dream. Alice asked, "What else can you tell me about your dream?" Frankie smiled, "I can't say anything else, but I am supposed to pray for you." Alice smiled, "Well, when are you supposed to do that?" Frankie laughed, "Right now!" Alice began, "Do you know that I went for a walk this morning, and I talked to God. He told me to come here and have you boys pray for me." Frankie answered, "Today, only I am supposed to pray for you. Tomorrow, both Samuel and I are supposed to pray. Are you ready?" Alice continued, "Yesterday after Samuel prayed for me, part of my memory returned. I had a dream about the fire. I still have some questions, but I was happy to remember that. Samuel, I wanted to say thank you for your prayer yesterday." Samuel smiled, "I prayed because I was supposed to just like Frankie is supposed to today. I believe you will remember more things today." Alice continued, "Thank you for being obedient to Jesus."

Frankie asked, "Are you ready now?" Alice answered, "Yes. I am ready." Alice looked at Seth and smiled. She closed her eyes. Frankie started with his eyes open, "This is how Jesus showed me to pray in my dream. Our Father, who is in Heaven. Holy be Your Name. Your Kingdom come; Your will be done. On earth as it is in Heaven. There is no pain in heaven, so there will be no pain on earth. In Jesus' name, scars heal in these hands. Pain go away. Thank You, Jesus, for the healing." Frankie was looking at Alice's hands. The scars disappeared in front of his eyes. Alice opened her eyes to see her hands no longer had scars. She did not have pain in her hands. She started to cry. Seth came closer and was amazed at the faith of his little boy. Alice cried out, "Oh my God. I have no more pain and I do not have any scars on my hands. Thank You, Jesus! Frankie, thank you for praying." She continued to cry and praise God. Alice suddenly started laughing. Frankie, Samuel, and Seth also started laughing.

Frankie asked Alice, "How do you feel?" Alice explained, "Since I woke up from this injury, I have never felt this good. I feel light and tingly all over my body. I feel like I could float away. I can move my hands and I have full mobility. I feel overjoyed and blessed. You have healing hands. Both of you boys do. Seth, your boys are a blessing." Seth was looking at Alice and was amazed at how blessed he felt. Seth answered, "I didn't know what to think. Both my boys have had a challenging two years and to see them praying for healing is a miracle." Alice stated, "Today is a miracle. It has begun, but it is not over. I know I will get more healing and so will your boys."

Seth was not sure what to think. He knew that Francie had always had something special about her. Seth also knew Francie had stewarded this gifting or anointing that his boys were now walking in. Yet, he had only experienced pain and crying for almost two years. He wondered, 'How could this be? They had stopped going to church after Francie had gone missing. Forgive me, Father; I have been so angry at You.' Seth did not know what to say. He was in such deep thought; that he had forgotten for a moment that he had a guest.

Alice asked, "Are you okay, Seth?" Seth looked at her bewildered, "Yes. I do not know what to say. I am in awe of how big God truly is. I have been so angry at God; I must have missed something." Alice smiled, "it's okay. We all get lost for a little bit." Samuel added, "Daddy, these things just started to happen. Don't worry, you did not miss anything. I think there is something about this place. It's like, God lives here with us." Frankie laughed, "God lives with us all the time. He just wanted to show off. God has been telling me that He has always been with us, and He is with mommy too. We were so hurt and in so much pain we were not listening." Seth hugged his boys, "When did you boys get so grown up? So smart, smarter than me." Alice could feel the love that Seth had for his boys. She wanted to join them in the hugging but did not want to cut into their family time. Suddenly, Frankie reached over and held Alice's hand; Frankie felt electricity go from his hand into Alice's hand. His eyes opened wide, and he smiled at her. Alice felt the same electricity come from Frankie. Suddenly, she felt the love that they were feeling. She felt a part of the hug without being hugged.

Seth looked over at Alice and smiled. Seth laughed, "I am so sorry. I feel you have been left out of this special moment." The boys leaned over and hugged Alice. Seth hesitated, "Alice, I feel that you are right. There is more healing coming for us all."

They spent the rest of the morning talking about Francie. Alice was very interested in who Francie was. They shared the story of the day she went missing and spoke about how difficult it had been for them. They shared dreams and visions they had. Seth watched Alice very closely. He watched her mannerisms and listened to her voice with the sound of kindness. Seth could tell that she was very kind and unique. He could not quite wrap his mind around it, but something was extraordinary about Alice, who had suffered a horrific accident.

Alice suddenly realized that she was not self-conscientious of her looks. She felt so comfortable around these boys. Alice noticed that the scarf that she usually wore to cover her face was on her shoulders. She was laughing at a story that Frankie was sharing about Buddy. She suddenly realized what time it was, and she had forgotten to feed Alpha. He seemed very comfortable while he slept next to Buddy. She hated to change the subject, but Alpha needed to eat. "Seth, could I trouble you for something for Alpha to eat?" Alice asked. Seth jumped up from his seat, "It would be a pleasure to prepare a steak for him. Unless you think fish is better?" Alice smiled, "Whatever is easiest." Seth laughed, "Steak it is." Buddy and Alpha continued to nap until Seth called Alpha to eat.

It was almost lunchtime when Alice realized how late it had gotten. She had to excuse herself. "I hate to leave, but I need to get home. They will be worrying soon. Thank you so much for everything. Thank you for the prayers. Seth, your boys are a delight. I hope to return tomorrow." Frankie answered, "You must come back tomorrow so both Samuel and I can pray together. God has another surprise for you."

Alice and Alpha seemed to float back. Alice felt blessed and could not wait to share everything with Valerie and Janie. As she entered the house, she called Janie, "I'm back. What's for lunch?" Janie peeked her head out of the kitchen, "I was hoping you would make it back for lunch. I am fixing chicken and biscuits." Alice replied, "That sounds delicious. Where is Valerie?" "I believe she went to the stables to look for Erik," Janie replied. "Is he doing, okay?" Alice asked. "I believe so. Since breakfast, he had not come in, so Valerie wanted to check on him." Janie answered and Alice replied, "Oh, okay. That sounds like a great idea. Are they coming in for lunch?" Janie smiled, "Yes, they are. There is something different about you, Alice. I can't put my finger on it." Alice grinned, "I don't know what you're talking about." "Shall I prepare Alpha something?" Janie asked. "He recently ate a steak, so I think he can wait a couple of hours." Alice continued, "I am going to my room to wash up. I will return in a few minutes."

Alice could hear Erik and Valerie talking as they entered the house. So, she sat down at the table with her hands on her lap. Alice was waiting patiently. After everyone was at the table, she asked if she could say grace, "Lord, thank you for this meal. Thank you for my friends. Bless the hands who prepared this meal. In Jesus' Name. Amen." Alice reached out to grab a biscuit as the food dishes passed around the table. Alice thought to herself, 'No one had noticed.' The conversation continued then Valerie asked, "How was your morning? Did you have a good visit?" Alice responded, "I had a good time." Erik looked at Alice, "Something is different. What is it?" Alice smiled, "I don't know what you're talking about." Valerie stopped and looked at Alice, "What's going on?"

Alice could not hold it in anymore, "I can't believe you didn't notice my hands." Alice extended her hands and displayed them, and they all stopped to look. They had not noticed until Alice spoke, "Didn't you notice that my hands no longer have any scarring?" Valerie reached out to Alice's hands, "Oh my! What happened?" Alice smiled, "Thank You, Lord, for the healing! I received a miracle from God today. He took away the pain and removed the scars." Janie stood up, "Oh my goodness! Thank You, Jesus! I have never seen anything like this." Erik came over to Alice, "May I touch your hands?" Alice laughed, "Yes! Feel how smooth and beautiful my hands are." The group wanted to hear every detail. Alice shared everything she could remember. She told them how young Frankie was and how well he prayed. Alice explained that he had a dream where Jesus told him exactly how to pray. She explained that she was to return tomorrow for more prayer. Alice explained the feeling she had when Frankie prayed. The feeling of electricity and floating. The peace she felt and how comfortable she was with the boys.

Alice told them that Samuel had prayed the night before, and she was able to have a dream about the fire. She explained that she was hoping to have some quiet time with Jack when he arrived so she could show him privately. Alice also wanted to speak to him about the fire. Alice decided that she should rest before Jack returned from work. She excused herself, "I will lie down for a nap before Jack arrives. Please call me when he is about thirty minutes away. Thank you, Valerie." She laid down to take her nap but could not fall asleep right away.

Alice finally drifted off to sleep. She fell into a deep sleep and dreamt about the day's events. Alice saw herself walking in the morning talking to the Lord. She could see the Lord walking next to her. He was enormous and very bright, dressed in a long white tunic-style clothing. She could not see His face, but a brilliance of light and glory surrounded Him. His voice was like thunder. She wondered if others could hear His voice as they walked and talked. She asked many questions, and He answered them all. First, she asked, "Have I known you before now?" The Lord replied, "Yes, for a very long time. I have known you since before you entered your mother's womb."

She asked, "Why don't I remember anything about my life?" He answered, "You had an injury to your brain, and I could not allow you to remember until you healed properly and became stronger." Alice continued, "Why do I dream?" He answered, "I am speaking to you through your dreams because I can reveal mysteries that you cannot hear when awake." Alice was afraid to ask the next question. The Lord spoke first, "Do not be afraid. I have not given you the spirit of fear. I have given you a Spirit of Power, Love, and sound Judgment. Ask

My daughter." Alice smiled, "Did I know Your Son, Jesus, as my Lord and Savior?" The Lord answered, "What are your thoughts on this matter?" Alice replied, "I feel like I did. My husband says we don't believe in this nonsense." The Lord spoke, "Jack knows the truth. Your husband also believes. You love My Son, and He loves you. He gave His life for you. That's how much Jesus loves you." "Lord, I dream of babies. Are they mine?" The Lord laughed, "Yes, they are yours, but they belong to Me. You will have them to enjoy for a short time on earth and eternity because of Jesus. You have loved and taught them well and you may be surprised at what they will teach you." Alice continued to ask questions, "Why do I dream about flying?" The Lord answered, "This next part of your life will be much easier. It will seem effortless. Do not lose focus. Keep your eyes on Me."

Alice could hear Valerie's voice calling her. She did not want to awaken; she wanted to continue to speak to the Lord. She wanted to have more questions answered, but Valerie's voice was so loud. Finally, Alice opened her eyes, "I want to sleep longer." She mumbled and closed her eyes. Valerie answered, "Alice, you wanted me to awaken you so you can prepare to speak to Mr. Alexander." Alice sat up, "Oh my goodness is it that time already? I had the most pleasant dream; I didn't want to wake up." Valerie smiled at her.

Alice sat up, "I think I want to change my clothes. I feel I am to wear pants, not sure why but I am feeling pants." Alice got up and started to look for the right pair of pants to wear. Alpha was picking out a pair. Next, she looked for a blouse to wear. Finally, she found a red blouse and as she lifted it said, "Hmm, I think this is the right blouse. Red seems right today." Alice dressed and then looked to her friend, "Would you join me in prayer?"

Alice sat in her chair. Valerie came and sat near Alice, "Let's pray." Alice began, "Lord, thank you for taking care of me. Thank you for Jesus, Your Son, Who gave His life for me. I ask that you give me Your wisdom as I speak to Jack. I thank You for the healing You have given me and will continue to give me. Lord, I need your wisdom today more than ever. Please lead me through this conversation with Jack." Valerie added, "Lord, as Alice prepares to speak to her husband, prepare Jack's heart. Soften his heart to understand Alice's need to know more. Thank you, Lord." The two ladies looked at each other and smiled, then in unison said, "Amen."

They heard Jack's car pulling up the driveway. Alice smiled and headed to greet him. As Jack opened the door, he was surprised to see Alice standing in front of him. He smiled, "Is everything okay?" Alice laughed, "Yes, welcome home. After you settle in, I hoped we could sit on the patio and talk." He looked at her puzzled, "Are you sure that everything is okay?" Alice responded, "Yes, it couldn't be too much better. Get comfortable. I will have Janie bring us some lemonade on the patio." Jack smiled at Alice as he passed by her to head into his room.

Alice headed to the kitchen. "Janie, would you mind bringing some lemonade to the patio for Mr. Alexander and I?" Janie smiled, "It would be a pleasure."

Alice was sitting on the patio enjoying the sun. Jack came out and sat next to her. He looked a little concerned, "What's going on?" Alice smiled, "I have great news to share." She began to share her dream about speaking with God. Jack sat back, "I think it's just a dream. Dreams do not mean anything. I do not want to see you hurt any more than you already are. I think you need to stop this nonsense." Alice looked at him, "This is true. Look at my hands. The neighbor boy had a dream about praying for me, and look, no more scarring."

Jack looked at her hands. He was shocked, "What kind of witchcraft are they doing?" Alice was feeling frustrated at his reaction, "What? Witchcraft? Are you losing your mind? This is a miracle from God." Jack continued, "If this is from God, then why not heal you all the way? Why did He not remove the scarring from your face? Why stop at your hands?"

Alice sat up, "Are you kidding me? You cannot see this as a miracle. All you see is why not do more? What happened to you that you deny God?" Jack answered, "There is no God! If there was a God, why did he allow this to happen to you? Why did my parents die when I was little? Why leave me orphaned? Why allow so much pain into a child's life? Answer me that?" Alice felt tears well up, "I do not know why you have been hurt. I cannot answer that. I do not know why this happened to me. However, I can tell you that after the first boy prayed for me to get my memory back, I had a dream about the accident. I saw everything that happened during the fire. I saw God or His Angel protecting me, leading me out of the cellar, which had a lock on the door. Why would I have been in the cellar with the door locked? That is the question I want an answer to." Jack erupted, "Why don't you ask God? You say He is the One that gave you the dream. Then He is the One to give you the answer. I don't believe that the door was locked, and why would you have been in the cellar?"

Alice was feeling desperate, "I can't believe I would have married a man that is so hateful. You are not behaving like a loving and understanding husband. What is your problem? I thought that you would be happy for me. This healing and remembering something are such a big step. Why are you so angry?" Jack realized that his reaction was not healthy, "Look, I am so sorry. This all has caught me off guard. Please forgive me. Of course, I am happy that you have some healing." Alice got up, "I'm sorry. I need time alone to process your reaction." Jack grabbed her hand, "Please forgive me, darling. I had an awful day at work. Please understand what I am about to say is for your good. I forbid you to continue to see these people, and you need to stop this nonsense for your good." Alice pulled away, "First of all, you can't forbid me to do anything. I am an adult, and I can choose to do whatever I please. I just need to go lie down for a little bit." She walked into the house and saw Janie, "Please forgive me, but I do not think I will be joining you all for dinner." Janie answered, "Alice, may I bring something for you?" Alice just continued to walk to her room as her husband's voice echoed in her ear. She did not want anyone to see her cry.

Alice closed the door behind her, crawled into her bed, and sobbed. Alpha jumped on the bed and snuggled with her. She cried out, "Lord, why? Why doesn't he understand?" She fell sound asleep. Valerie knocked on the door after dinner with a tray of food. There was no answer. Valerie peeked in, "Alice, are you awake?" Valerie entered the room and found Alice sound asleep. She placed the tray on the table and walked out.

25 THE MIDNIGHT VISITOR

Alice awoke to a dark room. She quietly reached over and turned on the lamp. She saw a tray with food. She smiled and thought, 'Janie and Valerie are so thoughtful.' She took a bite of her bread, and Alpha sat up. Alice handed him some meat. Alice whispered to him, "Do you want more to eat? Come on then, let's go find more."

She opened her door quietly and walked into the kitchen. Alice placed her tray on the counter. She found more meat for Alpha to eat. Alice turned to look out the window. She saw the moonlight shining down on what appeared to be the neighbor's cabin. She continued to watch. The whole cabin seemed to glow. She softly asked, "Do you want me to go there?" She heard a gentle voice, "Yes." She looked at Alpha and went back into her bedroom to grab a sweater. She locked the door behind her and left.

As she walked out of the house, she felt excitement. Alpha too, sensed the energy and leaped for joy. Alice walked across the meadow and sang a lullaby she did not recognize. As they approached the creek, she noticed someone walking alongside the creek. As she crossed the creek, the person came closer. Alice called out, "Hello?" Then, she heard a familiar voice, "Hello Alice. What are you doing out so late?" "Seth, I could ask you the same question." She laughed. Seth answered, "I heard a voice call to me to arise."

Alice smiled at Seth, extending a hand to help her cross the creek. Alice said, "That's very interesting. I was in the kitchen and saw the moonlight shining bright on your cabin. Then I heard a voice answer my question." Seth waited, but she was silent, "What was your question?" Alice smiled, "I asked the

Lord, Do you want me to go there? He said yes." Seth smiled, "I didn't want to walk too far away from the cabin. I wanted to be near if the boys awoke. So, I have been walking back and forth for the last thirty minutes." Alice responded, "That was about the time I had seen the light and asked my question."

As they walked toward the cabin, Seth held Alice's arm to support her. Alice asked, "Seth, were you dreaming when you were awakened?" Seth smiled at her, "Yes, I was. I was dreaming of my beautiful wife." Alice remained silent for a moment, "I can tell you love her dearly. I can feel your love for her." Seth smiled, "Yes, we have all been praying for her safe return. Why do you think the Lord sent you here tonight?" Alice hesitated, "There is something special about this place. I feel so much peace and comfort here, and I don't understand why but it feels like home."

Seth quickly reacted to Alice's stumbling and put his arm around her waist. "Are you okay?" He asked. Alice laughed, "I'm sorry, I didn't see that rock." Seth laughed, "I didn't notice it either. Your laugh is contagious." Alice tried to gather herself, "I guess we should be quiet, so we don't wake the boys." Seth laughed, "If they haven't already awoken with Alpha's greeting, they will sleep through any laughing. I believe they have already awakened." As they opened the door, Buddy jumped on Alpha.

The two pups played around in the small living area. Seth headed to the kitchen, "May I offer you a cup of cocoa?" Alice answered, "That sounds delicious." As Seth reached for the milk, he looked over his shoulder at Alice and asked, "Would you like marshmallows?" Alice answered, "I don't know if I have ever had marshmallows." Seth smiled, "Then tonight is a good night to try some." Alice asked, "Seth, would you tell me something about yourself?" Seth turned to face Alice, "What would you like to know?" Alice shyly asked, "Your wife has been missing for over two years. How do you not give up hope?" Seth watched Alice, "I have always felt she was closer than I knew. I smell her fragrance at times. I feel her presence, and occasionally I see her. At times I can almost touch her. When you love someone so deeply, you never give up hope. It's not just for me; my boys need their mommy more than I can imagine."

Alice had tears running down her face. She looked up at Seth, "You and your boys' give me hope. I dream of two babies, and when I awaken, I can feel them so close to me. I can smell them. I know deep in my heart that these two babies are mine and I know I have loved them. Jack says I have never had children. However, my body tells me different. My heart aches for them. I agree when you love so deeply, you will not give up hope." Seth watched Alice's face when suddenly he noticed that the boys were standing at their doorway listening.

He smiled at them, "Come on over, boys. I'm making cocoa." Samuel was the first to speak, "Mrs. Alexander, why are you here so late?" Alice turned to face the boys, "I saw a bright light shining down on your cabin. I then asked the Lord if He wanted me to come over, and He said yes." Frankie asked, "Are you going to have marshmallows in your cocoa?" Alice laughed, "I think I need to. They sound like they will be so good." Frankie laughed, "They are!" Samuel wanted to know more, "What did the light look like?"

Alice smiled, "It was a golden light and it looked like it was glowing around your cabin." Samuel continued, "What did the voice sound like?" Alice answered, "It was a faint, soft, calming voice but firm." Samuel continued, "How could you see the cabin? The cabin is so far away that you really can't see it from your house because we can't see your house."

Alice was surprised, "You know what? You are right! Normally I cannot see your cabin, but tonight, I guess I must have seen a vision. I saw your cabin as if it was only 100 feet away from where I stood. I didn't realize that until you asked me."

Frankie's eyes were huge with excitement, "We shouldn't talk about this anymore. Not until after we have our cocoa. I know God wants us to do something but not right now. We need to enjoy our cocoa first."

Seth filled the cups with marshmallows and served everyone a cup. Frankie was the first to comment, "Daddy, this is very good. I would love it if mommy were here with us." Samuel was next, "She is here. Mommy is always in our hearts. Mommy is here." Samuel reached out and held his little brother's hand. Seth smiled, "Mommy is in our hearts, so she is here even if she is not here physically."

Alice sat quietly, watching how the boys longed for their mom. She knew that wherever the little boys were that she dreamt about, they must have been feeling the same way. Alice was daydreaming of finding the little boys. Suddenly she realizes that Seth is speaking to her. "Alice, are you okay?" Seth asked. Alice smiled and answered, "Yes, I'm okay. I am just so impressed with the hope and faith you all have." Frankie continued with this cocoa, "I think the cocoa needs something. I think it needs snow." Samuel asked, "Snow? What do you mean, little brother?" Frankie smiled, "The last time I dreamt about cocoa, it was snowing." Seth laughed, "Please, no snow this time of year. I just want to enjoy our last days here. I want to fish and possibly go for a hike."

Alice laughed, "I can only imagine how snow would feel on my toes or even on my face." Samuel laughed, "No one would want snow on their toes! It is too cold. When it falls on your face, it tickles." Frankie was laughing, "It does tickle your face." Alice laughed, "What if we all close our eyes and imagine snow falling on our faces." Alice and the boys closed their eyes, and Alice spoke first, "I feel like it would be a brisk day. The wind would be blowing very gently. The sky would be a little cloudy." Samuel jumped in, "I can feel the snow. It is gently falling on my face, and I can stick my tongue out to catch some snowflakes on my tongue." Frankie giggled, "The snow tickles my cheeks. The snowflakes are cold." Seth was watching them as they imagined this scene. He was amazed at how calm everything was here at the cabin. He would love to stay longer, but he knew he must get back to work.

Suddenly the room was infused with the scent of roses. Seth closed his eyes, and he could see his wife. She was standing right in front of him, smiling at him. Frankie cried out, "Mommy! Where are you?" Samuel opened his eyes and looked around the room, "Can you smell that?" Alice still had her eyes closed, "I love roses." Frankie laughed, "Jesus, where is my mommy?" He heard Jesus speaking, 'Open your eyes and pray.' Frankie opened his eyes, and he saw something special. He could see the light shining down on Alice. Samuel looked at Frankie and nodded his head. It was as if they were speaking and saying, 'the time has come to pray for Alice.' Seth was so busy with what he saw that he did not pay attention as the boys moved toward Alice. They did not speak a word. They both placed their hands on Alice. Alice opened her eyes, but Frankie nodded his head; she closed her eyes.

Samuel placed his hands on Alice's head, and Frankie placed his hands on her shoulders. They began to pray. It was as if they had done this before; each took his turn to speak. Frankie started, "Our Father, who is in Heaven. Holy be Your Name. Your Kingdom come. Your will be done. On earth as it is in Heaven. Jesus, You gave me a dream, so here I am, asking You to make my dream come true." Samuel spoke next, "Dear Jesus, You gave me a dream. I did not know the lady in my dream, but I saw Frankie and myself praying for her." Frankie continued, "With the power given to me by my Jesus. I speak to the skin. Heal in Jesus' name. No more scars." Samuel continued, "With the authority given to me by Jesus Christ, I say to every muscle, line up now to the way God intended you to be." Frankie smiled, "Jesus' fire, please purify the face muscles." Samuel continued, "Jesus, heal the skin on Alice's nose and eyes." Frankie saw everything as they asked Jesus to heal; she was healed in front of their eyes. Samuel then started, "Thank You, Jesus, for the healing. Jesus, now give Mrs. Alexander her memory back. Thank You, Jesus." Frankie started to cry, "Jesus, show her who her boys really are."

At this point, Seth opened his eyes. Tears ran down his face. He spoke first, "Lord, you are the All-Mighty God, the God of the Angel Armies. Please give her memory back." Frankie said again with his voice cracking, "Jesus, fix her voice and make it the way it used to be before the accident." Samuel added, "Jesus, take all the pain away. You paid for it on the cross. Thank You, Jesus."

Seth fell to his knees, tears streaming down his face, "You are so beautiful." Samuel asked, "What do you remember?" Alice was crying, "I don't feel any pain in my entire body. I am tingling everywhere." She looked at herself and saw the scarring was gone. She was in awe of what was transpiring in her body. She stuttered, "I. I. I can remember a baby in my arms, but it was dead. I remember the pain I felt." Frankie was crying, "What else do you remember?" She looked at Seth and shouted, "I know you! I have loved you so much! Sammie, you are my sweet boy! Frankie, you are my sweet little one!" She hugged the boys so tightly. She did not want to let go. Seth ran to them, "You are back! Thank You, Lord!" The family hugged and cried.

Frankie was the first to speak, "Mommy, I missed you so much. I prayed every day for you to come home safe." Samuel added, "Mommy, I knew you were coming home. Jesus told me. He had me make a special gift for you. I will go get it." Samuel ran to the bedroom. Seth hugged his wife and spoke softly, "From the first day we met you on the mountain, I knew there was something special about you, but I couldn't put my finger on it. I watched your every move. You moved like Francie but had a different name. You looked beautiful to me every day I saw you. I felt ashamed, thinking that I was attracted to someone other than my Francie, but it was you all along." Francie had tears running down her face. Francie confessed, "I never felt I loved Mr. Alexander. I had no attraction to him. But I did feel connected to you and the boys. I just could not put my finger on it. Finally, the Lord brought me to you."

Samuel re-entered the room with a box wrapped in brown paper bags. Francie was so proud of his wrapping. Samuel placed the gift on her lap. "I made this when Jesus told me you were coming home very soon." Francie cried as she opened the gift, "Oh my! It is beautiful, Sammie. I will keep this close to me always." She held up the picture frame that had a picture of the four, and around the frame were the names of the babies that had gone to Heaven.

They cried for hours and held each other so tightly. Francie was the first to speak. "I dreamt of you almost every day. I just did not recognize it was you. God is so good. Thank You, Lord, for my family and getting me back home to them."

Seth listened as they sat and shared everything that had happened to them. They knew the Lord had never left them, even in their darkest days. Seth spoke, "The Lord was there holding and comforting us. As angry as I was at the Lord, He never left me." Frankie smiled, "Our faith in Jesus never changed. That is what made our promises come true. God gave us all our dreams and visions.' Francie softly spoke, "Please forgive me for breaking my promise. God never breaks His promises. I am home." Samuel was smiling, "Mommy, it was not your fault. God's love and grace brought you home. We just obeyed what He told us to do." Frankie ran to get the gold nugget and handed it to Francie, "Mommy, this is what God gave us for you."

Francie was in awe of what God had done. The way He had brought the family together. She started to remember the day she was taken. She had been baking when the doorbell rang. She took out the last batch of cookies and set them down. As she reached to open the door, someone forced their way in, and she was immediately knocked down and unconscious. When she awakened, she found herself in a small dark space. It was musty and filthy. She had stumbled around in the dark and could not find anything in the darkness.

Finally, she fell to her knees and began to cry out to God. "Papa, please get me home. I just want to be back with my babies and husband." She wasn't sure how many days she had been in the dark space, but she began remembering the sound of the fire. The fire made a thunderous sound as it ignited and burned the house. She had thought for a moment that she would never get out. That was when she found the door and tried to get out. Then she remembered the angel. He was huge. He had said to her, 'do not be afraid I am here to help you. Follow me.' The locked door flew open. He instructed her to stay close. An enormous beam fell, and she fell backward under the weight of the beam. She saw the angel pick her up and carry her to the steps. That was the moment that the firefighters came across her.

Francie looked at Seth, "I remember everything." He asked her, "Who was it?" She heard the Lord speak to her, "You must forgive and release the man." Francie said the following words carefully and with purpose, "As an act of my will, I choose to forgive the intruder. The man who harmed you, our babies, and me. I forgive him, so our family can heal." Seth repeated her words, "I choose to forgive the man who caused all this pain. I forgive him." Tears ran down their cheeks.

After being together, they decided it was time to make a few phone calls. Francie called her parents, Rae, Valerie, Erik, and Janie. The three friends rushed over to see her. They were all shocked, amazed, and in awe of the miracle before them.

Frankie, Samuel, and Seth did not leave Francie's side. Rae arrived a few hours later, and everyone had another good cry as the healing manifested in everyone. They praised and worshipped the Most-High God.

Dear Francie,

I am so sorry that I hurt you. I was so infatuated with you from the moment that we bumped into each other in the hospital hallway, and I set eyes on you. After the fire, I had to secretly institutionalize Alice for severe depression, suicidal attempts and starting the fire. I thought I could just give you her memories and my life. I deserve whatever punishment comes my way. Please forgive me for wanting you for myself.
Jack

ABOUT THE AUTHOR

Rachel is the daughter of EL ELYON, the Most High God. She is married to her husband since 1981, a mother of two sons, and a grandmother. She was born in Texas, grew up in Nebraska, and implanted in California. She enjoys writing, gardening, and travel. As someone who has traveled internationally, she desires to do more traveling to spread the love of Yeshua. So, the question is, where will she go next!

A Mother's Broken Promise